WRITTEN IN BLOOD.

The elderly bookseller had a metal spike driven into his ear. It was the kind of sight bad dreams were made of, but for Jack Journey it was simply the start. . . .

A Chicago newspaperman specializing in crime, Journey attracted trouble the way a magnet drew iron. A long-legged lovely named Laura, a bunch of bruisers in three-piece suits, and a corpse had all wound up at his door. They raised questions. Turning up answers led to New York, Paris, and the underworld capitals of Europe, following a trail of killings begun forty years before in Sicily, and leading to a set of missing diaries it would be extremely dangerous to find.

"THE STORYTELLING IS SO WELL PACED, YOU'LL SOON STOP LOOKING BETWEEN THE LINES AND GET ON WITH THE TALE."
—*Chicago Tribune*

BOOKS BY JAY ROBERT NASH:

FICTION

On All Fronts
A Crime Story
The Dark Fountain

NONFICTION

Dillinger: Dead or Alive?
Citizen Hoover
Bloodletters and Badmen
Hustlers and Con Men
Darkest Hours
Among the Missing
Murder, America
Almanac of World Crime
Look for the Woman
People to See
The True Crime Quiz Book
The Innovators
Zanies
The Crime Movie Quiz Book
Open Files
The Toughest Movie Quiz Book Ever
The Dillinger Dossier
Murder Among the Mighty

QUANTITY SALES

INDIVIDUAL SALES

THE
MAFIA
DIARIES

Jay Robert Nash

A DELL BOOK

Published by
Dell Publishing Co., Inc.
1 Dag Hammarskjold Plaza
New York, New York 10017

Dell ® TM 681510, Dell Publishing Co., Inc.

ISBN: 0-440-15163-5

Reprinted by arrangement with Delacorte Press
Printed in the United States of America
September 1986

10 9 8 7 6 5 4 3 2 1

WFH

This book is for my wife, Judy.

THE
MAFIA
DIARIES

I

The Cancellation

1

It had been a bad year for me and the United States of America; we were both going broke. Newspapers had folded out in Iowa and down in Georgia and they had taken my crime column with them, gone under cornfields and red clay.

More than money had drifted out of my life. A young lady named Eden Barce had quit my adventurous company when I got involved in a series of murders that had led to the arrest of the governor-elect of the state of Illinois. Of course, he escaped into retirement through legal loopholes pried open by an army of lawyers. My own lawyer, who had been involved, also escaped. Politicians and lawyers almost always manage to land on fat pillows, no matter how hard they fall. It was all scary stuff for Eden Barce and she went off to weld herself to someone safe, a commodities broker, I think, one of those fellows who shriek out potential ulcers in Chicago's trading pits and goes home tranquilized by commercial exhaustion for the rest of his life.

There had been other women since then, all of them great and lasting loves. I had gone with some of them as long as a month, models dieting down to starvation, actresses too good for any part, including the right part, even a women's libber who took pride in anything ugly. There was one who had lasted many weeks, a dark brunette named Laura Manville, long-legged with volcanic eyes of burning slate. A thinker, crafty, this woman, a lady of high finance who worked as a banking consultant. I would see her again, I was sure of that. I was reasonably sure I would call her someday, look down the shabby list, names check-marked and crossed out and reinstated, and pick out her name and call her.

My trouble was that I had lost interest or had other interests that held little or no interest for the ladies—crime, the dark side of the moon. That's my business, what I write about, historical crime and ancient felons.

I tried to think of Laura Manville, but she was too much for the sizzling day. It was blistering hot, a typical July day in Chicago.

As I walked along North Clark Street with my tie hiding the top open button of my shirt, I thought about a tall cold beer in a frosty mug, but it was too early for that. I could feel a trickle of sweat moving over my chest and it wasn't yet noon. The morning had been uneventful, offering routine paper work at home, fact-checking for one of my columns dealing with superstition among criminals. The day promised only long hot hours and more sweaty research, but before its end murder would once again slip slyly like a phantom into the hours of my life, real murder and real bodies. Some of these cadavers would be my friends.

Many people crowded about me on the sidewalk as I made a slow way toward my less than opulent offices. All around me people swooped and galloped and lolled, indifferent to the blotches of spilled ice cream, fragmented pretzels, and all manner of paper crumpled and shredded underfoot. There were those in the crowds, impatient with the pace, who suddenly stepped into gutters swirling with more debris and quick-stepped around slowly moving knots of barefoot teen-agers, inchworm elders in oppressive dark clothes, college girls, with round, pert behinds inside tight jeans and wobbling, tilted forward on four-inch open-back heels that had poured wealth into the limp-wristed hands of snickering, immaculate designers in far-off Paris.

The crowds were much too large, I realized, for this workday Tuesday, even with the out-of-school hordes. About me too were sullen men and hard-faced women who did not glance into the quaint cute shops selling exorbitantly priced antiques and beachwear or pause before hardier stores offering cut-rate paints and discounted lawn mowers. These trod grimly forward with steady gaze, workless people with nowhere to go on a workday, guilt upon their faces for an ethic made shabby by chatterbox politicians.

We were in a deepening depression but would not admit it, alone or altogether. That had happened before, in the thirties. That was the past and Americans knew that the past came but once to America. This was the 1980s, the jaded eighties. We were still the strongest nation on earth, weren't we? I slipped my hand into my pants pocket to reassuringly feel the folded bills nestled therein. It was a thinner wad of government paper than any Tuesday last year would have provided. In fact it wasn't a wad at all but a sliver.

Working against the onward flow of the street crowds, I edged into my office building, going up the narrow marble corridor to the small stairs and taking these slowly. I passed the janitor, Fredric, mopping the floor tiredly. "That smells awful," I said to him.

"It's the disinfectant," he replied in a tired voice, a sigh. "Gotta do it—the bums urinate in the hall."

"Why do you let them do that?"

"Me?" He straightened to lean on the mop handle. "I'm no cop, Mr. Journey. They get into the entranceway easy and go around the stairway and into this hall and do their number. There ain't too many people coming in here anymore. Most of the dentists have moved out. You, Mr. Lindquist, and your secretary are up and down these halls more than most, so I guess you get the worst whiff of the bums. That's why I lay down the disinfectant so hard, see?"

"Fredric," I said encouragingly, "I'm grateful for your vigilance and counterattacks against all those leaky bladders."

He shrugged and went on mopping. "That sounds pretty good, I guess." At the end of the long hall, stopping before my office door, I turned to see him mopping methodically, each stroke measured against the energy of his years and the lurking little pains of his work. I was glad to escape the overwhelming smell of the disinfectant by slipping into my office, where the clatter of Abbe Gessner's typewriter greeted me.

Abbe sat with her back to the door, a blazing red scarf wrapped around her head. She stopped and swiveled about in her chair.

"What are those?" I said, pointing to green plastic cylinders around which her dark hair was wrapped. She edged the scarf forward on her face.

"Curlers. Don't you know about them? They set hair."

"Isn't that something you do in the privacy of your own home?"

"Look, Jack, no one ever comes in here but you and

Charlie. So who does it bother? Besides, I put a scarf on to cover them."

"Isn't that scarf what you call a babushka?"

"If you're Polish."

I rummaged through the phone messages. There were several, all from the same person. "Lewis Lucan called *six* times this morning."

"That's him, the bookdealer, right? He's been calling since I got here at nine thirty. He's a pretty demanding guy and he was demanding to know your home phone number."

"He's a rare-book dealer, those fellows are sensitive. Did you give him my number?"

"Hell, no. The last time I did that, you popped your cork. I told him—politely—that your number was unlisted, so unlisted that even I didn't know it. But he knew I was lying. You can tell when people are on to you that way."

"I'm sorry you had to lie for my sake."

She wheeled about and went back to her typing. "No, you're not. You love it when other people lie for you, all men do."

"Thanks."

"I'll have the four columns you wrote last week ready to go this afternoon. And we got another cancellation."

I went to my desk, holding the phone messages from Lucan. "Where?"

"Altoona, Pennsylvania. The paper is closing down there."

"Good God, another one. Damn it! Damn the depression and television and especially God damn those eastern bosses with their inherited wealth."

"That's pretty radical coming from you," snorted Abbe without missing a beat on her electric typewriter. "Are you buying another library from Lucan?"

"A small one, from Europe. It was kept by a retired inspector of the Sûreté."

"French police?"

"Yes. He had about eighteen hundred volumes on historical crime going back to the 1850s."

She kept typing and talking, a display of ambidextrous concentration that had long since ceased to amaze me. Abbe didn't really read anything she typed, merely related the written symbols to the mechanics of typing, which left her free to jabber.

"Jack, you must have fifty thousand books already jammed into that town house of yours. Where are you going to put another eighteen hundred?"

"Closets, bathrooms."

The phone rang. Abbe reached it before the second ring. "It's Lucan again."

"Hello, Lewis," I said, taking the call. "You're running up quite a bill calling me today."

"Jack, I'm sorry, but that French library I arranged for you to buy is no longer available."

"What? Now, I paid for those books two months ago. You're talking about my property and I want that shipment."

"Yes, I know, but I'm helpless. Hugo Keimes in New York has written me that the library is no longer available. He's refunded my check and I'm going to refund yours. I just wanted to tell you personally instead of merely sending you a check in the mail. You're a good customer and I like to treat my clients with some respect."

"*Some* respect, Lewis, is not enough. I bought the library straight and clear and I want my books. I won't stand still for any cancellation."

"You'll have to, Jack. Keimes controls this in New York. But, look, I know you're disappointed on this, so I'll not only return your check but add the interest on the money it would have earned in a bank. That okay?"

"No."

"But it's the same as what the banks do. You'll get interest on your money, Jack. Now that's a hell of a deal. What bookdealer in the world would offer you a deal like that?"

"None, Lewis, including and especially you. It's all very odd. Have you made another deal on that library for more money?"

There was silence at his end and then he said slowly: "That's the kind of remark I would never expect from John Howard Journey—to be accused of shopping a client's purchase." He added in a low, hurt voice: "I'll send you the check, Jack, *with* the interest."

"Wait a minute, don't hang up."

Lucan hung up.

I sat studying the phone. Lewis Lucan offering me interest on my money for a library he could not or would not deliver. He was the most buck-squeezing bookdealer in town. But he was definitely honest. He would never sell a library out from under a buyer; that was bad business and would get around. No, something was wrong, terribly wrong.

Charlie Lindquist, my researcher and friend, barged into my office, coming from his own adjacent room. In his thick hands were pages of scribbled notes. "I found some more superstition among criminals." He put the pages down on my desk, staring at them as he talked in his usual staccato, words running into one another. "This is a pretty case here—these two fellows in England, hardcase thieves, had just robbed a car—Frederick Guy Browne and William Henry Kennedy—stole a car—"

"When?" I asked with little interest, my mind producing angry accusatory thoughts about Lucan.

"On or about September 27, 1927—"

"That's current," cracked Abbe as she continued to type.

"You stay out of this, Ms. Gessner," Charlie snapped back, "the name of the game is crime *history*, remember?"

"Who can forget? I must have typed up ten thousand stories about criminals who have been dead before the typewriter was invented."

"So?" Charlie looked at her, his large, red face gone sour. "That's what you get paid for." He turned back to his pages. "Anyway, Jack, these two bowler-hat types steal the car and are stopped by a cop named Gutteridge in Essex. Browne shoots the cop—"

"They call them constables in England," chimed in Abbe.

"Shoots the cop," repeated Charlie, ignoring her, "and as the officer lies on the ground, Browne gets out of the car and stares down at him and says: 'What are you looking at me like that for?' and then shoots out the cop's eyes, both of them." Charlie underscored a scribbled line on the top page of his research papers. "This guy Browne—he and Kennedy were picked up later and hanged—was really superstitious. He thought—now get this—he actually thought that his image could be traced on the cop's eyes after death! Imagine that one!"

"Yeah, it's an old superstition, and a good story."

"Well, it's true anyway." Charlie straightened, his enthusiasm for the discovery thinning. "What's the matter, not good enough?"

"No, no, it's fine, Charlie. I'll add it to what I dug up at home this morning." The library cancellation grated on me. "What do you think about Lewis Lucan?"

"Who—the used-book dealer?"

"That's him."

"What's to think about? He's a tightwad and as mean as

seven A.M. If he knows you really want a book, he takes it in back and *then* writes the price on the inside back cover. Ever notice that about him when you're down there in that cave he calls a warehouse? None of his books are marked with the price. First he sees if you're interested, *then* the price goes in. What a grubber."

"Lucan canceled that French library today and offered to return my money *with* interest."

"Lucan did that? He must have been up all night reading *A Christmas Carol*, or a wall of books fell on him and made him crazy."

"He's far from crazy, but if I don't get my books—" I stood up with the decision to confront my antiquarian friend. "C'mon, Charlie. We're going down to see Lucan."

"When am I supposed to finish on the superstition research?"

"I've got more than enough for a column." I faced my typist. "Abbe, call Lucan for me and tell him I'm coming down to see him." I was already heading for the door, Charlie following with a grumble.

It took twenty minutes to walk to the garage and move into heavy noonday traffic. Charlie carped all the way south as we snaked our way into the Loop. "What the hell do I have to go along for? I was planning to finish up early and catch that new outer-space movie."

"Why—you could hear the same weird noises in your own backyard—guys playing with piano wire, pneumatic drills stalling—that's no movie. Where's Roy Scheider, Al Pacino, where's Dustin Hoffman?"

"I like those Star Wars things because they're soothing, unreal and soothing. People don't really die in those movies, robots and tiny little spaceships, get it? It's a way of escaping from the lunatics and mad people you write about all the time, like those two British murderers— shooting the eyes out of a cop because they think he's got a camera in his eyeballs—I mean that's disgusting when you really think about it."

"True, but it happened. For a long time, maybe a few hundred years, it was believed that the retina of a murder victim actually did retain the last image captured, and one man worked most of his life in France to perfect a machine that would photograph the eyeballs of murder victims to capture that last image, unsuccessfully, of course. After decades of unproductive research into the matter the scientists discarded the notion. It wasn't fact so it became superstition. It was the same way when for three hundred years authorities implicitly believed that if a murderer was forced to touch his victim, the body would bleed. The last known experience of that type occurred in 1876 in Boston when a church sexton named Thomas Piper was brought into a room where the body of a girl he had murdered was lying. Piper was ordered to touch the body and did so with trembling fingers but it did not bleed."

"And that was the end of that scientific belief?"

"Pretty much, and the belief became superstition."

"How about this guy Piper?"

"Oh, they hanged him anyway."

"Jack, do you see that truck turning in front of you?"

"Yes, don't worry about it. Aren't you ever going to stop fidgeting in a car?"

"I take the El, remember, all the time. I don't trust this Loop traffic, I mean, what the hell is that truck doing on South Clark Street. Trucks like that aren't allowed on this street and where the hell are the cops to stop that bozo? Look at him drive, will you, cutting in and out of lanes like he was on a motor scooter. Where the hell are the cops?"

"Cops are for drunks and dead men, Charlie."

2

Luckily we found a parking lot that was not full and left the big Pontiac idling, walking over a block to Dearborn and on to Printers' Row, once the mighty bastion of hot-lead Linotypes and roaring presses that turned out the commercial print of Chicago. But this heart had stopped beating long ago when the computer age brought forth noiseless word-processors that showed copy in neat little lines on a green screen, justified margins, and did everything a printer could ever do. Now Printers' Row was nothing more than large lofts converted into overpriced studio apartments. A few die-hard shops with Linotype machines rumbled in ancient glory off Dearborn, one, in fact, directly above the two-story open warehouse owned by bookseller Lewis Lucan.

We noticed immediately upon entering Lucan's shop area that the floor above quivered and rattled and groaned under the weight of the dinosaur machines. I loved hearing them. I loved the smell of the ink from the proof presses above, seeping through the ceiling and walls, the smell of the hot "pigs"—long pieces of metal melting—to be reshaped by the machines into letters, burning letters that defiantly resisted the new age. But, in time, they would go. And the green screens would dominate.

Lucan's place was well situated, a small shop with dirty windows and dusty books jammed into high shelves on three sides, a false wall with a small door through which we walked into a two-story warehouse of books housing a half-million hardbound volumes.

The sight of Lucan's warehouse never ceased to awe me. It stretched for half a block, with enormous walls of books, row after row of them shooting upward like the sheer Dover cliffs along the British coast, two stories high with wheeled ladders running up to high catwalks. In the center, above it all, beyond the typesetting firm on the third story of the building, was an open shaft shooting to a five-story skylight that spread out light filtering downward through still dust, gradations of light that worked hard to reach the ground floor. To aid the eyes, there were very small lamps fixed to support beams and arching over each aisle.

"This place smells like your town house, Jack, only worse."

"It's musty with the smell of old books."

"Rotting books, you mean."

"It is the smell of literature," I told Charlie as we made our way down the center aisle. "Of Bacon and Marlowe and Shakespeare, who, of course, were all one and the same."

"It stinks."

"Such irreverence for the past, Mr. Lindquist. Someday your movie theaters will smell like this but they'll be empty except for that very large screen into which you have disappeared so often."

"Naw, the movies will never smell like this. Say, did you notice that Lucan's girl, what's her name, Ruth? Did you notice she wasn't up front when we came in?"

"Yes, and the door left unlocked, the shop empty, not like Lucan."

Charlie pointed upward. "Well, there he sits, you can tell him for me that I think he runs a lousy shop."

Lucan sat like Buddha, his large weight behind a broad desk that was perched on a platform in the center of the warehouse. He faced us staring, his mouth grim and silent.

"He's probably heard every word you've said, Charlie," I whispered as we approached the platform, which loomed up almost a story high, mounted on huge timbers,

a single goose-neck desk lamp arched over his paper
work, its glare giving the bookdealer a silent, almost grue-
some-looking face half hidden in shadow.

"Jack," hissed Charlie, "why doesn't he say something?"

"Lewis," I called, "wake up. Customers." I turned to
Charlie with a grin. "That ought to get him blinking."

We were at the foot of the stairs, and by then I'd realized that Lewis Lucan was not asleep. We moved to the
base of the platform and yet he sat facing frontward, staring into space.

"I don't want to go up there, Jack."

"C'mon." I jerked at Charlie's sleeve; I wanted a wit-
ness.

We went up the stairs to the open platform and stood on
either side of Lucan, looking down at him. His eyes were
open. His florid face was a mass of wrinkles and jowels and
mottles. I reached for the lamp on the desk and twisted its
neck so that the light shone on Lucan's face.

"Christ, Jack, there's dust on his eyes."

"Step over here to my side," I said, and as Charlie did so
I pointed to Lucan's right ear. Blood, almost black in a
hardened trickle, went from the opening, down the side
of his neck, where it had splattered onto his white shirt.
The ear opening was filled, a round metal stand blossom-
ing away from it, giving the illusion of a second ear, a
mechanical ear of welded steel.

Charlie shrank from the sight of it, stepping backward,
a grimace on his face, his eyes blinking. "What in the hell
is that?"

I flicked my index finger against the rim of the stand
and it emitted a bell-like sound. "The bottom of a steel
billing spike. It's been driven into his brain through his
ear."

In the shadows beyond the single desk lamp I saw Charlie's face tighten, the heavy cheeks draw inward as he sucked his breath. He took another step backward, a stagger, really. I looked back to Lucan and then his desk, studying it.

"Lord, Jack, I can't go through this kind of thing again," Charlie hissed.

"Don't touch him or anything here," I told him as I leaned forward to pull a pile of papers from under Lucan's limp hand.

Charlie was moving off the platform. "Let's get the hell out of here."

"Just a minute." I went through the papers and found a letter addressed to me, telling me about the canceled library. Attached to it was a check drawn in my name, a check for more than what I had paid for the library, Lucan's promised interest included. It was in the amount of $3,300. Lucan, incredibly, had added the $300, a whopping piece of interest for a man who had penny-pinched his way upward into the ownership of a half-million books. On the check's memo line Lucan had written: *Order canceled by Keimes, NYC.*

Charlie was off the platform, facing me, looking upward with a pained expression as he backpedaled toward the front door. "Jack, for Chrissakes, Jack!"

"Stop where you are," I said sharply. "You're going the wrong way. I need only a few minutes."

"Anybody can walk in here and find us. Then it don't matter. We're here with him like that and that means only one thing in this town—we did it! Us!"

"Perfect," I said, still rummaging through the papers, "we've been set up."

"Nobody knew I was coming down here," came Charlie's moan. *"You've* been set up, maybe, not me."

At the bottom of the pile of papers I found a letter from Hugo Keimes, the rare-book dealer in New York City who had handled the overseas purchase of my library. The letter was a curiosity. It read:

Dear Lew:

Simply cannot deliver the Frenchman's library. My Paris bookman, Rombout, has gone a little crazy, sending me the wrong books and I'm having difficulty reaching him. Since I can't get confirmation on Jack's order I'm returning your check herewith and including an interest payment. Terribly sorry.

Hugo

P.S.: There's something very strange about all of this; I received two phone calls in the last few days from people who would not identify themselves, asking me if Journey had gotten his books from Europe. Of course, I told them I did not disclose such information to nameless callers. Do you think these were Jack's people calling from his office in Chicago?

I took the letter and check addressed to me and the Keimes note to Lucan and folded them, slipping them into my coat pocket.

"For Chrissakes, *please*, Jack," Charlie cried hoarsely.

"In a minute." I took out my handkerchief and carefully wiped the areas of Lucan's desk that I had touched. I thought for a moment to turn off the desk lamp but reminded myself that the less we touched, the less chance there was of anyone knowing we had been there. I started to go, when the phone on the desk rang. I reached forward, covering my hand with the handkerchief.

"Don't do that!" Charlie shouted from below the platform.

I picked up the phone and heard Abbe Gessner's voice. "Hello, Mr. Lucan?" I said nothing. "Mr. Lucan, are you there?" I replaced the receiver in its cradle and then headed for the stairs leading from the platform.

"That was real smart," clucked Charlie.

"Just Abbe. I told her to call Lucan and tell him we were coming. She's probably been calling all the while we drove down here. That means he was killed only a few minutes after I talked to him."

"Yeah, and the guy who did it, maybe, was standing right next to him while you were on the phone with him. And that puts you right in line for a setup."

"No," I said, and motioned Charlie to follow me to the back of the warehouse. "I didn't tell him I would be coming down here."

"Reassuring," Charlie said, not too reassuringly. "Where we going?"

"Out the back, down the alley, and to the car."

We walked quickly down the long aisle toward the rear of the warehouse, the towering racks and walls of books looming eerily above us, the books all silent witnesses to the horrible death of their possessive owner. Above us the ceiling trembled with the movement of the typesetting machines, sending down waves of dust. At the end of the aisle we turned and went around another wall of books. At that moment there was a distant noise from the shop area.

"What's that?" whispered Charlie.

I slipped back around the corner and looked down the aisle to the doorway leading from the shop, almost the distance of a half block. Framed in the doorway with the light streaming from the shop area behind him was a faceless man in a business suit. Glancing over to Charlie, I saw him flatten himself against a wall of books. "God damn it, move out of the light, Jack," he whispered. "You can be seen standing there."

The man made no movement toward me. He stood rock-still facing me, silent as we stared in each other's direction. Then I took a step sideways and went behind the wall of books, pulling Charlie along with me as we went out the rear door, hurrying down the alley and to the street, where we walked with thick foot-traffic. Charlie moved with his head down, shaking it a bit, deeply troubled.

"He saw you," he said finally and solemnly.

"He saw what I saw, a shadow of a man."

"I can't take any more of this, Jack, not like last time when all those bodies started to drop out of the sky in that Ashmore case."

"Maitland Ashmore is a hermit, his wife is in an institution for murder."

"Yeah, and the cops warned you never to get involved with anything like that again."

I slowed as we entered the parking lot. "All I did was order a foreign library."

Charlie faced me squarely, his large face reddening. "Yeah, this time. You know what you're like—one of those —" He snapped his fingers. "Magnets, yeah—you attract murder. Researching for you is like touring morgues. Stiffs pop up everywhere. I can't take that. Now I hope you'll just walk away from this, Jack, for God's sake."

"I will . . . after I take a little trip to New York to see Hugo Keimes." I showed Charlie the letter Keimes wrote to Lucan. He held the single sheet in his trembling hands, studying it as sweat dripped from his forehead. The lot attendant brought up my Pontiac.

Charlie handed the letter to me. "It's gettin' bigger."

We got into the car and headed for the Lake Shore Drive. Charlie sat pensively staring forward, moving his mouth but saying nothing.

Finally he blurted: "Look, if you go to New York, you go alone. I'm out of this, Jack."

"You don't like New York? It's a wonderful town, like in the song."

"It's dirty and dangerous, full of strangers. A friend of mine just came back from there and said he was almost mugged in Times Square, and in broad daylight. Times Square! And this pal of mine tells me how really bad it is. Those two statues in Times Square, one of Father Duffy and the other of George M. Cohan—why, for Chrissakes, they got pigeon shit all over 'em. That's what New Yorkers think of two of their greatest heroes. Pigeon shit. You don't find any of that crap on our statues, no sir! Hamilton, Grant, Sheridan, clean as a whistle." We were passing Buckingham Fountain near the Drive. Charlie jerked his head in the direction of the fountain and its magnificent shooting sprays of water. "See that? That's Chicago, that fountain, clean and good-looking. Why you could drink out of that fountain, Jack." Then he said, without looking at me: "No, you go to New York alone if you have to, but I'm begging you not to."

"Why?"

"Because you'll get killed and I don't want to see that."

"Cut it out, Charlie. You can get killed in Chicago just as easily."

As I shot my Pontiac onto the Drive I did not realize the prophecy lurking in my words. I was thinking about the man who had entered Lucan's place, the long-distance shadow, and whether or not police were by then swarming about the motionless bookdealer, his open, sightless eyes no longer keeping watch over his beloved yellowing domain.

3

It was happening again, like a seizure. I felt a swelling anger at the thought that someone could murder old Lucan in that bizarre, comic fashion. He had been killed for show, with no more meaning than brains surrounding the stem of a billing spike. I thought of tomato wedgers, onion dicers, and egg slicers. It was on that level, this Lucan murder. He was meant to be a counter exhibit, a display item. For whom? Me? Yes, certainly.

All of this was swimming in my brain as I walked with Charlie back into my office. We stopped in silence to see two homicide detectives, old acquaintances, Frank Ackerly and Bill Brex. Ackerly sprawled his large frame in my chair, Brex stood leaning against the wall, holding some of my typescript in his hand as he glanced in our direction.

"Where've you been?" Ackerly demanded.

I walked forward and took the typescript from Brex, replacing it on my desk. "Wait till the paper comes out with it, Bill."

He gave me a weak smile from thin lips. "You don't believe all that superstition jazz those creeps pretend to believe in, do you, Jack?"

"I'm superstitious about people reading my copy before it gets into print." I stood next to Ackerly, looking down on him. "You're in my chair."

He glared up at me for a moment, then shot upward, bringing himself to his full height, using every inch so that he could look down on me. "I asked you where you've been."

I stood very close to him. "Don't try to strong-arm me, Frank. We've gone through this before, remember?"

He moved aside a few inches to let me pass. "We were down at Lucan's." Without taking his eyes from me, he nodded toward Abbe, who was sitting stiffly, watching with large brown eyes. "Your gal says she called Lucan for you, to tell him that you were on your way down there. She says that she talked to him and told him that."

I had it figured wrong, but why did Abbe call back when

Charlie and I were in the warehouse, standing next to that corpse? I couldn't ask her with Ackerly blowing garlic breath into my face. "What the hell did you have for lunch, Frank?" I fanned the air. "Your breath smells like a Burmese jungle at night."

"I don't want to know anything about Burma, just if you were down to see a Mr. Lewis Lucan, bookdealer."

"The late bookdealer," added Brex. "You *do* know he was killed today?"

"No."

Charlie started for his office.

"Where are you going?" menaced Ackerly.

"All right, stop it," I said. I jumped up so suddenly that Brex bounced away from the wall and Ackerly back-stepped, both genuinely startled. "If you guys have some sort of charge, make it, damn it! If you want to talk, be polite and don't order anyone around. Who do you think you are, the Gestapo?" This I said squarely to Ackerly, a man I deeply disliked even though he had once saved my life.

Ackerly gritted his teeth, showing long yellow incisors. "My old man fought the goddamned Nazis, Journey. Don't call me a Nazi!"

"Then stop acting like one." I turned to Brex, the good cop, which is the role he always played. "What do you really want, Bill?"

"You boys go down to see Lewis Lucan?"

I saw Charlie standing as if he had been stapled to a scarecrow pole. I waved him into his office. He shrugged and moved into the other room. "We went for a drive, but we never made it to Lucan's. It's a hot day and we stopped near Buckingham Fountain and took the air."

"Buckingham Fountain," snorted Ackerly. "You?"

I sat back down. "I've lived in Chicago for a lot of years now and I have never been to the Field Museum, the

Aquarium, the Planetarium. I thought I had better see Chicago before I died. I started with Buckingham Fountain."

"Prove it." Ackerly buttoned his summer sport coat, a mass of wrinkles, baggy at the elbows. He was all business.

"There was a balloon man there, guy with a long gray beard. He sold a balloon to a woman with a little girl and the girl didn't get a good hold of the string and it blew away but he gave her another one without charging the woman." This I had seen from the car while waiting for the light to change.

"We can check on that," Brex said.

"So check."

"What else?"

"The little girl was wearing a blue dress, the woman a bright red one. I didn't get their names. Sorry. But the balloon man is there every day, I suppose."

Ackerly squinted at Brex, who shrugged. "We'll check on the balloon man, Journey." He headed for the door, followed by Brex. I went after them. They turned in the hall. Ackerly stepped forward, as close to me as possible without touching, glaring. "You're getting to be a regular murder man, aren't you?"

"And that means what?"

"I'm never gonna forget that Ashmore thing, Journey." He shifted his weight and glared. "I still got a piece of bullet down there because of you." He pointed at his leg.

"I didn't put it in you."

"No, but I should of let the guy who did, the guy who wanted to waste you, do it." He straightened. "I don't like you any better now than I did then." He thought back on it for a moment. "A lot of bodies got collected because of your one-man investigation. You start that crap again, Jack, and I promise you a long future as a cripple."

I stood up to him, almost shouting: "Spell it out."

He pulled back slowly. "It's called 'the beating of your life.'"

"I've already had one of those," I said, tired but wary. I moved toward my office. "In Europe, by experts. And I'm still walking straight, my eyes are uncrossed, and there's no water on the brain."

"A cripple!" he snarled. Ackerly started the long walk down the hallway, his heavy body making the ancient floor creak. He grumbled as he went, distant thunder. He slapped the wall twice on his way, almost cracking the paint. Brex stood there with me, watching him go. When Ackerly got to the end of the hallway he turned and let me have a full blast, roaring: "A cripple, you arrogant bastard! God damn it, how I hate your guts! C'mon, Bill, c'mon, God damn it!" He marched around the corner, shouting for his partner to follow.

Brex looked at me quietly, then said: "We got a fingerprint down at Lucan's, Jack. We already checked it against yours and Charlie's and it didn't match."

"What the hell you doing with our prints? We've never been arrested—even for littering."

"We had yours a long time ago, from your service record. Got it during that Ashmore case. Charlie's is on file because he was once a deputy sheriff. Before he turned in his badge and threw away the piece he was carrying. Anyway, we have no evidence that you were even in Lucan's place. But your girl in there said you were headed down there. And we saw all those notes she wrote out this morning about his calls to you."

"Great. Just walk into a man's office and inspect everything you find."

"The messages were on top of the desk."

"How did Lucan get killed?"

"Devilish. Somebody drove a billing spike into his ear.

Can you imagine such a thing? Ever heard of such a thing in all your writing about crime?"

"I think that's new."

"We got a print from the murder weapon, sort of a print. Say, was Charlie with you all the time you were out of the office?"

"Every second."

"Charlie doesn't look too good, Jack. He doesn't have a drinking problem, does he?"

"Not at all, Bill. He can drink anything he gets his hands on."

"Well, you fellows might hear more from us on this Lucan thing."

"You've already told us everything we know. I bought some books from him, period. There's a couple dozen like that in Chicago."

Brex gave me his serious look. "If you were there and found him and left, which is what we think happened, well, let it drop and stay away from it. Don't get involved in this kind of thing again, Jack."

"Don't worry." The lie crawled out of my throat. "The only crime I'm involved with goes on paper, and from deep history. I've had my taste of blood in the streets. And that cost me too much."

He smirked. "Like what?"

"It cost me a good story and the love of a girl."

"I notice that you put the story first." Brex pulled out a pipe and jammed it into his mouth. He began walking down the hall. "I don't want to see you again, Jack," he said softly over his shoulder, "unless you're asking for a file that's at least fifty years old."

"So long, Bill."

He didn't answer. I went into my office and slammed the door. Abbe was looking at me, defensive, her brow wrinkled right up to the curlers in her hair.

"Well, what could I say?" she said. "Those clowns barged in here and started slamming things around and banging the desk—well, Ackerly did. The other one is kind of nice."

"And you told them I went to see Lucan."

"You did, didn't you?"

"Did you talk to Lucan?"

"Well, yes, sure I did. I called him like you asked me to and he was there and I said you were on your way to see him. And he hung up."

"Did you call him back after that?"

"Yes . . . but how did you—"

"What for, if you already told him I was on my way?"

"Somebody by the name of Walter Cubbedge from the Inter-Ocean Bank called you, said it was urgent that he talk with you, so I called Mr. Lucan back to see if you were there . . . to give you the message." Her words slowed to a shuffle. "Someone picked up the phone down there, Jack, but they didn't say anything."

"Then what happened?"

"You tell me." She shook her head. "I'm no sleuth."

"What happened?"

"Someone put the phone back without talking, *whoever* it was." Abbe turned away, spinning about on her swivel chair to face her typewriter. She looked down at the keys pensively. "Was that you, Jack?"

I walked to the door leading to Charlie's office. "Yes."

"Was he dead then?" Her hands rested on the typewriter keys, limp.

"Yes, we found him dead and left."

Abbe inserted a piece of paper into the typewriter. "I'm glad you got out of there." She nodded to her own thoughts. "Good. Let the police handle it." She began to type. "Good, you're not going to be involved in this." Her speed mounted. "That's a relief." Her fingers danced on the keys, high velocity.

Closing the office door behind me, I faced Charlie, who sat stiffly at his desk, his elbows crooked as he held a large book awkwardly before his face. "There's nothing to say to me, Jack. I heard what you told them about the balloon man and all of it, Jack. I'll back you up on that. I saw the guy too, the balloon man, I mean. And they'll check and find the guy and he'll remember giving away a free balloon, a free balloon they always remember, as you know. That was smart to see that for a second and remember it and use it. Now we're completely out of it and—" He slammed the book shut and then down hard on his desk. "That makes me feel just fine!"

II

Doubtful Victim

1

By 5:00 P.M. I was back in my town house, turning on the air-conditioners to ward off the sweltering heat and suck up the humidity. Henry, the dog I had inherited from my ex-wife, Leila, was mooning about, sad, black-rimmed eyes staring up at me as I paced the living room. Upstairs, the vacuum was humming in the master bedroom; Josephine, my cleaning lady, was busy with her weekly chores, a good woman whose cleaning mania encompassed all manner of work disdained by any upstanding domestic. She defrosted my refrigerator, dusted the thousands of books on all three levels of the town house, even did the windows. Some days, if the maternal spirit moved her, she would prepare a little dinner for me before going home. Sweet lady.

I sat in the living room with walls of books shooting upward, listening to the drone of the vacuum cleaner and pondering Lucan's death. Many of the books on my shelves had come from old Lewis Lucan, and as I battled myself over the prospect of involving myself further in his death, I tried to pick out the tomes Lucan had sold to me. I could not find a one, but I knew they were there somewhere on the shelves. I sipped some cold tea, then slid into my sandals, went out the back door, and walked to the rear of the town-house complex, where two great birch trees stood next to the lake that lapped at the shore of the private beach. I sat at the end of the concrete ramp that ran down into the water, listening to the gentle waves slosh over the thousands of smooth pebbles and rocks that had washed up over the winter months.

I looked east and saw a cloudless sky growing dark blue beyond where Michigan lay and I thought of several states to the east of that and of New York and of Hugo Keimes, a bookdealer I had known almost as long as Lucan. A quarter of my crime library had come through Keimes. He never missed, nor did his foreign dealers. And who would want to kill Lucan anyway? What was this, coincidence? My library canceled, a visit to Lucan, who is dead in a grisly joke murder. Linked to my library, it had to be. Why? Keimes would know. He might not know he knew, but he would have part of it, probably.

But I had promised myself, *ordered* myself, never to get involved again with this sort of thing. I'd leave that for all the bright young and eager boys on the papers who considered themselves investigative reporters long before their editors told them they were. All those boys who drank too much gin and beer at O'Rourke's, or Billy Goat Tavern, who boasted about being able to turn Bernstein and Woodward upside down.

Of course, none of these lads knew how to decipher a Chicago Police blotter, or read a ledger in the archives at 26th and California. Christ. They'd probably never been down to 26th and California, where the old police records are kept. I laughed and remembered how in the old days I stole records out of that place, stuffing them into my waistband behind my suit coat. No, the investigative reporters today stole nothing. Nor did they lie, cheat, and weasel in the ways of Ben Hecht and Ring Lardner. They also didn't get the stories anymore. They were hand-out artists, taking the releases from the crime commissions and the Bureau and rewriting these and presenting them as vital discoveries. Well, to hell with it. Oh, eventually it might mean a journalism award of some sort, sure, and a raise, and then, gracious fate, a career in broadcast journalism. TV, the ultimate destination, the ultimate reward. Begin as an investigative journalist and end up anchoring a big-city news program or, if the right people died, stepped aside, were run over or pushed down an elevator shaft, a network anchor job with a million-dollar salary, a yacht bobbing at Marina Del Rey, a Palm Springs club membership, and, most important, your own makeup man. I never had such ambitions, but then I knew that I was warped.

Sitting at the end of the ramp that ran down to Lake Michigan, I listened to the waves slap harder at the shore. It was about as peaceful as it was ever going to get. I looked around at the birch trees and the barren ground about them. It would be nice to have some flowers or shrubs over there, I thought. Maybe I would plant some. Fill the place in with some green and red and yellow. Give it some color against the coming dreaded iron-gray winter months. No, I wasn't going to go to New York. I'd stay right here in my own backyard and plant some geraniums. Why not? Lucan's death was just inside the periphery of my life. Let Ackerly and Brex and others who liked rolling corpses over at the end of their shoes do all the hunting and picking and pointing. It wasn't any of my business. These days it was give me a geranium anytime.

"Mr. Journey! Mr. Journey!" It was Josephine calling from the back porchway of the town house, calling down the long, narrow walk leading behind the other town houses to the beach. Then Henry, my little half German shepherd, half Basenji, came dashing out, leaping and running like a miniature deer, barking wildly.

Henry dashed down onto the large concrete shelf and made for the waves, snarling and snapping at them, biting them and gulping water, leaping and jumping after the waves that relentlessly attacked him. He fought them stoutly, idiotically, and got drenched for his heroics. Josephine came down the walk toward me. "There's someone on the phone for you, Mr. Journey." She turned a black face that glistened in the late afternoon sun to the beach area to see Henry exhausting himself at the edge of the waves, dropping back as the water rushed inward, charging forward as each wave rolled outward.

"Now I'm gonna have the devil's time getting that dog back inside. He ran right out when I opened that door, and Lord, that dog is dripping wet!"

"That dog is crazy, Josephine. But don't let it bother you. He doesn't mind. Henry, come here!" Henry ignored my command. "Who's on the phone?"

"A man named Cubbedge, he said Walter Cubbedge, from some bank."

I looked at my watch. "The banks are all closed and the bankers have gone home to their double barbecue pits."

She ignored me and went after Henry, going down to the beach area, walking slowly, smiling as she took a Milk-Bone from the pocket of her cleaning smock, holding it up to entice the dog. Henry went on attacking the waves. Josephine was calling him by name over and over as I walked up to the town house. I went to the kitchenette area and picked up the receiver.

"John Howard Journey?" came a piping voice on the line.

"Yes."

"This is Walter Cubbedge, vice-president of the Inter-Ocean Bank."

"Where's that?"

"In the Loop, Mr. Journey. We're one of the biggest banks in town."

"I guess bigger is better in your business. But I bank at the Chicago Guarantee and Trust, so don't count on my trade to boost your assets."

The high-pitched voice gave a professional chuckle, then said: "Oh, no, no. It's this terrible news about Mr. Lucan who banked with us. His secretary, Ruth Snyder, called in all of his outstanding checks and one of these is a check made out to you in the amount of $3,300. She didn't believe she mailed this check to you but felt that it might have been one of Mr. Lucan's last acts before his unfortunate demise."

"I've never heard of a murder described so delicately, Mr. Cubbedge."

"How so?"

" 'Demise' is something that happens to wealthy old ladies and retired admirals."

"Murder, then, yes, as described in the late editions of the papers."

"Yeah, I read them."

"The question is, Mr. Journey, do you have Mr. Lucan's check?"

"I don't know," I lied. "I'd have to look over today's mail."

"Could you do that, Mr. Journey—while I wait on the phone?"

"I don't get this," I said, suspicious. "If Ruth Snyder wants to know these things, she ought to be on the phone, not you."

"Well, of course this is not normal procedure. The bank is presently closed, but I'm trying to expedite Mr. Lucan's outstanding checks. He was a personal friend and I know how much he valued your patronage. He spoke of you often, saying that he provided a great deal of background material for your historical column on crime. Now that he has passed on, I thought to help his estate by clearing as many of his checks as possible before probate court took the matter over. So, you see, I'm really trying to do you a favor. Once the courts take over Mr. Lucan's estate, all of his money will be tied up."

"That's uncommonly kind of you, Mr. Cubbedge."

"Think nothing of it, Mr. Journey. Could you look through today's mail now . . . while I wait on the phone? If you have the check, I think I can get it through the bank in the morning before the courts tie up the account."

"Hold on." I put down the receiver and stood thinking, staring at the phone mounted on the wall. I smelled the police. If I said I had the check, they would want to see the envelope in which it was mailed and I would have to lie about that. They were trying to put me at the scene, all right. They had gone through Lucan's outgoing mail and found a series of checks, that was it, and one was missing. Ruth probably went through her stubs and found out that it was the one made out to me. Why the hell did I take that check? Bonehead!

I picked up the phone and said: "I'm sorry, Mr. Cubbedge, no mail from the deceased Mr. Lucan."

There was silence at the other end, silence and heavy breathing in the background that my paranoia imagined. I could almost smell Ackerly's bad breath steaming through the line.

Walter Cubbedge then blurted: "Oh, well, I suppose there's nothing to be done. I'm afraid you'll have to wait for your money until probate settles the matter, Mr. Journey. I'm sorry I couldn't help you."

"That's all right. I'll survive."

"If by chance the check does arrive in the next few days —we understand how impossible the mails are—please give me a call. There might still be something I can do regarding this matter."

"Sure, thanks." I hung up.

Going downstairs to my writing den, I eased into the worn-out black leather chair that had held my bones before my Royal manual for so many years and slipped from beneath the desk blotter the check from Lucan. Nothing unusual about it but I knew I could kiss it good-bye. I crumpled up the check and was about to throw it into the wastecan, knowing I would have to take my chances with probate. Then I stopped for a moment, holding the ball of paper in my hand, tossing it up and down. I decided to keep it because I felt it might mean something later; but then, I kept everything. That was my problem. I collected, incessantly, almost impetuously, as I approached my fortieth year, not only books and records and massive memorabilia but scraps of paper, lists, pamphlets on extinct birds, and dining guides for restaurants shut down decades ago. It was all important or it would be. Hell, I might as well keep this useless check, too, I thought. Just another bit of paper inside a hundred tons of paper that weighed down the town house.

Yes, Cubbedge was acting on behalf of the police, I concluded. Trying to put me next to Lucan's corpse. Vice-presidents of banks don't circumvent probate courts. That's dangerous and bankers never peek over the edge of any cliff, never. No, it was all put up by Ackerly. He would think having Cubbedge contact me very clever. My admitting to having the check would be almost as good as a photograph of me posing with the dead book-dealer, Lucan seated and staring, me with my hand resting on his shoulder, grinning like a country cretin, an Iowa farm boy heading for the photographer's studio the first day in town to make sure history recorded his arrival. Sorry, Ackerly, it didn't work. I folded the check flat and shoved it under the blotter just as the phone rang. It was Charlie, nervous, the image of the dead Lucan dancing about his words.

"We were lucky, Jack, don't you think?"

"I don't know."

"Then that was a cop who came into the store when we were leaving?"

"Could have been Ackerly, for all I know. Same height, I would guess. It doesn't matter. Forget about it. We're done with it."

"What if they pull me in?"

"You tell the same story I told. Why incriminate yourself?"

"I know these birds, Jack. They won't come up with anything except us and then they'll start."

"They don't have us there. Period. Now stop thinking about it. Go to a movie, go see that space thing."

"That guy Ackerly is nuts, you know. He won't stop."

He was irritating me with his apprehension and I hated the fear in his voice. "For God's sake—what would they come up with? That I drove a spike into Lucan's ear because he reneged on a library purchase? Sure, I've got nothing else to do but bump off bookdealers."

"Remember that fight you had with that used-book dealer on Lincoln Avenue?"

"Fight? That was no fight. He sold me a library with six doubles in it and all I did was take the copies of the same books and toss them back into his store."

"Yeah—overhand pitches straight to the bean!"

"Now don't start."

"If the cops find out about us being at Lucan's, well, they'll use anything to build a case."

"Go to a movie, Charlie."

"I can't. Too nervous. I'd gag on the popcorn."

"Then get a couple of drinks."

"Okay, that'll calm me down. Where do we meet?"

I didn't want a couple of drinks, but Charlie did and it was necessary. "I'll see you in O'Rourke's in two hours."

"Can we make it in twenty minutes?"

"You can, but I'll be there in two hours. I want to clean up." I hung up, then turned off the lights in the den and went up the stairs to the third-floor bathroom, which sparkled and gleamed from Josephine's cleaning. I ran the shower and stood beneath the hot spray, lathering, thinking about Lucan's funeral and who would attend. He had been a loner with no family to speak of, and few friends. I wondered if his good friend Walter Cubbedge would be there.

2

O'Rourke's was jammed. A hot summer Tuesday night and the place looked like the beginning of a weekend, crammed with young types gulping beer. In the beginning, twenty years earlier, this had been a hangout for writers, newspaper people. Nelson Algren used to come in, but it had changed. Most of the writers had died, moved off, or joined AA, at least the ones I knew, and now it had become a meeting place for lawyers, young and old. Everybody was a lawyer these days, more than thirty-five thousand new lawyers each year swimming frantically upstream to hopeful practices.

The legal people had replaced the idling writers and as I passed the small booths, working through the crowd, I could hear snippets of conversation, all having to do with this case and that case and motions and pleadings. Not the title of a book, an author's name, a poem, a piece of doggerel, only the overflowing babble of the courtroom. I stopped midway down the bar and ordered a beer, then looked around to see Charlie leaning against a wall, gripping a stein and looking downward at the litter-strewn floor.

Charlie looked up, startled to see me standing before him. He took a gulping swallow from the stein of beer, his lower lip going quickly over the top one to work away the foam. His hand trembled a bit. "This Lucan thing," he said in a quiet voice, and shook his head.

"He's gone. If it will help you to calm down, think some bad thoughts about him."

"About the dead? The Catholic Church tells you plenty about that."

"He was a tough old buzzard, Charlie. He's gone."

"Bookdealers are classy guys and they don't get killed like that."

"Yeah, Lucan had a lot of class. In the old days when he had a little shop over on Sedgwick, he burned bound copies of *Punch* in his stove to keep his place warm in winter."

"Let's talk about anything except Lucan, okay?"

"Fine. I was thinking tomorrow I'd knock off in the morning and go to some nursery and buy some flowers to plant out by the beach."

"Huh? Flowers? You?"

"Yeah, geraniums, marigolds, that sort of thing."

"You never planted anything in your life." A weak smile came to his lips. "How come your thumb gets all of a sudden green?"

"Something to do, bring some life into a patch of ground. Lucan dies, plant some geraniums, I guess. Life for death."

"I won't be telling anyone about that one. Christ, if it got out that you were planting pansies—"

"Hey, Journey!"

I turned to see Champ Rimmel, a labor columnist and friend, standing rugged before me in a blue working-man's shirt, a large fist encircling a stein of beer. "Hello, Champ. What brings you into this gossipy hangout?"

Champ's intense blue eyes sparkled and slivers of light brown hair fell over a clear brow. His Irish jaw jutted when he talked. "I'm getting married and I thought I'd treat myself to a one-man bachelor party."

Charlie grinned and moved quickly to the bar, saying: "Let me buy a round on that."

"You guys look awful glum standing over here in the shadows."

"Just talking business, Champ."

We moved over to the bar to stand with Charlie, who was having difficulty getting the attention of the lone, much harassed bar lady. "Come on down to the front booths," Champ urged. "Bud Bible is over there being interviewed by some guy from *Newsweek*."

"Aw, I'm tired of listening to that guy Bible drone on about the poor working class," Charlie sneered.

"He's colorful," I said.

"And funny," Rimmel added.

"And he should have drowned in his own vomit years ago," Charlie replied in a low voice.

"What have you got against *him?*" asked Rimmel with genuine concern, as if a city icon had just been destroyed. Bible, of course, was Chicago's self-styled street chronicler of ultra-liberal bent who fought on radio and TV for the oppressed masses—whoever they were—and made a fortune doing it, living in a small mansion and wearing old-fashioned knit ties, checked shirts, corduroy jackets, and suede shoes, the usual chronicler's costume.

"I can't stand that guy," Charlie told Rimmel through curling lips. "He goes around getting other people's stories and uses them to make big money and then touts himself as just a plain old beat-up Chicago guy squinting savvy out of both eyes." Charlie downed his beer and tapped the stein on the bar to get the bartender's attention. She gave him an angry glance as she hurriedly served lawyers at the end of the bar.

"You want to go down and talk to Bud?" Rimmel asked me, turning his back on Charlie.

"I don't think so, Champ. I don't want to interrupt his interview with *Newsweek*."

"Christ, that's all that old blowhard does is interview. Gets interviewed, gives interviews, takes interviews. Interview Ike, that's what he is." Charlie's voice rose in volume over Rimmel's shoulder.

"He's a joke, you know. The way he talks you'd think he was born in a child-labor sweatshop or was the hero in Upton Sinclair's *Jungle,* working down at the yards a hundred years ago with those poor, dumb immigrant Polacks."

"Poles," Rimmel corrected him softly.

"Forget about Bud," I told Charlie. "He gets Chicago national press and network coverage."

"What's that got to do with it? So did John Wayne Gacy."

"C'mon, Charlie," I soothed. "The fellow's harmless. I like to listen to him talk. There's old southside Chicago in that voice."

"He's a ham actor."

"So are you," Rimmel said. He turned to face Charlie. "Especially when you get a couple of beers in you."

I put my hand on Rimmel's broad shoulder. "Charlie's got a lot on his mind right now. We had a pretty bad day."

"So why take it out on Bud?"

The bar lady stood before Charlie scowling. "What's the rush, Lindquist?" She was pretty, petite and dark. "There are other customers, you know. What'll it be?"

"We're celebrating Champ Rimmel's impending marriage," I told her. "Give him anything he wants, as long as it's domestic beer."

Rimmel held up his empty stein to indicate a draft.

"I need something stronger," Charlie snorted. "How about a Black Russian? Make it two. Jack will have one, right?" He turned to me, blinking.

"Sure, make it two."

The bar lady went off to get the drinks.

"Who's the lucky lady, Champ? Do we know her?"

"No, she wouldn't come into the dumps we hang around. She runs a string of boutiques."

"She's not a lawyer, is she?"

"No, Jack, just expensive clothes."

"Where'd a mug like you run into something elegant like that?" Charlie snorted.

"She read one of my columns about the Union Label commercial, you know, all those nice old ladies singing on TV, and wrote a letter and I had a date with her. Met her over by the *Tribune* building."

"I thought you didn't date blind from your fan mail," I said.

"Well," smiled Rimmel, "I was crafty. I had her wait for me in front of the *Tribune* building and told her to wear a little flower on her blouse. So I'd know her. Then I stood down on those stairs going to the underpass, sort of hid, peeking up from the stairs so I could see what I was meeting. Well, she was a pistol, a real looker, and I was up there bowing to her in a minute once I caught a gander."

"What if the dame had looked like a shipwreck?" asked Charlie.

Rimmel shrugged. "Then it's down the stairs quick, home, and to hell with it."

"You mean you would have let that woman stand there waiting for you if she hadn't been good-looking?"

"Sure. Think I'm the charity ward in Cook County Hospital?"

"That's a goddamned cruel way to think." Charlie was indignant at the prospect of Rimmel or anyone deserting an ugly woman.

"Look," Rimmel said defensively. "I only did it once and it turned out okay. So where's the harm?" He shrugged and began to walk toward the front of the bar. "C'mon, Jack, let's say hello to Bud."

I jerked my head in the direction of Rimmel to signal Charlie.

"Naw, I don't want to hear any more stories about how bad off other people are. I *work* for a living, Jack."

"I'll send your drink down," I told him, and moved off with Rimmel. Midway down the bar a long leg came out and into the crowded aisle in front of us, at the end of which was an expensive Gucci shoe. Jammed against the bar by knots of people on both sides was Kelso, another columnist. He slumped on a barstool, his thin frame sagging. Like others sitting belly-tight against the bar on stools, he barely had room to move, crowds of standing drinkers pressing in a second thick rank against him and the bar. Kelso clutched a bag with a bottle in it, which rested at his crotch. Rimmel laughed at the sight of him.

"Look at this guy, will you? He comes to a bar and brings his own."

Kelso, his horn-rimmed glasses sliding down a long nose, lifted the bottle to his lips with elbows pushed into his chest by other drinkers. He took a long pull and snorted: "Who can drink the swill they serve here? This is good stuff." He patted the bottle in the bag. "Napoleon brandy."

"They've got that behind the bar, Kelso," I told him.

"Smart, tough guy, aren't you, Journey?" he said through slippery lips.

"He's gone," Rimmel whispered. "Sober, he's like the rich drunk guy in *City Lights* who makes friends with Chaplin, the little tramp. Drunk, this guy Kelso is as mean as the rich guy is when sober in the movie, kicking people around."

"He writes a terrific column," I whispered back.

"You know, Journey," Kelso said to me with narrowing eyes. "I'm getting tired of reading about all those criminals you write about."

"Everybody knows you only read your own column," I said.

He waved me away with a tired arm, moving only from the elbow, customers pressing against him on either side pinioning his shoulders. "Aw, go away, Journey. You're bad news."

"And you're old news," I gave back to him. I guessed I liked him, though I didn't know him, even after twenty years.

"Someday all those Polish readers who live and breathe by your column," Rimmel said lightheartedly to Kelso, "will desert you."

"Never," Kelso exclaimed with a short laugh.

"They will when I put it in my column that you're really Czechoslovakian."

Kelso's eyes blazed open. He tried to lean forward menacingly, but the crowd around him pressed him backward. "That's a goddamned lie, Rimmel! That's the worst thing you could say. Christ, that's like calling a Serbian a Croatian. They kill for that!" He leaned backward, exhausted by his own outburst, and the crowd closed around him so that we could only see his Gucci shoes, the heels hooked to the metal bar of the stool where he sat.

"Jack! Jack!" The bar lady, her small body hidden by the crowd, was calling. I could see in her upraised arms, barely visible above the heads of the customers, a stein of beer and a Black Russian. I walked a few feet down the bar where there was a small opening, using my shoulder gently to push to the bar. Slipping the money onto the bar, I picked up Rimmel's stein of beer and stepped backward to hand it to him. A line of people in front of those pressed to the bar on stools moved over and closed the gap like a wave covering a small reef.

"It's hell to get a drink in here," Rimmel said. "Look, someone's moving aside. There's your drink on the bar."

I began to move forward, and in that instant I saw a hand reach over my drink, hover for a moment, the hand of someone sitting at the bar whose body was shielded by the crowd behind him. The hand, wearing a large sapphire pinkie ring, fluttered for a moment over my drink and, in a second, dropped something white and powdery into the Black Russian. I reached through the narrow opening between a slim, attractive brunette and her well-suited escort and retrieved my drink, straining to look down at it, where I saw a grainy substance coating the ice cubes floating on top.

Turning to Rimmel and holding up the glass, I said: "Did you see that?"

"Yeah." The single word came out of him with long amazement. "Jesus, you just got a Mickey!"

"I want to see *this* guy," I said, holding the glass protectively to my chest, pushing hard into the standing couples so that they separated with startled looks. Sitting at the spot where the hand came from was a man in a conservative blue business suit and a head of thick gray-black hair, late fifties. I tapped him on the shoulder and he turned with a puzzled look on his face, which was wide with full cheeks and a heavy neck that bulged over a tight white collar. I looked down to see a sapphire ring on the little finger of his left hand.

"You just put something in this drink, pal." I held up the glass.

"What?" He glanced down at the drink and then up at me. "I don't know what you're talking about." He nudged a man, a bit younger, sitting next to him, dressed as he was, uncommonly businesslike for O'Rourke's. "I think this guy's drunk."

"He's not drunk," Rimmel said as he moved to my side. "I saw you do it too. You dropped some crap into his drink."

The businessman snorted. "Two drunks," he said.

Pushing the drink forward, I held it almost under his nose. "Take a close look at this," I said with plenty of anger. "What's the idea? I don't even know you."

Without moving his head, he looked down into the glass in front of his face. With the same even voice he said: "And I don't know you either. So that should end that." He turned slowly, swiveling on the barstool so that he faced the cloudy back mirror, as did his friend, casually lifting his own mixed drink to thick lips.

Standing sideways, I pushed in next to him and set the glass down in front of him. "You had better explain," I said, and it was an order. I found myself clenching and unclenching my fist rapidly as I rested it next to him on the edge of the bar.

"I don't have any idea of what you're talking about," he said. "Here, let me see that." He grabbed the glass and then turned around, holding up the glass to the dim light overhead, as if to inspect the murky liquid. "Looks all right to me," he said with an innocent voice, "whatever this is." He began to turn back, and as he did the glass slipped from his hands, crashing to the floor, shattering. He stood up slowly, a heavy tall man. "Oh, I'm so sorry," he said, a voice full of mock apology. As he slipped from the barstool he stepped on the broken glass, breaking the pieces into even tinier fragments. He threw his hands out for a second, as if it couldn't be helped. "Look, let me buy you another. What are you drinking?"

I glanced toward the opposite wall to see Rimmel talking to Charlie, who had just moved down the bar. Charlie was staring at the broken glass on the floor.

The businessman stood there with a stupid, helpless look on his face and a faint smile at the corners of his mouth, a look that angered me. "Anything you like, I'd be glad to pay for it."

"Keep your drinks," I said quickly, and shoved him aside with my shoulder. "I want to see tomorrow." When I pushed him away from the spot, he dragged one foot that rested on the glass, trying to keep it beneath his weight. One large piece of glass remained and I stooped and picked it up, holding it by a jagged tip. I pulled out my handkerchief and wrapped it thickly about the glass and put this in my pocket. "I'll know exactly what you dropped into that drink in a half hour."

The heavy man in the blue suit reached out and touched his friend's shoulder. "Come on, this place is full of paranoid crackpots," he said. The other man got up obediently and both of them began to work their way out of the bar, moving sideways through the crowd. I noticed that they raised manicured fingers to gently wedge their way along, tapping shoulders, murmuring "excuse me" as they went their very polite way.

"What the hell was it, Jack?" Charlie's face was flooded with apprehension. "That guy Mickey Finn you?"

"No, I don't think it was a knockout drop at all."

Rimmel shook his head: "I never saw anything like that. If I hadn't seen it and you told me about it, I would have thought that you were just off on one of your stories. But Christ Almighty, I saw it. Who was that guy?"

"Who was that guy, Jack?" Charlie repeated, anxious.

"I don't know. A total stranger."

"Maybe he was just screwing around," Rimmel guessed. "People do crazy things in this bar."

"Maybe he was just trying to put you on," Charlie suggested hopefully. "Sure, he probably just dropped some sugar into your drink, that's it."

"More like arsenic," I said while looking toward the entranceway, where the two businessmen were leaving.

"I'm going to find out about this," I said. I could feel angry blood pulsating at the side of my head. I made a move toward the front door.

"I'm not coming," Charlie said.

"Suit yourself."

"More goddamned trouble."

"I'll see you."

I plunged into the crowd, pushing hard toward the front door.

"All right," I heard Charlie say behind me, "let's go."

                              3

We squeezed through the crowd piled up in front of O'Rourke's and burst outside into the muggy night air. Crowds were flowing into the place as I stepped into North Avenue, busy with rushing traffic, to look down the line of parked cars. Almost a block east I saw the two businessmen getting into a long Lincoln.

Charlie came up behind me. "See them?"

"In that Lincoln."

"Look, Jack," he said breathing rapidly, "why don't you just forget it? Probably some crank pulling a practical joke, something for his friend. Happens all the time in that joint."

"No." I turned and began walking in the street toward

my Pontiac, which was illegally parked on the opposite corner, facing in the same direction as the Lincoln.

Charlie raced after me, standing on the other side of my car as I hurriedly unlocked the door. "What the hell you gonna do? I mean, if you could've caught them on the street and bopped the guy, okay. But now what the hell can you do?"

"I'm going to follow the bastard. I'd like to know where a practical joker like that lives." I kept glancing down the street to watch for the Lincoln; its lights went on.

Slapping the top of the Pontiac in frustration, Charlie nearly shouted: "This is something for the cops, Jack, not you, not again. Please!"

"By the time the cops got here O'Rourke's will be closed and the drunks will have taken over the sidewalk." I finally managed to unlock the door to the car. I jerked the door open, angry over my own nervousness. I could see the Lincoln trying to move out of its tight parking spot. I slipped into the car and unlocked the other door. Charlie opened it and bent downward, staring at me but not getting in.

"Those guys could be killers, Jack, did you ever think of that?"

"I thought you said practical jokers, which is it? C'mon, get in or close the door!"

He jumped in, slamming the door. "Why do I do this, why?" Charlie stared straight ahead.

"You do it because you love it," I said, starting the car and pulling it out into the street. The Lincoln had freed itself and had moved off slowly, stopping for a red light. I raced after it. "Yeah, my friend, you love it, can't get enough of it."

"Hate it, it's dumb, this going your own way like this, asking for trouble."

I kept my eye on the Lincoln, pulling up behind it. The

two men in the car were talking casually, it seemed, as they moved their heads slowly to look at each other. Muggy though the night was, they dangled clean hands encased in starchy white shirts from the open windows. Well, maybe Charlie didn't love it, but I did, reacting to what others did to you. Somewhere deep inside of me lurked a suppressed vigilante. Or a militiaman. Sure, why not? You'd have been at Concord and Lexington, right? Hell, Sam Adams got all those boys drunk, telling them that the British were coming to take away their muskets, whipped them up good. They all had the blind staggers when they moved out onto the green to pop away at those redcoated troops in neat file.

The Lincoln began to pull away with the green light. I followed slowly, keeping a long distance. It turned left onto La Salle and then again onto Clark Street, going north.

"Why don't we stop a cop if we see one along the way and have him pull those guys over."

I didn't look at Charlie as I drove, staring straight ahead at the crawling Lincoln, wondering when the businessmen would spot us.

Charlie craned his neck, jerking his head about. "I'm looking for a cop, Jack."

"And the *Robert E. Lee*. Forget it. All I want to do is find out where these characters live."

Gripping the dash, Charlie said: "If that guy did drop something in your drink, something that would do more than give you stomach cramps and the runs, then he meant to bump you, then it's got something to do with Lucan, right?"

"I don't know."

The Lincoln began to speed up.

"That's it, isn't it? Lucan gets croaked and before the day is out—because somebody knows we were in that damned warehouse—you get some crap dumped into your drink. Think that's it?"

I pushed my foot downward on the accelerator, keeping pace with the Lincoln. "I don't know, Charlie, but I think those people know we're behind them."

Charlie nodded his head and muttered, "Oh, Jesus."

The Lincoln raced up Clark, going right onto Lincoln Park West and then roaring away. I was right behind him. People in the park, walking dogs, jogging, spooning, scheming, suddenly stopped as both cars rushed past them.

"Should pick up a cop now," Charlie moaned. "You're doing forty in a twenty-five zone—and you just went through a stop sign!"

"So did they."

"Hey, hey, the guy on the passenger side is leaning out of the car. I think he wants to talk!"

"Not at forty miles an hour."

The Pontiac hit every bump and patchwork piece of road, jumping and jerking at the high speed. The Lincoln sailed on smoothly.

"The guy's pointing at me," Charlie said, leaning forward to see. "Christ, Jack! He's got a gun!"

"Get down, under the dash!"

"What are you gonna do?" Charlie put his head down, leaning sideways toward me.

"Run them down, smash them, if I have to."

I heard the shot, like the popping of a large air-filled plastic bag. Then another.

"They're shooting, God damn it!" Charlie had his head down toward me, but his shoulder jutted above the dash. "Now, enough is enough, Jack, Jesus!"

We were gaining on the Lincoln. People in the park were running into the wooded areas, diving behind bushes, shouting.

The Lincoln was fast approaching Fullerton Avenue. He would turn right and head for Lake Shore Drive, I knew. I was closing in on Mr. Businessman. Then, in a second, the windshield on Charlie's side cracked open, a thousand tiny cracks in the glass spreading like a miniature sunburst. Charlie lurched sideways, striking me.

"The bastard shot me!" He slid downward, turning his back against the seat, clutching his right shoulder. Blood appeared between his fingers.

"Hold on," I told him.

"I'm shot up, Jack!" He kicked the floor in pain and as he did his head lifted my hand from the wheel, which jerked to the right. I hit the brakes, but it was too late. We dove over the curb and roared into the park. I leaned on the horn, jamming it, grabbing the wheel again with both hands. A clump of bushes came up fast and the Pontiac flattened them and then another clump and another as we slowed. Behind the last high bush was a tree. We hit this at slow speed. I braced myself and held on to Charlie. He rolled forward and down onto the floor at impact. My arm, which I threw up at the last second, struck into the windshield.

We were stopped. The front of the Pontiac was crumpled, the hood bent backward, the radiator spouting. One of the headlights had been ripped upward so that it illuminated the tall oak we had struck. I saw the Lincoln turn right going at high speed toward Lake Shore Drive. Not a cop in sight.

I helped Charlie sit up, holding him by his uninjured arm. "Take it easy," I told him. "Rice Hospital is just a few blocks from here."

A squad car pulled up to the curb near the park and two officers came running.

Charlie gave out a long groan when looking at his shoulder, holding his hand tightly over the wound. "I can't stand looking at that blood."

"Don't look at it."

Several strollers in the park hovered about the car. I turned off the ignition. A grizzled man stumbled forward to stare at Charlie. He put his head into the car.

"Get the hell out of here," Charlie said to the derelict, wincing in pain.

"No, no, you guys got me all wrong," the old wino wheezed. "I'm here to help . . ." His words were slush as he weaved crazily before Charlie, steadying himself by holding on to the door where the window was open. "I'm helpin' ya . . . helpin' ya—jus' gimme the booze before the cops get over here! Hurry up, fellas, slip me the booze . . . I'll hide it, I'll hide it good." His smile was a toothless maw. He began backing away from the car, as did the large circle of people around us, as the cops approached, faces grim, hands resting on their gun holsters, unbuckling them.

"Gimme the booze," said the drunken old man, cackling. "They'll have to cut me open to find it." He cackled louder. "Jus' slip me the booze, boys, slip me the booze. . . ."

III

Blood Vow

1

"It's always me, never you." Charlie was lying on a hospital gurney, stripped, a sheet over him and a pressure bandage covering his shoulder. The gurney was against the wall, where several other gurneys before and after Charlie's were lined up with injured people, all waiting, as he was, to be rolled into surgery. He looked up at me with an expression of complete disgust. "Did you ever notice how it's always me who gets the whopping, never you? And it's you who gets us into these things?"

"Lie still and keep quiet. You'll only aggravate yourself." He had a point, but no one had ordered him to get involved. "And stop complaining. This is the first time you've ever been shot."

He turned his face to the wall. "And the last, believe me! God damn it, this thing hurts."

"If you're going to get shot, you couldn't pick a better spot. Take a look at the thing, will you? Hell, that's a Robert Taylor wound, a Hollywood wound."

Charlie worked his head onto his chest and looked sideways. "Crapola—in the movie it's a fake little blood blister with a tiny explosive, and it ain't real—this is real, God damn it."

"You heard the doctor, Charlie. Flesh wound, like in the movies. They'll have the bullet out of you in a half hour. You get to take a vacation for a few days—"

"And I'll have a hole in me for the rest of my life."

"There won't even be a scar."

"C'mon, no scar?"

"Maybe a little one. Everybody who's lived any kind of full life should go to his grave with a few good scars and at least *one* bullet wound."

Cops, dozens of them, were roaming up and down the large, long corridor of the emergency wing of Rice Hospital. It was to this place that all those under arrest, wounded in burglaries, robberies, gang fights, and domestic battles occurring on the great northside of Chicago, were brought. The corridor echoed with noise while the expressionless cops stood next to victims and attackers, taking officious notes for their reports.

The cops who had responded to our car crash had already taken the description of the Lincoln and the men in it and the man who had fired at us. I had neglected to tell them we were in high-speed pursuit of these two, stating only that one of them had dropped something into my drink and that we had followed them, were shot at, and were sent out of control and into Lincoln Park. One of the cops, Sergeant Roy Barker, I had known for years. His wife and my wife, when I had a wife, had known each other. He had been shocked to find me sitting stupidly in the car smashed up against that oak tree, but he had also been kind enough to drive us up to Rice so that Charlie could be treated, rather than waiting for an ambulance that might arrive in a day or so. I had given Barker the piece of glass I had pocketed at O'Rourke's, and he had gone off to the police lab to see what the well-dressed gent had slipped into my drink. His partner, a dedicated rookie, had stayed at Rice, writing out the report. He sat in the corridor on a wooden bench, scribbling on a legal-sized stenciled sheet, occasionally looking over to where Charlie sprawled and I stood.

Charlie began rolling his head back and forth. "Jack, ask that hatchet face of a nurse to get over here and give me another shot."

"Be quiet."

"Get me another shot, damn it, you know everybody around here."

"No, I don't. Take it easy. You've got a fat shot of Demerol in you and that will take care of you for now."

"Demerol? I thought it was morphine."

"Morphine is no longer the preferred choice and is used mostly on terminal patients, Charlie."

"How would you know that?" His voice was getting weaker.

"I've been on the terminal list, almost at the end of the line once, almost missed the last train from Madrid."

"Morphine is stronger, Jack. Get me something stronger like morphine."

"You want to turn into an addict?"

"I want to get out of this goddamned pain." He tried to turn his head and look upward and down the corridor to the swinging doors of the operating room where nurses had wheeled another patient inside, making Charlie next.

"Get me in there, Jack. I could be dying of lead poisoning."

"You're next. It's all fixed."

"I'm glad you knew that croaker, what's his name?"

"Pudvah."

"Yeah . . . Dr. Pudvah . . ." His words came slowly. He was groggy from the shot and the pain was driving him downward, ever downward into unconsciousness. It was the best thing for him. I felt bad about Charlie, and it was true, I had gotten him into it. I didn't have to ask. He was a loyal friend, the most loyal friend I ever had, one who would never have let me go off alone after two slick guys casually dosing my drink, not Charlie. That's why he was lying on the gurney, doped up and in pain, taking it for me. I felt like hell about that, but over that, like a heavy blanket, was a seething anger at the men who could pick me out of a crowd and junk up my drink and then shoot my friend. It had to do with Lucan, sure, but what did it have to do with Lucan? The man standing in the doorway when we left Lucan's warehouse—he could have been the businessman in O'Rourke's, about the same height and heavy build. He could have been.

"I've got this finished here," said the rookie cop, coming up to me. His nameplate read *S. Trubner*. "You want to look it over, Mr. Journey?"

"Sure." I took his clipboard and read the routine report, which detailed the shooting and the accident. Short, sweet, and with no real answers.

"Officer," came a voice with a thick Spanish accent. It was the man on the gurney behind Charlie's. He was reaching out feebly for the rookie. S. Trubner gave him a quick glance, then looked back to the report I held in my hand.

"Okay with me, I think you've got it all." I handed it back to him.

"Officer, please . . ." The man on the next gurney begged for attention.

The rookie turned his head, annoyed. "Yeah?"

"I gotta confess something," the man said.

"So confess," S. Trubner said without interest.

"That jewelry store robbery." The man raised his arm to a bandaged head. There were small cuts all over his hand. "The one at Wilson and Clark, you know, big jewelry store robbery." His words were like Charlie's, slowed by Demerol.

The rookie suddenly took notice of the man and moved close to him. "What about that robbery?"

"I might die inside that room over there," the man said with genuine apprehension. "I gotta tell it before that happens maybe so I don't burn in hell for killing that nice man, the owner, Mr. Spinoza, you know?"

Leaning close to the man, the rookie said: "I don't know. I didn't get the call. But go ahead and tell me anyway."

I looked over to Charlie. He had passed out. A nurse pushed open the doors to the operating room. Her olive-green scrubs were coated with dried blood.

"Poor Mr. Spinoza," rambled the man to the rookie. "I didn't mean to kill that poor old man, kind man who gave to all the . . . charities . . . bought presents for the kids . . . hid the ones without the green cards . . . got them work. . . . Poor old guy."

"Are you saying that you did the robbery and the killing?"

"I did it!" screamed the man on the gurney. "It was me!"

S. Trubner quickly lifted his clipboard, flipped the page containing the report on Charlie and me, and began scribbling on a fresh form. "Go ahead."

"Now I can . . . go to my Maker a clean man. You gotta go clean if you're a Catholic, officer, you go clean. If you go dirty . . . then you are in the mud for eternity, you know?"

"Go ahead—get it off your chest," the rookie urged him.

The man's hand slid across his bandaged head and fell lamely to his chest. The nurse who was coated with blood rushed to the man and felt his pulse at the carotid, then listened for a heartbeat.

"Is he okay?" The rookie's young face was squeezed into a look of deep concern. "Try to bring him around. I need to get the rest of his statement."

"I think he's dead," the nurse said with a tired sigh.

"Try to bring him around, can't you?"

"I have to get a doctor," she said, going down the corridor to the emergency room. "The doctor has to pronounce him dead." She gave me a quick look and said: "Your man is next." She pushed through the swinging doors of the emergency room.

"God damn it," gritted S. Trubner. "I almost had a good collar."

Another cop came down the corridor, and to his hand was manacled a burly black man, his face and arms covered with cuts and crusted blood. The rookie stepped into the middle of the corridor and stopped him. "Hey, sergeant," he said while pointing to the silent man he had been talking to. "This guy here just admitted killing a jeweler named Spinoza in a robbery over at Wilson and Clark tonight. You think the captain would mind if I took the collar for this one? The guy's dead but he admitted everything before he died."

The sergeant, a big-chested cop in his mid-fifties with a weathered face and a grim mouth, looked over to the dead man, then moved closer to scrutinize him. He straightened. Then he clucked his tongue. "You nuts?" he said to the rookie. "*That's* the jeweler, Spinoza." The sergeant yanked hard on the handcuffs holding his prisoner, who grimaced in pain. "This is the son of a bitch who robbed him!" He shook his head sadly when looking back to the dead man. "A tough old bird, Spinoza. This guy I got here hits the old man on the head with a gun butt and the old man drives him through his front window. Christ,

I saw it all, I was just driving by Spinoza's store when it happened. And you mean to tell me that Spinoza there told you that *he* did the robbery? Poor old guy must have been out of his skull." The sergeant turned full face to his silent, sullen prisoner. "Now, it's a murder rap for you, asshole." With a yank on the cuffs, the sergeant dragged the prisoner down the hall and into a waiting room.

The rookie turned to me, perplexed. "Why would Spinoza say he was the robber? Why would he do that?"

"To get into Heaven, why else?"

"Heaven's all right if you gotta go there," Charlie said, coming out of it briefly, struggling to speak like a man swimming upward from the bottom of the ocean, kicking against crosscurrents, upward toward the light and the surface. "I'm getting my exercise, Jack, really."

"You're doing a good job, Charlie. You look trim."

An orderly pulled the gurney that held Mr. Spinoza out of line and began wheeling it away from the operating room, toward the deep freeze. Other orderlies moved up the gurneys behind.

The nurse with the bloody scrubs reappeared with an intern, and they began to push Charlie toward the operating room.

"Okay," Charlie raved on, "so I exercise by walking only two blocks a day to the store and back, but that's more than enough."

"How do you figure that?" I asked him.

He smiled knowingly inside the drug that gripped his mind. "Add it up. In one week I walk a mile, in a year, fifty-two miles, in ten years, five hundred and twenty miles. Anyone who can walk five thousand two hundred miles will certainly live to be a hundred. See how simple it is?"

"Clear as a sleepy lagoon, my friend."

They were pushing him through the doors. I could see

Dr. Pudvah and others waiting beneath the hot white lights for him. Charlie looked at me, riveting his eyes on me.

I gave him a smile and a weak wave. "You'll be fine."

Then a light shone in his eyes and for a moment he was lucid, working his head upward. Before he disappeared behind the swinging doors, he shouted: "Buy another god-damned library, will you—anything—join the Book-of-the-Month Club!"

The doors swung shut. I started to walk up the hospital corridor, feeling miserable as the image of my friend going under the knife rushed to my brain. But it wasn't Charlie anyone wanted to kill, it was me, and whoever it was and for whatever reason, they would go on trying to kill me, I was positive. And I didn't even know what it was all about, like old man Spinoza who had just died back there telling a rookie cop, a stranger, that he was his own killer. I was no stuttering victim, I told myself, not me. If I was going to get killed, I was damned sure that I would know *why* before it happened, if it happened. And if it did, I'd take as many of the bastards trying to get me as I could. I'd take those two smug bastards in the blue serge suits first, one for Charlie and one for me.

I felt braver than I knew I would ever be. But my anger was real, stronger than bravery, and I would count on the anger to last beyond where courage evaporated. The anger would carry me and you could think about the bravery later when your knees began to knock and the nerves in your hands started leaping.

2

Sergeant Barker caught me just as I was leaving the hospital. The burly cop held a lab report in his large, gnarled hands, rubbing his thumb nervously up and down the side of the page. We stood in the lobby foyer, where attractive receptionists softly answered incoming calls, their voices hardening when asking if the callers had medical insurance.

"This is bad, Jack," Barker said, turning the report over to me as if handing me a urine sample, holding the single page by its corner, squeezed between thumb and forefinger. "The boys found a few grains of sodium cyanide on that sliver of glass you gave me. I guess those guys meant business."

"Charlie thought they were practical jokers."

"You wouldn't have died laughing." He thought for a moment, removing his hat to reveal a high forehead with wrinkles. "You know, I saw a woman once who had been poisoned by cyanide . . . her husband, an insurance broker, had been feeding the stuff to her slowly. When she died she bent her body like a bow. The pain must have been terrible."

I slipped the report into my inside coat pocket. "What have you got on those two fellows?"

Barker shrugged. "Found the Lincoln parked near Belmont Harbor. A rental which was stolen from a couple in from Des Moines, staying at the Americana Congress. It was stolen right out of the hotel parking area." Sergeant Barker gave me his most solemn look. "This is very serious, Jack. These guys went way out of their way to nail you. What kind of people you been writing about lately?"

"Only dead ones. This doesn't have anything to do with my column."

"Charlie gonna be all right?"

"Yes, he was lucky, the bullet chewed up the meat of his shoulder, no bones smashed."

"That guy was always lucky," Barker said with a slight smile. "Now if that had been me, the way my luck is, I would've gotten that slug right here." He jabbed the middle of his forehead with his thumb. "By the way, that homicide guy, Ackerly, wants to talk to you. He left word over at our precinct. Says you should call him."

"What for?" I knew what for; Ackerly was still figuring that I had seen Lucan before the body was discovered when he learned about Charlie getting shot and the cyanide dosing; he was putting something together. He was no slouch.

"Well, hell, Jack," Barker said in a half-apologetic voice, "Charlie gets shot, you almost get poisoned—that's attempted murder. And that's homicide, Ackerly's job, you know, homicide. You'll have to give him a report, probably. It's routine."

"I know about these routine reports. Some years back I was writing a column about some Mafia thugs in East Chicago and I received a call, a death threat against the piece I was writing. The usual thing—if you publish that story we'll cut your throat in the middle of Rush Street—I was naive in those days and contacted the police to report the call. Two detectives from homicide sat in my office, bored to tears, writing down everything. When we finished, I asked them: 'What happens now?' One of the plainclothes guys replied: 'Simple. If we find your body in the middle of Rush Street or floating in the Chicago River, we'll have this report to start with.' "

Barker looked away from me as I talked, fixing his gaze on the attractive receptionists, listening to me and shaking his head. I put my hand on his shoulder and concluded: "I now realize, Roy, that it is best not to bother the police with unimportant matters . . . while you are still alive."

"Aw, Ackerly's not like those guys," Barker said.

"Sure he is. He's the one who took the report. I've got to get home, Roy, got to call a cab. I'll talk to Ackerly later."

Barker patted my back reassuringly. "C'mon, I'll take

you in my squad. It's the least I can do for a guy who almost had his back arched like a bow." We started out the hospital entrance, toward the circular drive where his squad car was parked. "Did I ever tell you about this dingey waitress over on Division Street who went nuts one morning and dropped a whole bottle of lye in a big pot of freshly made chili? Christ Almighty, her customers were dying and had the runs at the same time." He made a sound that was between a gasp and laugh. "The old broad was getting even for every tip she never got—what a mess when I ran in there. Customers rolling around on the floor, screaming and going in their pants and this old broad is just standing there, nonchalant as can be, making out their checks behind the counter. Course, I was just a green kid then . . ."

I knew exactly what I was going to do before I went through the front door of my town house. Barker's last words to me when dropping me off in the front parking area were about calling Ackerly, a firm request instead of a polite order. It was the same thing. This was police business and I had better cooperate. But it was now my business and my life. I immediately raced downstairs to my lower den and retrieved the check from Lucan and the Keimes letter. Reaching for my desk phone, I got my secretary, Abbe, in three rings. I asked her to take Henry for a few days. She grumbled but said she'd come right over. Then I went up the two flights of stairs to my bedroom, where I slid back the large doors of the closet that ran along the entire wall. From the shelves high above the suit and shirt racks I dragged down a suitcase and a hang-up bag, throwing these on the king-size bed and opening them. I packed hurriedly, throwing underwear, socks, a few ties, and toiletries into the case, then several pressed slacks on top and then shirts from the hangers, folding them while listening to an all-talk station. It would be on the damned news, I was sure, as soon as it hit the hour. In ten minutes a woman announcer with crisp *R*'s and sharp *T*'s was reporting the shooting of Charlie Lindquist, researcher to John Howard Journey. There was no mention of the poisoning attempt. With her next breath the female announcer—I imagined her to be a hot-looking brunette, but she was probably a grandmother with lumbago—was reporting the mysterious murder of Lewis Lucan. The shooting and the murder were treated separately, unrelated violence in a sprawling city where such news was terribly common.

I finished packing the case by neatly folding my shirts, squaring them off, collar frontward, and placing them on the doubled slacks. My former wife, Leila, never could pack shirts well, I remembered then, but I had had experience packing. I had been packing all my life, ever since I had traveled with my mother, way back there in the forties when she was singing cross-country in garish cabarets and theaters that smelled of ammonia. The suits and sport coats I put on hangers in the hang-up bag. Then I went to the closet where my two tuxedoes were hanging, pushed these aside, and looked at the .38 hanging in my old service shoulder holster.

Don't touch that, I told myself. It's a keepsake only, a memento, nothing you walk around with. It had been in the closet for years, hanging behind the tuxedoes. It had been more than a decade since that holster was strapped across my back and that was in another country, at a time when I had had the authority to wear it or as much authority as you were allowed in counterespionage, which was no authority at all from the country in which you did your bizarre business. American authority was enough in those days of Pax Americana.

I lifted the holster and held it, slipping out the .38,

checking it. I had kept it clean all these long years, out of habit, or an old promise never to use it again but to keep it and remember that I had used it. Put it back on the wall behind the tuxedoes, I told myself lamely. You're not in the service of your country now. You're like every citizen now, without arms and wars and revolutions. You are in a civilized land of laws and police. You are protected. I slid the holster and revolver into the case beneath the underwear, then took a box of ammunition from the bottom drawer of my bureau and put it in the same place before zipping the case shut.

I took the bags downstairs. Henry was waiting, staring upward with those huge brown eyes, panting, mouth open in what could almost be a happy grin. The house was hot and humid and I turned on the air-conditioner. Next I put through a call to O'Hare Airport and booked a flight leaving for New York in forty-five minutes. Just as I put the phone back on the hook the front-door bell rang. It was Abbe, fuming.

"This isn't really part of my job, you know, Jack?" She slammed the door closed and marched in, dressed in a low-cut cocktail number, looking more elegant than I had seen her in years.

Henry pranced and jumped around her, curled tail wagging so hard that his hindquarters went out of balance and he flopped on his side before jumping up again.

"What's wrong with this dog?" Abbe said, sidestepping the front paws that went up to greet her.

"Probably hungry." I went into the kitchenette and dug out Henry's food, filling his bowl. He scampered after it.

"How can you treat a dog like that, Jack? You can't forget to feed an animal. They eat regularly, like humans, you know?" I threw some cans and dry food into a bag and handed it to her.

"This dog lies around on thick carpet all day, has a

dozen toys to play with, listens to stereo, has its own bed—" I pointed to an alcove where Henry's bed was wedged between two bookshelves. "And gets walked three times a day in the most exclusive vacant lots on the northside of Chicago." I handed Henry's leash to her.

"How exclusive?"

"Of course, Henry's a lone Democrat in a herd of pampered Republican canines. But he deals with snobbery by exhibiting marvelous indifference to poodles wearing rhinestone collars, poodles whose owners spend thousands on them each year, buying them gourmet food and having Korean manicurists visit them in their penthouse pads." She was staring at me as if I had gone mad. "No, it's true," I continued. "And the owners walking these haughty little bitches exhibit the same snooty temperament. There's one woman who walks her dog to the lot wearing diamond bracelets and sparkling necklaces. Her dog also has a diamond collar—"

"What? Diamonds on a dog? What kind of woman is that?"

"Merely the standard neighbor around here, but if you must know, she is the kind of woman who buys a pedigreed dog, walks it on a diamond-studded collar, and then looks the other way when her Pekingese poops."

"Do you realize that I've got a date tonight and he's outside in the car waiting, and now we've got to take Henry over to my place, where he'll probably go all over the floor?"

"Henry's too well mannered to do that. Besides, Josephine walked him a few hours ago before she went home. Who's your date?"

"A wealthy young podiatrist." She bent down and slipped the collar onto Henry, who had finished his meal. "A *normal* human being who makes his living without wallowing in crime."

"And grew rich slicing off ingrown toenails, I know."

Abbe clipped the leash to the collar and headed for the door, holding Henry's bag of food.

Opening the door for her, I reminded her to "give him a can of food each day and mix that high-protein grain, no more than two good handfuls, with each bowl. He gets walked before you leave for the office, when you come home, and about ten o'clock at night. And give him plenty of water."

"You sure you don't want me to sing to him before he goes to sleep?"

"Just a couple of bars of 'Rose of Washington Square,' I'll be in New York for a few days, at the Algonquin."

"Did you make reservations?" She stood at the door, the leash taut as Henry pulled against it, wanting to dash out to the small patio that led to the stairs going to the parking area, where a new Cadillac sat idling, lights glaring.

"They'll let me in when I show up. I know them, they know me."

"Who do you think you are—Alexander Woollcott? They don't know you that well. I'll call and get you a room when I drop Henry at my place. What's this all about, Jack?"

"I had a little trouble tonight. I'm going away for a few days to rest up."

Henry was pulling hard at the leash and Abbe had all she could do to hold her ground. "What kind of trouble?"

"Someone tried to poison my drink in O'Rourke's. We followed him in my car, someone shot at us and Charlie was slightly wounded."

"What—wounded?" Her eyes widened with fright.

"He'll be all right. He's over at Rice for a few days. Visit him. Take him a couple of books on the movies." I handed her the card of the towing service that had hauled away my Pontiac from Lincoln Park. "The car was a little bent out of shape when we were forced off the road when this fellow shot Charlie."

"You call that a *little* trouble?"

"Pick up the car when it's ready. I'll call you from New York when I get to the Algonquin."

Abbe puffed up her cheeks and blew out the air slowly. "Mr. Journey, working for you is like walking up and down a dark train tunnel, waiting for the express to flatten you." She walked into the patio, jerking Henry in her direction, saying to the dog: "Come on, pooch. I'm taking you to someplace sane." Then, over her shoulder to me: "You're not kidding me. You're going to New York because of this Lucan thing." She was down the stairs, turning to face me for a moment. "I hope your insurance is paid."

"I've left everything to Henry with you as guardian. If anything happens to me, get him the usual stuff—diamond slave bracelets and winter booties with platinum tips. So long, sweetie."

I closed the door and then called a cab. While waiting for it, I made myself a cup of tea. Then I checked my cash and credit cards. All were in order and waiting to be exhausted. The phone rang and I told myself not to answer it, but I did and wished I hadn't.

"Journey, this is Ackerly." The tone of his voice was not dissimilar to that of the hangman greeting the condemned man stepping slowly onto the scaffold.

"Look, chum, I've had a very tiring day, so let's talk later. I'm about to turn in." I forced a yawn and let him hear the after-moan.

"No you don't. Stay out of that bed. I'm gonna be over there in twenty minutes. You've got a lot of answers I want. Your employee gets shot after you chase a guy along the park at floorboard speed. You crack up your car and could have run over a dozen people who were lying on the grass. And you're gonna turn in? No way!"

"I'll talk to you only if you promise to put a guard in front of Charlie's room at Rice."

"Don't hand me that concerned crap—nobody's after *Charlie* and you know it. I heard all about that cyanide stuff in your drink at O'Rourke's. I talked to the lab people, and that Sergeant Barker, that pal of yours, he's got a lot of guts driving you home. I told that asshole to drive you down here to headquarters. He's gonna lose a stripe for that, maybe more."

"I'm not under arrest and Barker knew it. You give him trouble and I'll give you plenty of the same. I'm the victim here, God damn it!"

"Victim, hell, when you step out of your house nobody's safe! You stay put—we're coming over to see you right away. And you better be there when we show up, Journey. If you skip, you can order a bed next to your pal at Rice!"

"Aw, you don't mean that, pal."

"If I'm lyin', I'm cryin', Journey, and I ain't your pal. Don't move, don't budge. Understand me?"

"How about that guard on Charlie's room?"

"Okay, but don't go anywhere."

The front-door bell rang again. "Hold on, will you?" I put down the phone, going to the door. It was the cab-driver. I pointed to my two bags and he picked them up and carried them out to the taxi. I went back to the phone. Ackerly's voice boomed over: "You there, you stupid bastard—Journey? Journey?"

I sipped some tea and then answered: "Yeah, I'm here, bullyboy, and when you drop by make it snappy. I'm as tired as Hillary coming down the mountain."

"Hillary—the guy who climbed Everest—yeah, I know. Cute. See, Journey, you ain't the only guy who reads."

"You're no dummy." I could hear the cabbie honking his horn. I looked at my watch. I had about a half hour to catch my plane and had to go across town to O'Hare to do it.

"That's right and you be there when we show up," Ackerly said in a threatening voice, a voice that promised severe punishment.

"My word on it, Ackerly, you can put it in a bank and collect interest." He hung up and so did I. Going to the front door, I turned and locked both bolts, then ran down the stairs to the waiting cab.

3

The cabbie made O'Hare in record time, cutting across town to the Northwest Tollway and then, twenty miles above the speed limit, to the airport. As we drove up to the departure area, it was swarming with police. At least twenty squad cars were at the curb, light-racks blinking red, white, and blue.

"Looks like a bomb threat or something," the driver said. "Is this the line you want, buddy?"

I thought for one quick moment that Ackerly had done this. He had found no one at my place and put out a call to the airlines and unearthed my reservation. All for some questions, but he would do it, all right. He'd show me who was boss, that was his way. And he'd build a hell of a charge into my slipping out of town. He'd be in love with that, charging me with something, anything where I'd have to post bond, go through questions from reporters from the paper running my column, people I knew.

"Keep going," I ordered the cabbie, "I don't want any part of some mad bomber. It would be my luck to land on a plane being hijacked to Cuba."

The driver swung the cab into the outer lane and

zoomed past the cop cars. "Naw, they don't take 'em there anymore. Those nuts take 'em to Algeria, those big planes, someplace where they can sell the goddamned plane. Really, they sell the plane. You know, maybe a million or more. I read about it last week. So where you wanna go? Home?"

"Go down the expressway to the Loop, take me to Union Station."

"Gonna take a train?" The driver was startled.

"What's wrong with that?"

"Okay by me, it's only that nobody goes by train anymore, do they? I mean except short distances?"

"Do a favor for me, pal," I asked him. "Call your dispatcher as we go and tell her to book a bedroom on the Broadway Limited for me to New York. Under the name of Journey."

He looked at me through the rearview mirror, then wagged his head. "Ain't supposed to do that."

I reached forward and dropped a ten-spot on the seat next to him. He reached for the hand phone to call his dispatcher.

Luck was with me; I caught the Broadway fifteen minutes before it was scheduled to leave, and got a bedroom in the bargain. For ten minutes I sat in the compartment with the blinds pulled down, half expecting to hear the sound of heavy flatfeet slapping down on the concrete ramp next to the idling train. A minute or two before we pulled out, I did hear the sound of someone running along the ramp, but in high heels. I leaned forward and separated the blind a crack to see a shapely pair of legs encased in light brown hose, beige pumps, and, above the knee, a tan skirt. Opening the blind farther, I could see a woman with a voluptuous figure and long black hair. She had her back to me as she talked to the conductor and I admired her summer business suit—tasteful, subdued, expensive. I knew that figure somehow, or wanted to. As the conductor pointed to the car in which I sat, she pivoted on one heel, revealing a familiar profile. It was Laura Manville, my banking-executive friend.

"It's this way, ma'am," I could hear the porter tell her as they passed my compartment, going down the passageway, then stopping. Then, after some movement of baggage, I heard the porter say: "Thank you *very* much, ma'am, and I'll be sure and bring you coffee and juice in the morning, nine A.M." Then I could hear the closing of her compartment door, three or four doors down the corridor from mine, I estimated, and the porter walking back to his own small room at the head of the car.

Laura Manville on the same train. It was a happy accident or providence, but her presence comforted me and made the lonesome feeling of the train station, the idea of departure, seem more distant. I'd see her soon enough, I told myself, and then I told myself that I was sweating like a hog on butchering day. I flipped on the switch of the overhead fan, entered the lavatory and ran some cold water over a washcloth, rinsing it and then flattening it on my face to cool off. Glancing into the mirror, I could see a darkening jaw and a tired face. I dug out my shaving kit and went to work cleaning up as the train jerked forward and began to roll out of the station.

There was a soft knock on the compartment door. I opened it with the lather still on my face, my shirt collar opened and doubled under. The porter stood in the corridor, smiling, a big man but slightly stooped.

"Anything you'd like, Mr. Journey? Pillows? A writing table?"

I fished into my pocket for some money and handed it to him, asking him to get me some cigarettes and a small bottle of wine.

"The bottles of wine, sir," he explained, "are those tiny little things they serve on the planes."

"Five or six of them, then."

He glanced up the corridor. "Excuse me, sir." He took a step into the compartment to allow someone to pass in the corridor. It was Laura, stopping at the door to talk to him.

"Is the lounge car this way?" she asked.

"Yes, ma'am, three cars up."

"Thank you." She looked over to me and then broke into a laugh. "Jack?"

I nodded, embarrassed at my appearance.

"Is that you behind that foamy face?"

"Guilty."

The porter backed into the corridor, saying, "I'll get those items for you, sir." Laura stepped into the compartment. Sweeping the small towel draped over my shoulder into my hand, I wiped away the lather. "Come in. Have a couch." I closed the door.

She sat down, a wide smile on her full red lips. She crossed her lovely legs and looked up at me in amazement. "This is a bit more than unbelievable, meeting you on the Broadway like this."

"Just research," I lied. "I'm doing a series on historical train-murders—murder on wheels I'm calling it—and I wanted to get in the mood."

"How far are you going for this research?"

"New York."

"Exhaustive research, I should say." She moved over to the window, sliding up the blind, looking out at the grimy tenement buildings of Chicago's southside. She pulled down the blind. "Nothing short of a bomb threat could have compelled me to spend sixteen hours on the train."

"What bomb?"

"My God, didn't you hear about it? I was scheduled to fly out of O'Hare Airport tonight for New York, but most of the flights have been delayed indefinitely until they find a bomb. Someone called the airport to tell them that he had planted a bomb on one of the planes scheduled to take off—he didn't even have the good grace to specify the airline—and they stopped all flights. Dozens of bomb specialists are going through every plane looking for the awful thing. They told me it might be hours and hours before they could clear any flights and I've got an urgent meeting tomorrow afternoon in New York." She looked about the compartment, then spread her slender fingers outward. "This seemed like the only way to get there."

I cursed my paranoia, to think that Ackerly would have called out half the police force to prevent me from going to New York. The cabdriver had been right after all. The more I looked at lovely Laura, however, the more I felt glad to have been so impetuous.

The porter knocked again and delivered the cigarettes, tiny wine bottles, chilled, and two cups. I poured out two bottles and handed Laura a glass. She took it, and held it up to me in an exaggerated toast. "To lovely fate, Jack."

"To mad bombers," I replied, toasting back. We drank, looking at each other over the rims of the cups, each thinking about being together on a train laboring eastward.

"Will you excuse me while I shave? Then we can dine."

"I'd love it," she said in a low voice.

Stepping back into the washroom, I again lathered my face and began working the razor down my cheeks, talking to her through the open door. "You know, I met Alfred Hitchcock once," I told her, "and he loved trains. I guess I do too."

"Yes, but in his movies, isn't that correct? He really didn't travel on them all the time."

"Yes he did, or at least until the old Twentieth Century went off. He liked that slow luxury."

"I read a new book about him that describes him as a monster, how he was always doing sadistic things to his actors and friends."

"The author misread his temperament. If Hitchcock had been an American, he would have been labeled a practical joker. But being British and doing practical jokes is sadistic. It's all a matter of nationality. Hitchcock's humor appealed to me." I turned for a moment to see that she had put up the blind again and was looking out at the dark open country we were now crossing, flat plains with lonely farmlights twinkling.

"You found him *funny?*" She didn't look at me, but gazed into the darkness.

"He made fun of Ernst Lubitsch once, another director—"

"I know, 'the Lubitsch Touch.' "

"He said to me"—and I did my poor imitation of Hitchcock talking as I finished shaving—" 'well, *my* films on trains were considerably more expressive than Lubitsch's love scenes. He once showed Jeanette MacDonald and her leading man on board a speeding train. And when they kissed, Lubitsch cut to the train's pistons going in and out, in and out. Not what I would call an innovative shot.' "

Laura laughed huskily.

I finished shaving, wiped my face, splashed it with my cheap cologne, unrolled my shirt collar, and tightened the knot of my tie. Stepping into the bedroom, I took my jacket from the hook and slipped it on, then sat next to her on the long couch, holding the glass of wine.

She turned away from the window, examining my face, then slowly ran a soft cool hand down the side of one cheek. "A new man . . . a handsome devil with a 1920s face." She held up her glass to mine with another toast.

"Here's to pistons going in and out, in and out . . ." We didn't drink, but leaned forward, kissing fully, lips opening slowly, a hot moist kiss that told me that I was the luckiest man in the world.

IV

Shadowmen

1

We stepped out of the compartment on our way to the dining car. A heavy, creaking noise was behind us as we moved down the narrow corridor of the Pullman, and I turned to see the porter pushing a two-wheel cart piled high with luggage.

"That's all right, sir," he said to me in an apologetic voice, "you're goin' the correct way to the diner, straight ahead. Don't mind me back here—have to move these bags forward." Suddenly the small wheel on the cart bent inward under its heavy weight and the cart collapsed sideways, wedging itself against the wall awkwardly. The porter cursed under his breath.

"Do you think you should help him?" Laura said.

"Do you need any help?" I asked the porter, without enthusiasm.

The porter pushed hard on the cart, but it would not go forward. Then he pulled it and it groaned slowly backward. "No, thank you, sir, I jus' gotta pull it back to the next car now—only way it will go."

At that moment laughing fortune presented itself with the widest woman I have ever seen, fat from head to toe and certainly all of four hundred pounds, coming our way down the corridor followed by a line of grumbling passengers, unable to get by her. She took one look at us and the porter and his stopped cart and let out a deep sigh that seemed to send the already muggy temperature in the corridor upward several degrees.

Her body, sheathed in a flowing polka-dot dress that looked like a tent, occupied the entire width of the corridor, her flab pressing mightily against both walls. "What in God's name do I do *now*, tell me?" She said this to no one in particular, but the porter took full responsibility. "That's jus' fine, ma'am," he soothed, pulling his truck backward and waving her toward us. "You come ahead." Then to me: "Sir—would you mind, sir, you and the lady, if you jus' step into Room D next to you so's the lady can pass and you can go on. Nobody in Room D, sir."

I pushed the door of Room D open and backed inside, drawing Laura with me. The fat lady glided by, passengers behind her flowing forward with grateful looks. The porter had been wrong. Downward and to my left were two men, well dressed and silent, looking upward at us with annoyed expressions.

"Sorry," I mumbled, "the porter said no one was in this room." I nodded to the fat lady working her way by us. "It's only until the poor woman gets by."

Both men were dressed in conservative business suits, had short haircuts and manicured fingernails. The knots of their bland ties were tight against their collars, which must have been uncomfortable, since the air conditioning in the car was not working. Yet they were not sweating. Both were in their early fifties, it seemed. They had fleshy pink faces. One wore glasses. The other, who seemed younger, clucked his tongue in disgust at the sight of the disappearing fat woman.

"It will only be a minute," I reassured them.

They both looked away from me without a sound. They sat in an identical pose, legs crossed, hands folded at the knees. It was then that I noticed something peculiar. Both wore the same kind of ring on their right little fingers, something like a signet ring. I had seen that ring somewhere else but could not remember it. All I felt upon seeing those rings was a twinge of unexplainable fear.

Laura said nothing to either of them, merely looked into the corridor as we waited for the line of people, which now appeared to be the entire population of Lafayette, Indiana, to pass down the corridor after the fat lady. I glanced back to the couch to see the younger man looking at Laura's shapely legs. I stared at him until he caught my look; he quickly turned his head to stare out the window with his companion.

The procession in the corridor finally vanished and we stepped out of Room D. Before closing the door, I told the two men: "It's a distinct pleasure. I don't know when I've enjoyed a conversation more." I closed the door and followed Laura up the corridor.

"I don't think they appreciated your sense of humor, Jack."

"What kind of humor?"

"Insulting."

"Mannequins, the both of them . . . Amtrak plants to make the clientele appear to be the classy sort."

"Funny." She chuckled and swished forward on those long and beautiful legs, which I watched in delight.

We sat in the dining car sipping coffee that jiggled in our cups. It was jammed, and the ancient, harassed, and ill-tempered waiters lurched up and down the aisle as the train raced over decaying roadbeds. We had ordered the chicken but had no great expectations; the days of the old dining-car galley with foreign chefs and freshly made meals were long over. Now the meals were unfrozen by microwave ovens.

Across from us at the table sat an elderly man, balding with taut pink skin and shocking blue eyes that looked out from beneath a heavy brow. He wore rimless granny glasses and peered downward with concern at the goulash he spooned between thin lips. Next to him was a woman of indeterminate age, salt-and-pepper hair swept backward to a severe bun, a lean face, and narrow nose. She, too, picked at a plate of goulash, or maybe it was pot roast or beef stew, a dish of stringy meat swimming in yellow sauce. I tried to avert my eyes from their meals, looking out the window into the inky blackness that was Indiana.

"How is it?" the lean-faced woman asked the old man.

"Tasty." He did not smile or look at her but kept working his spoon. He looked up at Laura and me. "You ought to try this beef dish," he encouraged us.

"We've ordered," I told him. Now I knew it would start, struggling introductions, the forced conversations. Well, at least he wasn't Bruno in *Strangers on a Train*.

The old man stuck out his hand while staring into my eyes. "I'm Professor Michael Handler, University of Chicago, archaeology."

I shook his hand, which felt like papier-mâché, saying: "Harold Bissonette, editor in chief, *Morticians' Monthly*." *That* ought to turn him off, I told myself with tired caprice. Laura gave me a sideways glance and a little smile to go with it.

"I'm Wanda Stulka," the lean-faced woman said. She did not offer her hand and said this directly to Laura, adding: "I'm also at the University of Chicago, instructor, archaeology."

Before Laura could open her mouth, I introduced her as "Esther Blodgett, my editorial assistant."

"*Morticians' Monthly*—ummm," hummed Professor Handler. I could see that academic brain of his quickly sifting facts that might contribute to some intelligent conversation concerning the murky art of undertaking. "I didn't know such publications existed," he finally said. "Whatever would you run in such a magazine?"

"The usual," I said, and sipped my tepid coffee. "Articles on stiffs. Essays on eternal sleep, odes in honor of Charon and his nightly beat trips to the Isle of the Dead. Rather humdrum reading fare for the general public, but it's heavy with undertakers."

The lean-faced woman looked queasy, inching her plate away from her. Professor Handler never stopped lapping it up, relishing, it seemed, each morsel of his meal. When he finished, he carefully daubed his mouth with a paper napkin—linen, as well as the old heavy silver coffeepots and other charming accoutrements of the great trains, had also vanished. The professor gave me a wide grin that showed large teeth, separated, yellowed, and flat at the tips.

"Fascinating to me, such material," he said in a high thin voice. "I work with the dead too." He nodded in the direction of his companion. "We both do. The deep, long dead, ages before embalming fluid was invented. When was it invented, by the way?"

"Sometime in the 1890s, I believe," I told him. "At first it contained a great deal of arsenic, which confounded police in determining the guilt of poisoners." I found myself going like a programmed tape, listening to my own voice and wondering why in the hell I had begun this ridiculous conversation. "A man named Johann Otto Hoch poisoned about fifty wives with arsenic, had them embalmed quickly so that his poison would be thought

part of the embalming fluid then used, in case any of the
bodies were later exhumed."

"Clever," mused the professor. "So how did they ever
detect this man Hoch?"

"One of his victims survived and turned him in, the
usual way such killers are caught."

"Isn't that kind of material a little off the line for your
publication?" asked Wanda Stulka.

"Not at all," Laura joined in. "Morticians lead such dull
lives—they appreciate any kind of levity, no matter how
dark, to liven up their reading."

"Do you write for the *Morticians' Monthly*—ahh, Miss
Blodgett?" asked the Professor. He was still smiling idiotically.

"No, just correspondence and proofs. Mr. Bissonette
here does all the writing." She changed her face into a
look of hope, lifting eyelids as she looked at me. "But
someday, Mr. Bissonette has promised me, I will be allowed to work on the history of casket-making, a large
editorial project on which Mr. Bissonette has been laboring for years."

"Where do you start?" inquired the professor, reaching
for a glass of water and drinking.

I replied in a serious voice: "You see, it's broken down
into various ages—wood, iron, steel, copper, brass, silver,
gold, and platinum." At that moment I saw the two silent
businessmen who had been in Room D come into the
diner and take seats, speaking to no one, including each
other.

"Platinum caskets?" puzzled Wanda Stulka. "Isn't that
awfully expensive?"

"Only in Alabama."

The waiter who had been serving us, a bald-headed
black man with thick glasses, came over, checked the

professor's written order, and then put a dish of ice cream in front of him. It had melted to soup.

"Happens every time the air conditioning breaks down," the professor murmured, glaring at the ice cream. "And the air conditioning breaks down every time I ride this train."

"Why ride it, then?" Laura asked in a voice that was unconcerned about an answer.

"Nostalgia. I'm a train buff, or perhaps I'm addicted to anything old, aging, forgotten. I suppose it's the archaeologist in me." The professor turned to me. "Very interesting, this *Morticians' Monthly* thing—Mr. Journey—even though you made it all up. I'm a reader of your crime column and I recognized you from the little picture that runs above it." He pushed the melted ice cream away from him. "Amusing what one can do with one's whims. You're a pretty good storyteller."

"Sorry."

The waiter returned, putting out plates of chicken and rice before us. Laura picked at the pieces of sauteed bird. Wanda Stulka had a cross look on her face.

"I don't think it's funny to dupe people, Mr. Journey."

"Then tell me what you think is funny and I'll talk about it."

She pushed her chair backward until it struck the chair behind her, causing a heavyset man in work clothes to give her an annoyed look. "You didn't fool me, either, Mr. Journey. I knew who you were all along. We both did, didn't we, Michael?"

The professor's jaw muscles tightened as she addressed him so intimately and his bony cheeks flushed in embarrassment. "Pleased to meet you, Mr. Journey," he said hastily, pushing back his chair to slide across the seat vacated by Miss Stulka, who waited unsteadily in the aisle for him. He stood up to a surprising height, six six maybe, and rail-thin. He cracked that cadaverous smile again. "I also enjoy the movies, as you must. Harold Bissonette is a name used by W. C. Fields in *It's a Gift.*" He nodded in Laura's direction. "Esther Blodgett was the heroine Vicki Lester in *A Star Is Born.*" He gave me a cavalier wave of the hand. "Amusing." Both moved down the aisle toward the next car.

Laura wiggled her shoulders. "Cold fish, aren't they?"

"I wonder where Mrs. Handler is?" I said.

"You mean that crotchety old man and his assistant are off on an affair?"

"He was wearing a wedding ring."

"Some men wear wedding rings after their wives die."

"Only widowers who inherit their wives' fortunes."

"Why, he must be ninety." Laura took a dainty forkful of chicken and rice upward to luscious, full lips. "And she's about forty-five."

"That should be about right, don't you think? What's a forty-five-year difference in ages between two dirt shovelers who don't get excited unless a bone is a million years old or more?"

She gave me a slow turn of the head, her long black hair falling over her shoulder. "Did you ever think that two people like that might be examining your bones centuries from now?"

"I'd rather have you do that during my first hundred years."

Laura didn't blush; she wasn't the kind boldness could fluster. Though every curvacious inch was a lady, she knew the world well and herself and her own desires and ambitions and made no excuses for any of it.

Raising her eyebrows slightly in anticipation, she whispered: "Lead me to the tomb. I'm ready to dig."

We finished the meal hurriedly and then headed back to our bedrooms. We passed the two gentlemen from Bedroom D. They sat stiff and mute, both staring downward into two plates of beef in yellow sauce. They were not elated.

2

The lounge car was packed, smoky, and hot. Almost every vinyl seat was taken by teen-agers in torn jeans, elderly couples, and small-town families with excited children. They ate sandwiches from the snack bar or gulped beer. Peanut shells and candy wrappers littered the threadbare carpet. It was a sad sight, because I had seen in that long-ago day of my mother's glamour the elegant lounge cars of the past, deep-cushioned chairs occupied by passengers who would not dream of being there without smart attire. Perhaps the past had made a snob of me, but the memory of my mother making up her face in our compartment thirty years earlier, so that she would be presentable in a lounge chair, doubled my vision. It was a small shock of recognition that yesterday's nicety was today's inconvenience.

I purchased several small bottles of white wine and held two plastic glasses loaded with ice. As we stood looking about for a place to sit, Laura nudged me, saying: "There are two seats in that booth." We headed for it but realized that the archaeologists were sitting opposite.

"Keep going, beautiful," I said quietly to Laura, who was walking ahead of me. "I'm not up to a dissertation on the ancient tombs of Egypt. We'll have the wine in my bedroom."

From the back I saw her head bob up and down in a nod of instant agreement. Professor Handler and Wanda Stulka darted quick glances upward at us as we passed. The old man nodded, nervously smiling. I could have been nicer to him, I reminded myself. How many train rides did he have left? Professor Michael Handler was probably the only real gentleman in the car, including myself.

Laura went on to her bedroom, telling me that she had to "freshen up," which could have meant, as in the ways of all female statements, that she had to brush her teeth, comb her hair, add or wipe off mascara, spray on cologne or perfume, change her panty hose, or merely massage two tired feet.

"Yeah, I'll freshen up too," I told her as we entered our separate bedrooms at the same moment. "I want to shave my eyebrows."

"See you in a few minutes," she said, low-voiced, and wiggled her fingers at me as we went inside.

I poured a glass of wine for myself and drank it quickly. The fan was off and I had not remembered shutting it down. I flicked on the operating lever and stood thankfully beneath the breeze. As I looked upward at the slowly gyrating fan, my eye caught the flap of my case. The case was high above in the rack, jutting halfway into space. I had not unbuckled the flap and now it was hanging loose. I pulled the case down and unzipped it, carefully opening the top.

Everything seemed in order, the same folded shirts, the same flattened-out slacks beneath. Reaching downward, I pulled out the holster and gun. The flap on the holster was unbuckled and I was sure that I had buckled it. Placing the shirts and slacks in a neat pile on the couch, I pulled back the underwear to discover that the box of ammunition I had placed there at the last moment in Chicago was gone.

Someone had paid my bedroom a visit during dinner. I dismissed the idea of the porter going through my luggage. Train porters are the most trustworthy of men, always have been, always will be. They were the last great remnants of the old trains. It could have been anyone passing down the corridor, kids maybe, teen-agers. There was no way to lock the bedroom door once you left the compartment. The porter was supposed to look after things, but my porter had been busy with a broken luggage cart. But that would be risky business for any larcenous kid, not knowing where the occupant was and when he or she might return. No, someone who knew I was in the dining car did this. I thought of the two men in the next compartment, Bedroom D. It didn't make any sense, a couple of misplaced strangers doing that. And why not take the .38, instead of just the ammunition? Why? So you can't use the .38, dummy, that's why.

I rang for the porter and hurriedly repacked my bag, putting it back on the rack. I stood beneath the fan and waited for several minutes, ringing again and again for the porter. He was finally at the door, explaining that he was having a problem with luggage. I gave him some money and asked him to get a large bucket of ice. He returned in five minutes, handing me the ice-laden bucket.

"Is that all, sir?"

"No." I studied him for a moment, then asked: "What about those two men in Bedroom D? I thought you said the room was vacant."

He shook his head. "Terribly sorry about that, sir. Those gentlemen got on at Gary, went into their bedroom, number D, the conductor put them in there while I was busy with that load of luggage. They bothering you, sir?"

"No, I was just curious. Thought they might be stowaways."

"Oh, no, sir, those gentlemen are gentlemen." He pushed his lips together in a frown and added: "But you know, sir, we do have a problem with some of these youngsters, young people with guitars and such. They get into a bedroom and lock it before the conductor checks their tickets. Pretty stupid." He grinned. " 'Cause we got keys, you know, and we open it up and shoo them out and they pay or get off at the next stop."

"Not like the old days."

"Nothing left of them good old days, sir."

"Except you."

His grin widened. "There's a few others, old men jus' working our ways down on the trains, poor old tired trains."

"Thanks for the ice."

"Anything else I can get you, sir?"

"Air conditioning."

"I'm terribly sorry about that, sir. We got somebody working on that right now. Maybe in an hour or so he'll get it going on this car. He's working his way down from the diner. These old cars, you know, they jus' give out . . . one thing goes . . . another." He shrugged.

A few minutes after the porter left, Laura entered, sliding the bolt to lock the door. She wore only a thin blouse and skirt. Hanging from her arm by a strap was a small bag, which she tossed on the couch. "My nightie."

"You won't even need your skin in this heat." I poured her a glass of wine, using the ice cubes the porter had brought. She sat down with me on the couch and sipped the wine. "Oh, that's a bracer. I wish we could open the door."

"And let in the hot air."

The thought that someone had rifled my bag nagged at me. It had to be the two men next door. Got on at Gary? What would two Rotarian-type white businessmen be doing getting on the train in that steel city in the middle of the night? Cops? No—they were too soft and pink and well laundered to be cops. And they had manicured fingernails, lacquered and filed down. Yes . . . just like the man who dosed your drink in the bar.

"Jack—what is it?" Laura's voice seemed a long way off, calling down a tunnel. "Are you listening to me?"

I had been looking into my glass of wine, the ice cubes now melted down to tiny chips. "The heat, I guess. Go on —what were you saying? Something about your bank?"

"I was telling you that it seems I spend more time in New York than in Chicago these days."

"Why is that?"

"My job is really with the Haley National Bank—"

"Isn't that one of the biggest banks in New York?"

"In the world—I'm an executive vice-president, special accounts, working with our Chicago affiliates. But it seems I'm mostly in New York these days. I thought I told you that months ago."

"No, we didn't talk much when we met at that party— where was it? Evanston? At the home of Farly Ballinger, the rich poet, ex-beatnik, I think, who married the muffler heiress. No, we didn't talk about much at all those weeks we were seeing each other. Just sex."

"I don't remember it as being as crass as all that." There was injury inside her words, little-girl hurt.

"I was only remembering what was best between us in a relationship without commitments."

"That's the way you like it, don't you, Jack?"

I didn't dream of answering that one; she was angry now. There had to be more to it than sex, sex, sex.

"I suppose it was your first wife who did that to you?"

"Leila? Like any other marriage dropped down a well. It's something you can remember as worthwhile or rotten when it's over, depending on how the memory works for you. I was no different from any other middle-aged male suddenly set free."

Laura had turned fully on the couch, drawing up her

legs in a bent position, resting her back against the rattling wall of the compartment. She searched my face the way one might inspect fresh fish at a market stall, lifting the gills to see if the flesh beneath was pink or brown, sniffing for the slightest trace of rot. Hell, be honest, I told myself.

"After my divorce I moved into the lakeside town house. I did my work as usual but went a little crazy with women, a natural thing to do."

She brought the glass of wine to her lips and then said: "How many women?"

"I can't remember. A hundred maybe in the first year."

She smiled, but it was an angry, chastising little smile.

"It might have been two hundred," I said, feeling ridiculous for being honest. "I didn't keep a list, phone numbers only, written on the inside of matchbook covers, napkins, bar coasters, on the backs of envelopes. Some even had cards. I would stare at these numbers, many without names, and wonder who all these women were. I had met them when I was drinking—I don't drink hard stuff anymore—and I would try to envision them, their faces, their voices, their bodies. It drove me a little crazy. But I didn't stop any of the relentless womanizing for a long time."

Laura smirked and said: "You don't really care about *me* at all, do you?"

"I do—very much."

"No you don't, or you wouldn't tell me all this truckdriver gossip."

The heat and the wine were making me drowsy, but I plunged on, hoping to exhaust my memories of that first year of promiscuity. "So it came to pass that fear instead of lust won out."

"You became frightened of sex? Oh, come on, Jack!"

"Of women—too many women." Hell, I just didn't care what I told her at that moment. "I awoke one morning after a whirling night in the Windy City to find a blonde in bed. The phone rang and there was another woman on the phone, shouting out dinner reservations for that evening, and then, downstairs, my front-door bell rang and a loud female voice called out to me through the open second-story window. In those desperate seconds I realized I might not have long to live if I kept up that maniacal pace. I was going to get killed—shot, stabbed, strangled in my sleep by some affronted darling who placed monogamy before murder."

Laura began to laugh. "Three at once—in bed, on the phone, at the door? Jack, you're suicidal!"

"*Was*. I stopped that day, retreated into silence, social oblivion. I stayed with my work and became *very* selective about companions."

"But how did you get rid of the three ladies?"

"By following the maxim of any Hollywood entrepreneur—lied, cheated, and weaseled. I told the blonde in the bed that the lady on the phone was my secretary reminding me of an important meeting that morning. I told the woman on the phone in guarded terms that I would keep the appointment, which I didn't, and then I ran downstairs and told the redhead at the door that I could not see her, since I had broken out with a highly contagious rash."

Bringing her feet up to the couch, Laura rubbed my thigh with her toes. "What can you communicate to me?"

"*Amour.*"

She swiveled to a sitting position, stood up, grabbed her small bag, and said: "I'm going into that tiny little washroom over there. Why don't you have the porter make up the bed?" She went into the washroom and closed the door. I rang for the porter and he made up the lower berth while I stood in the outside corridor, wondering if he could hear Laura in the washroom. When he had gone, Laura stepped from the washroom wearing a short nightie. She slid beneath the fresh bed sheet and I quickly undressed. I turned out the overhead light so that only a small blue night-light in the wall above the bed shone on us.

"It's so hot," Laura said, and wriggled so that she could remove her nightie, which she tossed on the floor. I moved close to her, wedging my body to her side on the narrow bed the Pullman Company had obviously designed to thwart the act of lovemaking in any position. She curled an arm under me and I moved over on top.

She stared upward at me with those amazing slate eyes. "Do I look bad?" she asked. "I must look terrible . . . all this heat."

"Right now I'm enjoying the heat," I said, moving against her. "You're . . . just . . . fine."

"Please—I look bad . . . don't I?" Her breath came in shorter spurts as we worked our bodies back and forth in awkward movement, trying to find the center of that bed, which seemed to grow smaller with each thrust and take.

"I told you . . . you're okay." I tried to keep my mind on it, keep the lust up, but her words, like those of a woman chatting as she sat in front of her vanity, worked against the desire, thinned the passion.

"Why don't you . . . tell me . . . the truth. . . . Go on . . . you can say . . . it."

I stopped for a moment, trying not to put all my weight down on her, resting my elbow on the pillow. I studied her and said in a flat voice: "I've always been enchanted by wattles, liver spots, bags under the eyes—women with character—maybe a dueling scar. No—you're too beautiful—you just won't do."

Her milky arms went around my neck, drawing my face to hers and a deep kiss that had an appreciative laugh at the end of it. "Can we start again?" she asked.

"If my legs don't cramp up in this god-awful space."

"Let's start again."

"Only if you promise to moan a little." I covered her with my body once more, arms still on either side of her lovely face.

Laura flicked off the blue night-light. Then there was only the sound of our panting, the rhythmic hum of the fan above, and, a little later, Laura, softly moaning.

3

Penn Station was thronged with commuters. The Broadway Limited had pulled into New York late as usual. It was almost 4:00 P.M. when we arrived tired, hot, and yearning to breathe the city's air. It had taken mechanics most of the night to correct the train's defective air conditioning, so that we had spent a miserable morning and afternoon on the tedious run east. The merciless freights, given the right-of-way over the passenger trains, had broken down the roadbeds so cruelly over the years that our speed had been laughable, except that we were too frazzled to laugh about it. Only the professor of archaeology, whom I spotted in the dining car at breakfast, held on to a smile.

The two men in Bedroom D were not on the train when Laura and I had breakfast. The porter told me that they had gotten off at Harrisburg, and I dismissed my sinister thoughts about them. But that still did not explain the missing box of cartridges.

Redcaps carted our luggage through the massive station, up an escalator, and to the curb, where cabs zoomed forward to swoop up the best-dressed passengers.

Laura took out a pencil and small note pad from her purse, scribbling hastily. "Here's my phone number. Call me, Jack."

"I will." I took the paper and slipped it into my pocket without looking at it. "Maybe dinner tonight."

A cab pulled up and the redcap put her luggage inside. She leaned forward and kissed me lightly. "If you don't call me I'll tie up the Algonquin switchboard tracking you down."

When her cab pulled away, the last in line, another redcap rumbled up to the curb with a cart loaded with neatly wrapped boxes. At the redcap's side stood Professor Handler and Wanda Stulka. "There'll be a cab along any minute now," the redcap told them. "But this gentleman is ahead of you." He pointed to me.

"Hello, Mr. Journey," said Professor Handler affably. He looked upward at a slice of blue sky between skyscrapers. "New York's given us a fine summer day, don't you think?"

"It's as hot as Chicago," Wanda Stulka grumbled.

"Weather goes east," I said to them. "We moved with the front. Yesterday's weather in Chicago is New York's muggy today. . . . Sort of like living in the past."

"Interesting," Professor Handler murmured.

I was sure that he didn't find such comments at all interesting. I looked down at the boxes to see that Handler's name was in the upper left-hand corner and that the addressee was the New York Archaeology Association. "Having an exhibit?" I pointed to the boxes.

"No, no. Merely some small items for study."

"I can't imagine you really having an interest in our science," snapped Wanda Stulka.

"Oh, but I do," I said sincerely, then said: "Just the other day while doing a bit of arcane research I came across an entry in Admiral Byrd's diary when he was at the South Pole or within a reasonable vicinity. Byrd describes how he found a mastodon frozen in the ice and how he thawed out the giant carcass and found that the body had not putrified. In fact, the meat was fresh—this beast from millions of years ago—and so Byrd cut himself out a steak, cooked it, and consumed it."

Professor Handler moved a few steps closer to listen to me, fixing his blue eyes on my face. "Yes—go on."

"I don't see the point," Wanda Stulka said under her breath but intentionally loud enough for me to hear. Then she turned to the redcap and asked: "Don't you have a whistle or something to get us a cab?"

"No whistle, lady, sorry. Gotta wait."

"And so Byrd dined on mastodon steak," Professor Handler said, encouraging me to finish the story.

"Yes. Isn't it amazing when you think about it? Here you have this giant, hairy beast from the Pleistocene period, millions of years old, surviving to the twentieth century intact only to be carved up by a hungry aviator. That probably makes Admiral Byrd, as far as I know, the only man in history who ate an epoch."

The professor cracked a wide smile and laughed.

"That's idiotic," Wanda Stulka said, looking desperately up the street for a cab. "Not funny at all."

Professor Handler continued to laugh, then said to her: "Yes, it is humorous, Wanda." He turned back to me. "You have a strange mind, Mr. Journey, curious, intriguing." He removed a card from inside his suit jacket and handed it to me. "If you're in town for any time, call me at the association. We might have lunch."

Several cabs suddenly turned the corner and raced to where we were standing. I pocketed the card and insisted that the Professor and Wanda Stulka take the first cab, which they did, carefully instructing the redcap how to put the boxes onto the front seat. They carried their own luggage inside; their boxes full of artifacts were no doubt more precious to them than shirts and dresses.

"Byrd ate an epoch," the professor said to himself softly

as he entered the cab, shaking his head. Wanda Stulka jumped inside behind him, angrily closing the door and handing some coins to the redcap through the open window.

I took the next cab to the Algonquin. The hotel was the same, the overstuffed chairs and couches and antique lamps and little tables in the front lobby, dining rooms in back and to the left as you entered, the tiny Blue Bar to the right with old Freddy behind it staring into yesterday to see the ghosts of Beatrice Lillie and Dorothy Parker. Abbe had faithfully booked a room for me with a sitting area where I could work. The desk clerk handed me several messages from her, and, only minutes after I was settled in, I put through a call to my office in Chicago.

Abbe's voice was edgy: "Jack, what am I supposed to send out for this next week's column?"

"There are ten backup pieces in the top drawer of my desk," I told her. "Use those."

"That fellow from the Inter-Ocean Bank, Mr. Cubbedge, called again. Asked that you phone him from New York. Said you could call collect."

"How's Charlie?"

"He's okay—complained about the hospital food this morning. He's used to greasy spoons, I guess. The doctors there said he'd be okay in about three or four days. He says the minute he gets out he's going on vacation, some little town in Iowa that has six movie houses where he intends to spend all his time."

"He's got a big-screen complex—tell him hello for me and I'll call him at the hospital tomorrow."

"One thing more, Jack. Your friends Ackerly and Brex were up here and were awfully burned up. They went to your place last night to see you and they were shouting— Ackerly was—about you skipping out. I told him I didn't know where you had gone but that you'd be calling in probably. I hate this lying routine, Jack."

"Tell them I went to the Montevideo Music Festival."

"Where's that—South America?"

"Uruguay."

"C'mon, Jack. That's too far. They won't believe that."

"Tell them I called and that's where I said I was and they can take it or leave it. Is Henry all right?"

"Oh, let me tell you what a time I've had with that dog—"

"Can't now, pal. Very busy. I'll call you in the morning. Remember—Montevideo."

"Sure," she said unenthusiastically, "or Rangoon . . . or the Borgo Pass . . . or—"

"Bye-bye."

I next dug out my address book and called Hugo Keimes. The phone at his end rang twice before a recorded voice came on to state that the number had been disconnected and that there was no new number. Keimes's office was in a run-down building on Lexington Avenue that I intended to visit later. His book warehouse was somewhere in Brooklyn, God knew where. I called information for the bookdealer's home phone but was told that he was not listed in any of the boroughs. Hugo Keimes, for any purposes suiting me, had dropped through space.

A legman was needed. I didn't have any contacts on the New York newspapers, none of them ran my column, only papers upstate. But I did have a stringer in Greenwich Village, a wild, brilliant writer named Carlisle Cashe who occasionally did some research for me in the city.

Cashe was in his apartment when I called, making dinner, he said, Italian sausages and green noodles. I could hear the sausages frying as we talked. He said he'd meet me in the Blue Bar in an hour. Next I called Laura at her office in the Haley National Bank and told her I'd meet her at the San Remo bar in the Village. She complained about my taste for common bars but agreed.

I showered, shaved, and dressed before going down to the Blue Bar. I spent my time sipping beer and talking to old Freddy, who did most of the talking, recounting bizarre tales of bygone actresses and Broadway producers. Freddy wanted to write a book, he said, and I told him everyone in the world would want to read it if he could publish the book without libel. He didn't think he could do that. "Aw, they'd sue me," he groaned while rinsing out some glasses in the sink behind the bar. "Everybody sues today. They got nothing else to do but run to goddamned lawyers."

The Blue Bar never changed: same little tables and wooden chairs, enough to seat twenty-some people comfortably. There were eight stools at the bar. Christopher Plummer, the actor, came in briefly, had a drink, swapped stories with Freddy, then left with a smile still on his face. The afternoon sunlight faded slowly as it slid through the small French shutters on the window. It was almost two hours before Cashe arrived. We moved to a small table with two bottles of beer and talked in comfort.

Cashe was a tall, lean man with dark curly hair that was graying and thickly shot out from the side of his head. His hair was passé, long at the back and flopped over the collar of his jacket. He wore a much-washed cotton checked shirt and threadbare slacks. His black shoes were scuffed and the soles were worn thin. He talked with his hands expansively, every sentence a dramatic delivery. Carlisle Cashe was a poet who had to make a living as a journalist, which, of course, was far beneath him. Legwork was lower still.

"Hugo Keimes, a bookdealer on Lexington Avenue," I

told him, "has had his phone shut off and I can't locate his home address. I want to find him quickly."

"This have something to do with that column you write?"

"No, I want to find him on another matter."

"He owe you money?"

"No."

"Good, because the hardest guys to track down are those who owe people money. They're good at disappearing. So what's it all about?"

"I ordered a library in Chicago from a dealer, who bought it from Keimes, who bought it in Europe. Now I can't find Keimes. I want my library."

"Wait a minute, Jack," Cashe said with suspicion. "I read just this morning about some bookdealer in Chicago who got killed in a really bizarre way—somebody stuck a billing spike into this guy's head. Is that the guy you dealt with in Chicago?"

"No. Just coincidence."

"Yeah?" He leaned back in his chair with a very wise look on his long face. Then he sat forward, shrugging. "Well, it doesn't matter to me. Sure, I'll look up this guy Keimes."

I pushed a slip of paper across the table to him. "Here's his address. I want you to call me as soon as you've located him."

Cashe drew the index finger of his right hand rapidly toward him.

"Okay. How much?"

"A hundred now, another when I run this character down for you."

I pushed a fifty-dollar bill across the table and said: "Another fifty when you find him."

Cashe took the fifty and studied it, snapping it between his hands. "Jack, I realize that you're not asking me to find

Nixon's missing minutes, but this is last year's rate for such a job. I got to take cabs—" He kept snapping the fifty. "I mean, man, leave me some dignity and enough for a deli stop."

"Okay. I'll give you a hundred when you finish up."

He stopped snapping the fifty and looked at it with a sigh. "How about more now?"

"You can use a limousine with that."

"Man, you're turning into a piker, Jack. I'd never thought that of you. Why, when you came into town before, everybody got what you had, you know what I'm saying?"

"Yes, but the buck's leaner for me as well as you this year."

He stood up, affronted but accepting the offer. "If I have to shell out any of my own dough, you make up for that, is that a deal?"

"Deal. Find Keimes."

Cashe gave me a short little mock salute, long bony arm jutting from the sleeve of his jacket. "Yessuh, massa."

He walked quickly out of the bar. I moved over to Freddy to pay the tab.

"What's that?" He nodded in the direction of the door.

"Poet friend of mine."

"Those poets," Freddy said, taking the bill and my money to the till. "They never got a dime. Fancy words, yeah—but a dime, never. There was this guy Max Bodenheim used to come in here—ever hear of this Bodenheim? Christ, in the forties. Never had a dime. Wore a cloak, dripped a lot of words nobody could understand. He was a poet. But everybody bought him drinks. I could never understand that. . . ."

V

Stiletto & Co.

1

As I was leaving the Blue Bar the clerk at the desk waved his hand, signaling me. He had a message for me from Laura. She had called and asked that I meet her at the Plaza Oak Room bar. It took twenty minutes to get there by cab. Five bucks. Another dollar for the doorman. I found myself counting dollars spent.

Laura was in the center of the room, at a table with one of the most distinguished gents I had ever seen, right out of an ad in *Esquire.* His thick black hair was gray at the temples, just enough gray, almost as if brushed on. His white shirt was lightly starched, not a wave, with a long tapering collar and black silk tie with small dimpled knot, a tiny diamond pin holding it neat and flat against his chest, and surrounding this, a dark blue suit with almost imperceptible pinstripes. A light blue, perfectly folded handkerchief peaked fashionably from the top pocket. He was placing a single peanut into his mouth as I approached, and showing on a thin wrist was a glinting paper-thin gold watch, handcrafted by Cartier, no doubt. He had a tanned, pleasant face with full lips and prominent chin.

Smiling and lifting her head in my direction, Laura waved me over. She was wearing a low-cut, extravagantly expensive cocktail dress. "Jack—I'd like you to meet Mr. Jacquette, Darnley Jacquette, president of the Haley National Bank." She spoke this introduction as if heralding the Emperor Charlemagne. Maybe he was; his bank certainly had more capital than Charlemagne ever possessed, and most likely wielded more power and influence. Jacquette stood up to about an even six feet, showed a perfect set of gleaming white teeth, and shook my hand in a hearty clasp.

"Good to meet you, Journey. Laura's been telling me about you." He sat down, motioning me into an empty chair across from Laura. "Crime columnist, is that it?"

"Historian of sorts."

"Oh, yes, crime *history*." He held up a copy of *The New York Times*, which was folded in half. "It doesn't run in here, so I'm afraid I don't read the column. Where does it run?"

"In Staten Island and badly."

"Do they have daily newspapers in Staten Island?" He nudged the copy of the *Times* toward me, pointing at a story encircled with pen marks. "You did, however, make it into the *Times* today."

I looked down to read the small headline at the bottom of the page: CRIME RESEARCHER SHOT IN CHICAGO. The story was a brief one, telling how Charlie had been shot by an unidentified man and that he was a researcher for *John Howard Journey, a Chicago-based crime historian and daily columnist for chiefly midwestern newspapers*. That irked me. I looked up from the paper to see Jacquette watching for my reaction.

"The *Times* should know better," I said to him.

"Isn't it correct?"

"No—my column runs in New Jersey, Massachusetts, all down the Eastern Seaboard."

"I meant about the shooting—you were there, were you not, Mr. Journey?"

"Yes, on the spot." I gave him some corn: "Set up for the knock-off."

Jacquette turned to Laura with a patronizing hum in his voice: "You're right, he does talk like the kind of people he writes about."

"He's merely having fun, Darnley." She looked at me with a generous smile. "Jack seldom means what he says, or just the opposite."

"That would be impractical in my business."

"I can imagine," I told Jacquette, "where you bankers might be if you used pedestrian terms to explain exactly what it is you do for the public."

His brow knitted in curiosity. "Explain what?"

"How bankers get everything and the public gets less than what they invest, how you can manipulate a good five-cent cigar into a dollar stogie, how you've put this country back to 1933, a cesspool of mortgages that have choked off the small businessman, interest rates that have cut the throats of a whole generation of young lovers wanting no more than a four-room bungalow with a lawn the size of a beach blanket. How they can break their backs for it and lose it in a month. Explain that."

Laura's face was solemn, a hurt stare. Jacquette clung to his smile. "Surely, Mr. Journey, you can't paint us as black as that. We're strictly governed by federal laws. We don't create the economic conditions, merely react to them."

A waiter, stiff and formal, stood next to me, waiting for an order. "White wine—Graves if you have it, if not, Chablis will do."

"Chablis, sir." He was off, slipping through the crowd.

"Yeah, I know, you're such a civilized lot, bankers," I said. I hated his cultured guts and didn't feel guilty about it, not a bit. "You use those interest rates like a strip barker uses a cooch dancer. Get the crowd inside then sock it to them with overpriced drinks and a show that wouldn't intrigue an achondroplastic."

"I'm not quite following your vindictiveness," he said coolly, still smiling.

"You drop your interest rates—like a group of price-fixers on a spree—just long enough for everyone to get together their life savings to buy a house, invest in a business. By the time they jump in, the loan interests have zoomed upward." I held out my hand and made a slow fist. "And then you've got them for a lifetime or two—usury, call it what you want, but I could take out a better loan from the Mafia and pay less juice each month than what you'd demand."

"Oh, please, Mr. Journey—you know it's all a matter of how the federal government acts—federal loans, federal release of money. We don't control anything." His voice dropped to low shock: "But to be compared to the *Mafia*, well, that *is* gutter logic. Nothing pleases us more than to see American citizens get ahead—"

"Sure, and deep in your debt."

He pointed a stiff finger at the table and jabbed the worn surface for emphasis. "We are the backbone of this nation—"

"*Backstabbers*, you mean."

The waiter arrived with the wine. I sipped it and waited. Jacquette stood up slowly without a single wrinkle on his tailor-made suit. He put out his hand and I shook it once.

"I'm sorry you're feeling out of sorts, Mr. Journey. Good night." He buttoned his suit coat and then walked quickly away.

Laura sat toying with the swizzle stick of her drink and watching the ripples it made in the glass. Without looking at me she said: "That should just about destroy my relationship with Mr. Jacquette, I would think." She stared angrily at me.

"Don't worry about it. He's the type who will write me off immediately as the usual truculent journalist taking advantage of an obviously popular target, bankers in general. I know the Jacquettes—it's windy at the top, they remind themselves while ordering lobster and brandy. Some blocks from here there is a very old, exclusive club with huge windows that look down from the second floor. The Jacquettes sit in the windows looking down, impervious to the humanity thundering at their feet, and unconcerned with retaliation for financially raping the country. After all, the glass through which they view their victims is bullet- and bombproof. Who knows, if you faithfully serve their system long enough, beautiful, they might let you sit in one of those windows, as their token female banking mogul, that is."

"That's all nonsense, Jack, and you know it. I don't know what brought on this disgusting display of bad manners, but it's inexcusable. Darnley Jacquette is one of the most distinguished businessmen in this country with a reputation as upstanding as the President of the United States."

"Which president?"

"That kind of barbaric conversation might amuse your Chicago cronies, but here it merely brands you a social misfit." She stood up abruptly.

"What about our dinner at the San Remo?"

"I'm not in the mood for spaghetti and insults." She pushed her chair forward so that it struck the side table, hard enough to topple my glass of wine, which spilled in my direction. I met the flood with a large paper napkin and saved a soaking. Laura began to walk out of the bar.

As the waiter came running with a bar towel, I stood up, threw some money down, slipped the folded copy of the *Times* into my pocket, and followed her. She went down a hotel corridor and turned the corner and then another, going toward the main foyer. She was walking fast on her high heels and I barely managed to stay twenty feet behind her. As I edged around the corner of the check-in desk, I saw her cross the main lobby. A second before she went through the revolving door, a man came forward, out of the doorway of a small shop, and stopped her.

They spoke only for an instant. He talked, she barely responded. The man, in his fifties, conservatively dressed, with a pink face and glasses, seemed familiar. I recognized him as one of the two men from the train, in Bedroom D, a man who had supposedly gotten off at Harrisburg, Pa. Laura seemed surprised when this man stepped in her path, and, deadpan, said his few words. When she turned to speak with him, her back was to me and it was impossible to determine her reaction. It was only a matter of seconds before they parted or, rather, before she brushed past him, going through the door.

The businessman wheeled about and walked down another corridor that led to the busy dining room. I half thought to follow him, but I went across the lobby and out the revolving door after Laura. She was gone. I looked down the street, to see a taxi going away from the curb where the doorman stood.

"Did a young dark-haired woman get into that cab?" I asked him.

The doorman gave me a squint.

"She was wearing a black cocktail dress," I helped him.

"Didn't you just arrive a short time ago, sir?" he said to me.

"Right."

He nodded. "Yes, a dark-haired woman in a cocktail

dress went away in that taxi." He signaled for another cab, which came forward along the curb. He opened the door.

Pressing a dollar into his hand, I shook my head. "No thanks. I don't want to follow that cab."

The doorman closed the door and jammed the dollar bill into his pocket. Maybe it pays to tip well after all, I reminded myself. At least you get an answer if not a destination. She was probably off to see Jacquette, or home to a diet plate, wherever home was.

I was more tired than I wanted to admit. The train ride had sapped me, used me up, turned me into a crank. That outburst against Jacquette had been stupid all right. What good had it done, smart guy, except get you a lonely bed? Bankers. What was worse—doctors or lawyers, all money-grabbing, power-sucking fraternities that shielded members against the demands of the have-nots, the social strata that survived and flourished as American aristocracies.

I began walking down Fifth Avenue, past the elegant stores, windows now dimly lit to show emaciated mannequins in chic apparel. Yeah, it was a caste system now in America not dissimilar to India's, only it was built on earning power and staying power and control power, not religion. The workers, whose children would never enter Harvard anymore—had they ever outside of a 1930s dream?—would be forever lost inside that strata of strangling debt owed to the Jacquettes of the world. And the Jacquettes stayed sleek and myriad-times-over solvent because of that debt. And they lived longer and longer, the Jacquettes, and got richer and richer.

"Hey, mister, mister."

I came out of my walking daydream to look into the garishly made-up face of a young hooker who stood stoically in front of me, tugging at my arm.

"What do you want?"

"To show you a good time, what else? Ain't you been listening? I been beating my mouth on you for five minutes."

I pulled gently away, but she held on, a firm grasp of long fingers with hideous bloodred talons at the end of them, wrapped about my arm. "No, thanks," I said.

She held on. Looking down the street, I was amazed to see that for blocks and blocks Fifth Avenue teemed with prostitutes, young and old, black and white, and many of them transvestites, the males in female clothing having broad shoulders that almost burst through cheap blouses, hipless, without buttocks.

It should have come as no surprise to me. I had written about the invasion of prostitutes in New York City, how in recent years they had swarmed out of that pesthole that was 42nd Street and Broadway, once Winchell's "beating heart" of the city, and spread out through the better areas. And now they had reached Fifth Avenue, plying their coarse trade in front of Tiffany's, Rockefeller Center, and, God forbid, St. Patrick's Cathedral.

"Come on, mister, I'll get you good and hot," the young lady cooed.

"I'm plenty hot already," I said to her.

"I'm not talking about the weather, baby."

"I told you no thanks." Reaching over with my free hand, I pried one of her hands loose from my coat sleeve.

"Now, God damn it, you listen to me—you ain't never gonna get a piece—"

"Off you go, lady!" I worked her other hand loose and gave her a gentle shove. She fell backward, exaggerating her movements, so that it appeared that I had struck her hard.

"Why, you bastard, if my man was here, he'd cut it off!"

I started to walk away from her as she screamed after me. A few feet away, on the corner, I spotted a cop staring at me. I went up to him as the girl continued shouting her homemade obscenities.

Jerking a thumb in her direction, I said to the cop: "What about that?"

He gave me a serious, disapproving look. "What'sa matter, mister?"

"Did you see that?"

"Yeah. So what?"

"Are you a cop?" I looked him over, from cap to heavy black shoes, resting my eyes at his badge.

"What the hell do I look like, a messenger from Western Union?"

"New York's finest," I growled, and began to walk away.

The cop turned and walked along with me, a tough young dark-faced fellow clutching a nightstick. "I'm gonna give you some advice, friend," he said with intimidating concern. "Since you sound like you ain't from the city . . . you should know that you don't act like that with these people."

I didn't look at him and kept walking. "Go ahead—tell me all about it."

"You don't push 'em away, you hear 'em out, see? You're polite, see, nice to 'em, 'cause they're just tryin' to earn a livin' like anybody else. You're lucky that was a young broad you pushed, new around here. If it was someone else, you'd maybe get carved. These people got knives, razors, guns, some of 'em, and they're all nuts, so you listen and then thank 'em and then quietly walk away. You got that, fella?"

We stopped inside the same footstep and I looked him in the eyes. "Some cop—what do you get? A buck a trick?"

With animal quickness he jumped in front of me, spreading his legs, snarling: "Who the hell you think you are?" He brought his nightstick horizontal to his chest, gripping it so hard that his knuckles whitened. His eyes opened to bursting. "I oughta crack you on the head!"

"You're in my way," I told him, but I didn't move forward.

"If you weren't wearin' a tie an' dressed up like that, I'd crack you good." He blinked quickly, then lowered the stick. "Try to give a guy some advice and what does he do? He accuses you of bein' a whore like all the other god-damned whores. You know how many whores we got in Manhattan, wise guy?"

"A little over fifty thousand, high and low, from five bucks behind packing crates to five hundred at the special clubs, for an hour or a night, I know."

Now he looked *me* over. He blinked rapidly again. "What are you—somebody from the commission? Huh?"

"You're in my way," I repeated.

The cop stepped aside, talking rapidly as I passed him. "You're from the vice commission, huh? Well, I'll say it was entrapment, buddy, that's what I'll tell 'em if I get pulled in."

I kept walking, twenty feet, thirty, and he talked after me, his voice growing distant.

"I'm one guy down here, alone for this whole area . . . how am I expected to handle all these creeps? . . . one guy . . . jus' don't pull any of that entrapment crap, buddy . . . 'cause they know I'm jus' one guy . . . all alone . . . down here."

I turned briefly to see him standing in the middle of the wide sidewalk, hands on hips, shouting out his lungs at me. The night creatures around him in their stilt-like heels and grotesque dresses moved away from him rapidly, fearing no doubt that he would take out his anger on them, and *arrest someone.* "You think a guy alone . . . can handle all these people? . . . God damn it! . . . Like to see you do it, smartass . . . there must be a thousand of

'em . . . a million of 'em. . . . A buck a trick, huh? . . .
So that makes me a goddamned millionaire. . . . Ha, ha!"

The cop twisted his head about, realizing scores of eyes
were upon him, looking like hovering nighthawks from
the doorways of shops and the mouths of alleys. He spun
on his heel, walked to the curb, and slammed his nightstick against a hollow steel lamppost that rang out with
what sounded like the death knell of a great city.

Before I turned away and headed for the Algonquin, I
saw the cop raise his arm in my direction and give me the
inevitable finger.

2

Upon returning to the hotel I went immediately to my
room and, weak from walking and no food, ordered dinner sent up, a club sandwich and lobster bisque soup. I
read the *Times* story about the Chicago shooting and saw
that someone had underscored in pencil the line reading:
*John Howard Journey, crime historian and Mr. Lind-
quist's employer, was unavailable for comment.*

I turned on the TV and waded through a half-dozen talk
shows before I hit an old movie, *All Through the Night*,
with Bogart looking for Nazi spies. As I lay on the bed fully
dressed I dozed off, hearing that marvelous gravel voice;
Bogart would track down the agents, Conrad Veidt, Peter
Lorre, Judith Anderson, the whole rotten bunch, and
bring them to justice. He always did.

Into sleep I took with me the unshakable conviction
that the two men on the train had been cops after all, that
they had tailed me to New York and had gotten off at
Harrisburg to throw off suspicion. Funny-looking detectives, though. They didn't fit the physical mold. Maybe
they were federal. Why would federal agents become
involved in a local murder in Chicago? Well, it was no

trick to get off a train at Harrisburg and then fly to New York. They probably thought that was clever. What did they have? A box of cartridges? If they were federal agents, they could have pinched me for carrying a weapon across a state line. No, that applies to cars, transporting stolen cars across a state line.

The man who had gone up to Laura in the Plaza lobby didn't look like a cop, didn't smell like one. What could he ask her about me that would mean anything? She knew nothing, other than the fact that I had been on the train to research an article, if she believed that bilge, which she probably didn't. Did she get up in the middle of that wheel-clacking night? Do you remember her getting up and going to the washroom? Yes, dimly, and how she looked at your jacket, the inside pocket, remember? Did she do that? What's the difference? It was a natural thing for her, to check the name of my tailor, which was on a label on the inside of the pocket. It was the kind of snobbish curiosity that would fit her personality. Laura Manville would not have slept with just anybody on a moving train in a space-cramped bed, not wearing an off-the-rack suit. No, it didn't make sense, but she did look into the pocket as she came out of the washroom before getting dressed and going back to her own compartment. Did she really do that? Did she?

I struggled upward out of sleep, opening my eyes with great difficulty. The TV was buzzing and pictureless. Bogart, William Demarest, and Frank McHugh had captured the Nazis and gone home. I stood up and went to the chair where my jacket was draped. I pulled out my wallet and checked the contents. Money, cards, everything was there. I reached inside the inner pocket and took out Lucan's check and the Keimes letter to Lucan. Nothing had been touched. No, Laura had merely been checking the tailor's label.

The phone rang shrilly, piercingly loud, it seemed. Laura was on the line. "Jack—I'm sorry I walked out on you. Are you all right?"

"I'm okay, tired, that's all."

"Oh, I knew it was that," came her soothing low voice. "I told Darnley it was from that terrible train trip, that you weren't yourself. He understood."

"He did?"

"You may not believe this, Jack, but Darnley Jacquette admires your work. He could be a good friend. He's a wonderful and dedicated man. He told me he understood your conduct and to forget what you had said."

"When did he tell you that?"

"Oh, I caught up with him at the Plaza and we talked briefly."

"When you left the table?"

"Yes—and I'm sorry about spilling the wine. It was childish."

"You talked with Jacquette before he left the Plaza tonight?"

"Yes, in the lobby."

Her lie was senseless. But then, Laura had not known I had followed her, seen her alone, talking only to the man from the train in the lobby.

"It was sweet of you, beautiful," I told her, wanting to hang up as soon as possible.

"We all get out of sorts, Jack. I understand. Give me a call in the morning at the bank."

"Sure. Good night."

"Bye-bye, handsome."

So she hadn't seen Jacquette at the Plaza before he left. She had seen him later. Her call was probably made from his home, whatever mansion that was. He was more than a boss, than the president of a powerful bank, to Laura. But what about the guy from the train? I didn't know. I didn't know much about any of it and I was in New York, off my beat with slim contacts and not much hope of ever tracking down Hugo Keimes, unless Carlisle Cashe came through. On that score I was not optimistic.

I left an early wake-up call and sometime later the phone jarred me awake. I called Chicago and talked to Abbe at home. Everything was all right, meaning that Henry was not sick, the cops had not put out a dragnet for me, and Charlie liked it so much in the hospital he was thinking of staying on for another week. I told Abbe I would call her later that day.

After standing for twenty minutes under a hot shower, I felt fresh, ready to go, destination unknown. I ordered up some breakfast, croissants and coffee. Then I called Laura. She answered the phone after I went through three male secretaries who spoke annoyingly precise English.

"How are you this morning?" Her voice was cheery.

"Fine. I'm sorry about the diatribe last night." I wasn't very sorry.

"You're forgiven."

"Thanks. That makes me feel a whole lot better. What about a make-up dinner tonight?"

There was a pause, as if she were checking her schedule and then she said: "Sounds good."

"We'll go someplace special—have any favorite restaurants?"

"Any place French will do."

"I'll come by the bank and pick you up around five."

"Can you make it about six? I've got a crushing day."

"Six it is, Haley National Bank."

"Main entrance," she said, and clicked off without a good-bye.

I called Carlisle Cashe at home but got no answer. After an hour of killing time, reading over the morning *Times* that had been delivered with my breakfast, the phone rang and Cashe was at the other end of the line.

"I'm downstairs," he said. "I'll be sitting in the lobby under a 1928 lamp covered with a 1931 shade. You can't miss me—I'll be on the third overstuffed couch to the right."

Cashe looked awful, red-eyed, his unmanageable hair looking wilder than the day before, shooting upward and outward as if attempting to escape his scalp. We sat sipping coffee on a couch in the lobby, which was almost deserted except for an elderly woman in a print dress and an enormous hat who was reading *The Wall Street Journal* and an old man dozing in a wing-back chair.

"This guy Keimes is a runout, Jack," Cashe said, shaking his head.

"What does that mean?"

"It means he's taken off, flown the coop, beat it, as they might say in Chicago, scrammed. I went over to his place on Lexington this morning. The damned elevator was out, so I had to hike it up six floors—in this heat! The office is locked up like City Hall on Christmas. Down the stairs I go, to the super, who tells me Keimes has paid off his rent and moved out, desks, cabinets, everything."

"I don't suppose you found out where he shipped his equipment?"

Cashe gave me a forced smile. "Think I'm a regular clown, don't you, that I'm lazy. Oh, no, you're paying, so I'm doing the job. Yeah—he shipped it all to this address in Brooklyn." He handed me a slip of paper with an address on it. "I don't know where he shipped himself."

"So you have to go to Brooklyn."

Cashe took a gulp of tepid black coffee. "Maybe not so far. I find out from the super that Mr. Hugo Keimes had all his stuff shipped to Brooklyn except four big boxes that went over to an address on Ninth Avenue. And here's that address." Cashe handed over another slip of paper with his scrawl on it.

"It would be a good idea if you went over to Ninth Avenue, Carl."

Cashe shrugged. "That's a real divey area—wonder what he would be sending over there, fruit maybe."

"Fruit?"

"That Ninth Avenue address is surrounded by fruit and vegetable stands. You know, outdoor tables loaded with grapes and zucchini. No bookstores over that way, nobody reads books in that district, only labels that tell you which side of a tomato box is up."

"I've got a few more bookdealers we could check in the city who might have heard from Keimes," I said. "Maybe you could check them out for me. My address book is in my room. Come on."

We went up to the room and as we walked into the small sitting area, I saw, through the open bedroom door, a hotel valet on his knees, smoothing wrinkles from the bedspread.

"What are you doing?" I asked the valet.

He jumped up, surprised, then sauntered out of the bedroom. His nameplate read *Franklin*.

Cashe walked to a chair and sank into it.

"What do you want?" I asked the valet, who was heading for the door.

"Apparently, there's a mistake, sir," he said quietly as he continued walking to the door. "We got a call that you wanted some clothes pressed, but when I went to the bedroom I found nothing laid out."

"I didn't call the valet," I said.

"Apparently not, sir." He looked disapprovingly at Cashe and his crumpled clothes. "They probably got the room numbers mixed up downstairs. Happens sometimes." He went out the door, nodding his bald head.

"Yeah," Cashe said, yawning and stretching before standing up and following me into the bedroom. "At the Algonquin it's service whether you want it or not."

Standing at the small desk next to the window, I picked up my address book and began to jot down phone numbers and addresses of some New York bookdealers I knew. "Maybe some of these fellows will give you a lead or two on Keimes," I told Cashe without looking at him.

"I'll need some more moola, Jack."

"I know." I turned and reached into my pocket. Cashe was at the side of the bed.

"I'm really bushed," he complained tiredly. "I could use a nap." With that he grinned and impulsively threw himself sideways and downward on the bed. As he flopped down, there was a metallic clicking noise, a hideous tearing of fabric and flesh. In that split second Carlisle Cashe was dead. I saw his last motions of life quiver away through his hands and feet as he sprawled spread-eagled, a look of amazement on his angular face, his eyes bulging to the point of leaving their sockets. Through his chest protruded a steel spear and from its point ran Carlisle Cashe's human gore.

The minute I moved to his side, I knew he was dead. I checked beneath the bed to see that the spear had been somehow ejected from a spring mechanism placed beneath the bed, released the moment the weight of his body hit the mattress. I reached over and closed the lids of his eyes.

3

"A man—a good friend of yours, you say—gets impaled with an eighteen-inch steel spear sent up through a bed from a spring trap and you sit there and tell me you don't know a damned thing about it?" The man asking me this question was a chubby lieutenant of homicide, who leaned back in a wooden chair, jabbing a pencil into the side of a fleshy cheek.

"I was in the room, saw it happen, that was all."

"And you got no explanations?"

"I could give you a dandy guess."

He nodded once.

"Okay, the spear was meant for me. I've already told you that a valet was in the bedroom smoothing down the blanket on the bed when we came into the room."

"Yeah, we got that. A valet named Franklin, but the hotel says that no one by that name works here."

"That was the name on the little plate pinned to his uniform. But he wasn't smoothing down the blanket."

"What was he doing?" The lieutenant looked at me deadpan.

"He was pinpointing exactly where I had lain on the bed, noting the depression my body made on the blankets, figuring I would go back to that same spot. Most people do. And he centered the spear device right beneath that spot, knowing that when I hit the bed again, I'd lie down in the same place and the spear would do the rest. Only, Carl went on the bed instead of me and took the spear."

"Don't you think," said the lieutenant, drawing out his words as if talking to a child, "that if someone wanted to kill you they'd just put a bullet into you? That's the convenient way, you know, the safe way. Why all this elaborate spear stuff? Who's after you, Mr. Journey? Aborigines?" He snorted.

"I don't know."

He leaned forward on the worn-out desk in front of him, placing his elbow at the corner and resting his chin in his hands. "Somebody shoots at you in Chicago, and some of the homicide guys in your town tell me that they also tried to poison you, and you come here, and now somebody tries to harpoon you like a salmon. What did you do to deserve all this attention, Mr. Journey?"

"I don't know." I thought for a minute and then blurted: "Maybe I've got something they want."

"Why not give it to them?"

"I can't do that."

"I don't understand." The fat lieutenant squinted and his eyes disappeared into heavy folds of flesh. "It's your life. Nothing can be worth more than that. Give it to them, whatever it is."

"One more time—I can't."

He clucked his tongue. "Back to you—why?"

"Because I don't know what I've got that they want."

"What?" He sat up straight, hands on his knees, leaning toward me as I sat in his bleak office. The door was open and the noises of the precinct house drifted inside—officers walking, hollow-sounding conversations, distant commands and responses. "Let me have it again—just say I'm a dumb cop and you have to spell it out for me, Mr. Journey."

"It's true. I don't know what they want, so I can't give them anything. You see how damned simple that is, don't you?"

"I see that it doesn't make any sense."

"Nothing has made any kind of sense for the last few days."

Pointing a fat finger at me, the lieutenant cautioned: "You're in trouble."

"I had nothing to do with Cashe's death."

He grimaced and two enormous dimples presented themselves. "We know *that*, but we also know that we don't want you getting killed in New York."

"Is Chicago all right?"

"The cops in your town said you were a wise guy. Okay

—sure, go back to Chicago and get killed. Or go over to Jersey and get it done there. You might enjoy dying in Jersey, a lot of people do. Is that wise-guy talk enough for you?"

"I'd like to be going."

"Where are you going, Mr. Journey?"

"Back to my hotel."

He cleared his throat. "Maybe you ought to move to another hotel while you're visiting our wonderful town. How about the Sheraton or the Waldorf?"

"I like the Algonquin. They've given me a new room."

The fat lieutenant stood up when I did. "How long are you going to be here, Mr. Journey?"

"A few more days maybe."

"You know, we'd really love it if you could make it a few hours."

"I've got business to do."

"What kind of business?" Suddenly he held up his hand. "Okay, okay, I know—freedom of the press, First Amendment, journalist on parade." He walked with me to the door of his office, his gigantic frame lumbering forward. He put his arm on my shoulder and said with Dutch-uncle wisdom: "I'm gonna tell you something, journalist. Unless you figure out what these maniacs want from you and turn it over, you're in for more of the same and what they tried this morning—the spear thing—is nothing compared to what they might do tonight." He grinned grotesquely. "These guys are really inventive."

I moved from under his arm, which fell heavily to his side as I stepped into the hallway. "What do you suggest I do about it?"

"Go back to Chicago. Whatever it is started there and you should finish it there, got me?"

"And wind up on Chicago's homicide books instead of yours."

"Watch yourself," he said without conviction. Then he closed his office door and I walked along the grimy corridor, down the creaking wooden stairs of the precinct building, and out into the bright, hot afternoon.

I knew from the moment I hailed a cab and got into it a half block from the police station that the cops would be following, that the fat lieutenant would make sure that wherever I went in New York, detectives would be five breaths away. Leaning forward in the cab, I watched through the rearview mirror as an unmarked cop car pulled away from the curb and followed the taxi at a respectable distance. Two men sat in the car, heads stiff, faces staring straight ahead. No, the police would try to see to it that I did not litter up their morgue.

"What are they?" the cab driver said, following my gaze in the mirror.

"Cops."

"Really?" He was an old man with a huge nose and gnarled features. "Geez, you do something, mister?"

"Only minding my own business."

The driver turned quickly to look at me and then back to his driving. "You some sort of dignitary, star maybe?"

"Yeah," I said indifferently. "I'm the Big Boy Rocker from Australia. Rock's my life. You know how it is— swarmed over with fans. The police want to make sure I don't get injured by those who adore me."

He looked me over again in the mirror. "Big Boy Rocker, huh? I thought youse guys all wore long hair and painted your faces."

"Not in Australia. The rock people all have short hair, wear suits, and carry their instruments in large paper bags. We're very discreet."

"Geez, and you don't even sound like an Australian guy."

"We all sound like Americans now."

"Not British at all anymore, huh?"

"Not a tad."

"Just goes to show you—you never know who gets into your hack. I had Lauren Bacall in here once. Baby, you know. She was nice."

"Nice."

Then his litany began. "Let's see, singers—there was Mel Torme, the Velvet Fog, some years back, mind you— and Frankie Laine and Allan Jones, also many years back. Those were terrific singers, not rock stars, though, Mr. Rocker."

"Too bad."

"Yeah, well, them rock people usually take limos, you know."

"I prefer cabs, less ostentatious."

"Yeah, you're right, cabs is less costly, sure."

The police stayed behind us, about a quarter of a block. I had told the lieutenant that I did not know what the killers wanted, but I could have volunteered real suspicions. I could have showed him the Lucan check and the Keimes letter—it had to be that—items that were tied to a string and wrapped around a library I never received. It wasn't the check or the letter, I then concluded. It was what they represented, the damned library. But I didn't have a single book from that collection. As far as I knew, it wasn't even in the United States. For God's sake, who would be killing anybody for the sake of some musty old books?

"Is this the address you want, Mr. Rocker?"

"Where are we?"

"At the address you gave me—on Ninth Avenue."

The street was alive with crowds of seedy shoppers and smelled like Old MacDonald's farm. Produce of all colors and sizes, from cabbages and king-size corn, was piled high on long, open stalls and milling about these were pushing, grabbing customers.

I looked at a doorway that said 106, which was the address Cashe had given me, the place where Keimes had sent the four large boxes, an unlikely destination.

"You really want to go here, Mr. Rocker?"

"Yeah, sure." I handed him some money and got out.

"It ain't a place I'd ever figure a big-shot rock star would wander around," said the cabbie.

"I'm a vegetarian," I assured him as I closed the door. "I only eat fresh onions and beans."

"There's a lot of strange types around here," he warned.

I nodded up the street in the direction where the black unmarked police car had pulled over. "I've got the cops to keep me company," I said. And *that* was reassuring to me.

The cab pulled away and I went inside and up the steep stairs. There was a single overhanging light at the top where a hallway split in three directions. To the left, fronting a long wooden railing, was a row of cheap offices with opaque glass doors. I walked slowly past these doors to the end office. All of the doors had stenciled names on them, mostly in large print and centered on the glass. The end door bore, at the bottom of the glass and in small letters, the name HUGO KEIMES BOOKDEALER.

I tried the doorknob, and with incredible luck, felt it turn all the way. I stepped inside to see a long, littered office, a few old desks, paper strewn about. Three windows facing the street were open and let in the noise of the hectoring shoppers below. To the right was another office with more opaque glass that ran from a waist-high wall to the ceiling and a connecting door that was closed.

Keimes was either a sloppy character or someone had ransacked the place. Books, holographs, white papers in brittle folds, coated the floors; books stood on end, opened to bent pages. It appeared as if someone had been literally walking on the books. At the right-hand corner where two desks formed an L, four heavy wooden crates stood ripped to pieces. Almost tiptoeing around the carpet of books, I went to the crates and inspected them, pulling out one book after another. They were all in German and dealt with a single subject, archaeology.

Picking up the lid of one of the crates, I could see that the boxes had been sent from Paris by Jean Rombout, Keimes's book contact in France. The addresses, clearly stenciled in the center of the lid, held me in shock for a moment: JOHN HOWARD JOURNEY, C/O HUGO KEIMES. Beneath these words was Keimes's Lexington Avenue address. I went to the other opened crates, yanking out book after book. Every book dealt with archaeology and all were in German. It was stupidly bewildering. What the hell—I could hardly read German and I hadn't ordered a library on archaeology. As I held the heavy crate lid in my sweating hand, I lost my grip and the lid slipped over the box and down behind the two desks. I walked around the desks to retrieve it and saw, face downward, the short, squat body of a man wearing gray slacks and a white shirt. In the middle of his back was a long stiletto, driven three quarters into the flesh, spreading blood in a bursting-sun pattern.

Kneeling, I turned the body sideways by the shoulders and trembled at the sight. Although half the man's face had been eaten away by what appeared to be acid, I still recognized the dead man as Hugo Keimes. This was torture, no doubt, slow and agonizing, and finished off with the knife. "It's a rotten end," I found myself saying, letting go of the shoulder so that the body fell back on its face. I had liked Hugo Keimes, a good man, conscientious, fair. Maybe that's why he's dead, I thought. Christ, that's insane. Nobody, but nobody, dies for the sake of a book.

Next to the body was a large can of kerosene and some rags. I lifted the can and found it heavy. Dangerous stuff to have around paper and books, I thought. It wasn't for the books, I then realized; the kerosene was for Keimes. They had tortured him and stabbed him to death, after getting whatever information he had to give, or getting nothing at all, and then had intended to burn him and the whole place, to cover it all up with fire, accidental tragedy. This was the way the mob did things, I reminded myself, this was *their* modus operandi, and so were the acid and the stiletto, all mob.

But the job wasn't complete. Why? Because you walked in at the end. I felt Keimes's neck and hands. He was still warm. Nice. You had walked right in on it while they were finishing up. They hadn't had time to use the kerosene, to burn up their victim. Smart guy you are, barge in anywhere, help yourself to murder, maybe your own. I wondered where the hell those cops were who had been tailing me. Oh, down the street, sitting in their car, eating egg salad sandwiches and swilling pineapple soda.

There was a sudden scraping sound, like metal tearing at metal, coming from the adjoining office. I wasn't alone with the dead Hugo Keimes. A large, bulky shadow loomed behind the opaque glass of the next office, going upward. Someone had been hiding there, crouching low behind the waist-high wall. I stood up, went around the desk, and headed quickly for the hallway door as the shadow moved down the wall of glass toward the door leading to the main office.

I had gotten the hallway door half-open when the door to the adjoining office burst open. "Remain where you are, Mr. Journey." Coming toward me, an automatic in his hand and aimed at my midsection, was the familiar face of the older man who had been in Bedroom D on the train. His stare was tranquil and he moved his large body gracefully around the books underfoot. He glanced down at the debris and then back to me as he stalked forward.

"What are you? A cop?"

A trace of a smile flickered on his thin lips. I was dripping sweat at the moment, frozen in the door, looking vainly down the dark hallway for another human being. He, on the other hand, was cool.

"Oh, no," I volunteered, "not a cop. A book collector shortchanged on an order. That it?"

He kept coming, silent, only a few feet away now. He reached out, as if to slam the hallway door closed, and at that second his heavy foot landed halfway on the spine of a book that put him off balance and sent him sideways. I helped him along by jerking the door inward at him so that the wooden frame around the glass struck him hard and square in the head. He fell into the wall with a surprised look on his face and I dove through the open doorway, pulling the door shut after me.

Once in the hallway, I held on to the doorknob but stepped to the side of the wall. I knew what was coming and it did—several shots, fired straight through the center of the heavy glass. As I had hoped, the heavy glass caused the bullets to implode rather than crash through and shatter the glass.

With three shots fired, the gunman tried the doorknob, but I gripped it with both hands, still pressing my body to the side of the wall. He pulled and yanked, but I held on. He stopped. Now he will step back and let me have a few more bullets, I thought, this time he'll shoot downward at the knob in an attempt to blow away my hand. I let go gently and dashed down the hall, spun in a semicircle at the end of the railing, and went down the stairs three at a time, thinking I would miss a step any second and pitch forward to break my neck at the bottom.

I heard two more shots, distant, muffled. He was firing

through the glass again, his bullets mushrooming as they struck that heavy plate, I knew. It was the mob, all right; nobody but a mob gunman would be stupid enough to keep firing through glass that didn't shatter, to fail to realize what was happening. They work like automatons. You point them and they torture, stab, burn, and shoot. As I neared the bottom of the stairs I slowed my movement by stretching out my arms and, touching the narrow walls on either side, using my palm-outward hands to brake. My momentum carried me into the door at the bottom, which I flung open.

Glancing upward, I saw the gunman appear at the top of the landing. He knew it was too late for a clear shot and he scooted back around the railing corner, no doubt looking for the back stairs. I had to shove my way outside into the crowds of shoppers.

Wedging my way outward, I managed to work myself around the front of a stall, past shoving wild-eyed women shouting Spanish. The vendors shouted back at them. I got to the end of one stall and was thrown inward against the wall of the building by a well-dressed heavyset man whose head seemed tiny, out of proportion. He held a large bag into which he was dumping fruit.

As I tried to go around him, the eager customer shoved me back again, reaching for some overripe cantaloupe and grunting: "Lemme at them melons, bud."

In that split second, as the eager customer pushed me aside and stepped into my space, he was showered with a liquid that I instantly identified as kerosene. Looking upward, I could see that we were directly beneath the open windows of Keimes's office.

Immediately following the kerosene shower a burning rag came downward. The expression on the man with the small head was one of utter confusion. He looked upward so that his face, dripping kerosene, met the burning rag. I jumped backward against the wall of the building as the shopper burst into flames.

The blaze raced down his clothes, following the kerosene. He screamed and spread huge arms, also lighted, going backward on his heels through the crowd; all jumped and ran from him. Pandemonium broke out, women and men fleeing, stumbling, diving onto open-air fruit stands to avoid his burning path. His screams were incoherent cries for help, but no one could help as he spun inward and bumped the stalls, his entire body a mass of leaping flames that, as he moved away from me, shot upward to ignite the colorful awnings that overhung the stalls.

Scores of people ran into the street; some were struck by moving cars. Traffic came to a standstill. A woman stood at the curb throwing out clenched fists to the fleeing throng, shouting: "Someone help him, *please!* Oh, God, someone help him!"

He was almost a black hulk now, a quarter of a block away, stumbling and crashing into the stalls, igniting anything he touched that would burn. The two cops who had been following me appeared, getting out of their car and jogging toward the burning man. They watched him with open mouths and bug-eyed stares, helpless, utterly powerless to do anything except wait for the poor creature to burn himself to death. His energy gone, the burning man tripped forward. Strange strangling, guttural sounds escaping his charred face. He collapsed on a stall as a vendor, tall and robust, reached upward and ripped away a piece of burned awning and covered the man with it, pressing it downward on him. His arm jutted from beneath it and the crowd that closed in on him walked slowly forward in wonder and shock.

"Get away, get away," said one of the cops, flashing his badge and going to the dead man. Shopkeepers along the block were tearing down smoldering awnings; some had lugged out hand extinguishers and were crazily spraying foam in all directions. Two men who had run pell-mell into the street and had been struck by cars were being lifted up with bruises and cuts.

I looked upward to Keimes's open window, to see that the gunman had fled. A cop from the tail car came up. His face was white, his hands shook.

"I saw it, I saw it all—mister, you're a walking disaster."

"That kerosene was meant for me. The other guy shoved me aside and caught the load." I could hear my voice, oddly calm. "It came from the open window up there."

"I saw that, I saw that," the detective repeated.

"I was just up there and found a body, tortured with acid, stabbed. Hugo Keimes, a bookdealer I've been looking for. His killer was in the place, tried to shoot me—you'll find the bullet holes in the glass door of Keimes's office."

The detective turned shakily to see his partner fold the burned man's arm beneath the awning. "I saw the whole damned thing from the car—wait a minute." He came back to me, stepped close. "There's another one?"

"Upstairs, dead. The killer intended to burn him but I walked in, then ran out, and he tried to burn me with the kerosene."

His eyes darted about in their sockets as he went over every square inch of my face. "You say it so goddamned simple, like going out for a pack of cigarettes. You ain't got any emotions, mister."

"I've got them, same as you," I said, looking downward at my hands, which were strangely calm. "I'm just afraid to let them out right now, if you don't mind."

"Oh, that poor son of a bitch," the detective said as he

looked back at the dead man, and I didn't have a single doubt that he would have preferred to see me lying there, immolated, a cinder. Someone else clearly had the same wish.

VI

Meet the Mafia

1

I was back in the fat lieutenant's office, sitting at the same desk in the same hardback chair. This time the fat cop was holding his head in both hands, exhausted at the sight of me. I had already spent an hour describing my assailant, the man who had obviously murdered Keimes and burned the shopper by mistake, described him verbally to the lieutenant and, in detail, such as I could remember, to the police artist, who did up a skimpy composite sketch. There was nothing else that could be done except to hear out the lieutenant, to take his expected lecture in silence. After some hurried glances at my watch and a remark about how I had to get going, he jumped off on cue.

"You're what they used to call a pip or a corker." He clucked his tongue. "I call you a jinx." He gave a great sigh and then pointed his finger at me. "You're leaving New York, Journey."

"Only a few hours ago it was *Mr.* Journey."

"That was then, when we had only one corpse on our

hands. You ain't been in town for more than twenty-four hours and one man gets a spear through his chest, another is burned with acid and punctured with a stiletto, and another becomes a human torch that burns down half of Ninth Avenue. *Three* people are dead since you came to our fair city." He held up three fingers and shook them at me for emphasis. *"Three* human beings."

"I can count."

"You're leaving town, Journey, today."

"I'll leave when I'm damned good and ready."

He straightened his body in the chair, shifting his girth. "Today!"

"You're supposed to protect everyone in this city, lieutenant. That includes visitors."

He snorted a laugh. "You ain't a visitor. You're a plague. You're leaving today."

"And you don't run citizens out of town because someone around them gets murdered. What if I were a resident here instead of a visitor? Would you run me out of town?"

He spoke his words slowly: "If I had to get your citizenship revoked, yes!" Then he tried patronizing kindness. "Look, you're an intelligent fellow, Journey. Some very mean people are trying to kill you. But you've been lucky and some others haven't and they've been killed. You can't go on like this or the murder rate of New York City will double before the week is out. Now, I don't know what your business is, but will you please get on with it and leave? We'll give you a man to stay with you."

"I don't want any chaperons, thanks."

"We got a good man. He knows karate, expert marksman, wears a bulletproof vest, never sleeps, and is close-mouthed. Until you leave town."

"No—besides, I know some karate myself."

"Oh, great, great." He reached into a side drawer of his

desk. "I suppose you're a marksman too." The fat lieutenant pulled out a .38 in a holster, throwing it on the desk. "Ever see this before?"

"It looks like mine."

He arched his eyebrows, which sent ribbons of fat up to his hairline. "It is yours, Journey. We took it out of your suitcase at the hotel."

"You had no right to do that without a warrant."

"To hell with warrants! We are talking about three dead people."

"The gun is empty, as you found out, but it's mine. Hand it over."

"What do you want to carry around an empty gun for?"

"It's a memento from my service days. It's registered in Chicago and I'm not carrying it around."

He shoved the .38 toward me. "G'wan, take the thing. Put it back in your suitcase and keep it there. Now, what about this man of ours?"

"I told you, I don't want any bodyguards."

"Cooperate."

"I am, by not taking this guy on I'll probably save his life."

"No—you don't get it. He's supposed to save your life."

There was a lunch bag on the lieutenant's desk. I reached for it, dumped out some sandwiches and an orange, and shoved the .38 and holster into it.

"You got a goddamned nerve, you know that?" He looked at me with mad piglike eyes. His whole fat face was beet-red with anger.

"So have you. You went into my suitcase without permission."

"Nobody stole your socks."

"I'll need this bag to carry the weapon. I can't go around Manhattan showing a .38."

"Considerate of you. I can't tell you how much we appreciate your consideration."

I stood up. "I'm going now."

He didn't move, only rolled up his eyes to look at me without moving his enormous head.

"And don't put your karate expert on my tail."

"We don't need to do that to know where you are," he said in a tired voice. "We'll just follow the trail of bodies."

As I turned to go a short, muscular fellow stepped into the office. His shoulders were wide and his legs were so thick that they almost burst the seams of his slacks. His black hair was cut short, almost to a crewcut. He looked at the lieutenant, then me, asking his superior: "Is this the guy?"

"That's him, Jimmy."

"You put this besock on me," I told the lieutenant, "and I'll be in court with an expensive lawyer getting an injunction before nightfall."

"If you think you're gonna do anything alone, you're crazy. And I know what you're thinking, Journey."

I walked to the door, past the would-be bodyguard, into the corridor. As I made my way toward the stairs I could hear the karate expert complaining: "What do you want to help out a guy like that for? Hear what he called me—a besock? The guy's a nut from Chicago and we stick our necks out for him? Why? What the hell is a besock anyway?"

I stopped for a moment to hear the fat lieutenant's response: "Something they grow in Chicago."

2

The tally was grim and my side was losing. Four were dead and one wounded and I still didn't know the name of the game. What I did know added up to pennies. Someone wanted me dead, someone wanted the library I had never gotten, or, specifically, wanted something that was in that library. I speculated wildly on this while cabbing back to the Algonquin.

As I'd understood it from Lucan when I bought the library two months ago, the collection had about eighteen hundred volumes on historic crime, mostly French with some obscure tomes from Corsica and other Mediterranean islands. Some of the books dated back to the middle of the last century. The library's owner had been an inspector of the Sûreté, retired, then dead. His widow had put up the collection to pay off some debts and Jean Rombout in Paris had purchased the books.

I had no idea what the collection might contain. It was standard practice to buy such private libraries blind, but I had figured that it would yield some valuable works, many I did not already possess, since my research on French crime history was thin. My understanding of French was also shabby, but my secretary understood the language well and could do the necessary translations. What would interest anyone enough to murder over the contents of a library having hundred-year-old books? There was something in the collection, had to be, but what? The inspector's files? No, the French were extremely meticulous about such matters. The Sûreté checked and rechecked their banks of information. It was all computerized anyway and anyone desperate enough could go into the live computer banks without all this savagery. And they'd do it in Paris, not here.

Well, they—whoever "they" were—didn't know where the library was any more than I did. But they did think that Keimes had it. So did I. All he had, however, were German archaeology books. Yes, but they had been sent to me care of him by Rombout, the *wrong* library. And Keimes had been killed over that? I felt like returning to

Chicago, but I knew it would only start all over again and wouldn't end until I knew why I was marked for death or until I was dead. The answers weren't in Chicago. Now that Keimes was dead they weren't in New York, either.

I got one of the answers, a big one, when I returned to the hotel. There was a message waiting for me from a dead man—Hugo Keimes. The murdered man had mailed a letter to me the day before he died, or so the postmark informed me. I took the letter to my room—the management had moved me to a new, small suite—and read it behind the locked door. I noticed with curiosity how my hand trembled as I held the message. It read:

Dear Jack—

I called your office when I heard that poor Lucan was dead and your secretary told me you were at the Algonquin, and so I am sending this in care of the hotel, hoping it will reach you. Quite by accident, we are in deep trouble. It's got something, God knows, to do with the European library I purchased for you via poor old Lucan in Chicago. The dealer in Paris, Jean Rombout, sent me your books, except they are not your books. He has *your* library, I would think, still in Paris somewhere. I put through a call to him, several, in fact, which were expensive calls, only to find out that he's vanished—a man I've done business with since the end of World War II—imagine? Disappeared, gone. And the police there are looking for *him*.

I read about Lucan's death and your researcher being shot and now they're on to me, whoever the madmen are who are doing these things, and I don't know a thing! They've called me *twice*. Threats. I don't even want that mistaken shipment from Rombout around so I'm shipping it to my old offices on Ninth Avenue and I'm clearing out for a while. I can't stand threats, Jack. I was a prisoner in Germany during the war, and it was threats, threats, threats. No more of that.

I urge you, for safety's sake, to *leave this alone*.

Hugo Keimes

P.S. The second call came an hour ago. The caller mentioned the name "Giuliano." Who's that?

Giuliano? I stared at the name as Keimes had written it, stared and tried to remember. It was a Mafia-connected name, I knew, but long ago, and not in the United States. I thought about the name and only the name, sifting every brain cell in my memory, the memory I had always counted on, my reserve battalion, tough and ready, but it wasn't there. I ordered a large pot of coffee and a sandwich from room service and thought about the name. I paced and thought. I called Chicago, got Abbe on the line, and told her to punch up the name on our small computer. It yielded nothing.

"Well, Jack, we've only been working with this electronic toy for about nine months. Not all our index cards from the old system have been transferred onto disks."

"Check the old card system." I waited several minutes before she came back on the line.

"We have a blank here, Jack," she finally reported. "Nothing in the U.S. on this Giuliano fellow. Has he got anything to do with all of this madness?"

"I don't know. How's Henry?"

"Your dog is fine, eating me out of my savings. Don't you want to ask about Charlie?"

"I know, he plans on staying in the hospital for a month."

"No, he's out, as of this morning. Came into the office

wearing an arm sling, then told me he was going on vacation and *might* be back in a few weeks. I gave him his check. That okay?"

"Fine."

"Everything going all right? You coming back soon?"

"A lot of problems here. You'll be reading about it, maybe see it on the six o'clock news."

"Network news? About you?"

"Me and some others. There were some more deaths."

"Oh, my God, Jack, come back, come home. You can't go on with this."

"I'll be all right," I told her, but I didn't feel all right. "Look for me in a few days. Has Ackerly been calling?"

"No."

I hung up and thought about Detective Ackerly in Chicago. He didn't have to call my office. He knew from the New York police exactly where I was and how much trouble I was in and was probably happy as hell about it, downright joyous. The police in Chicago and New York knew I had been singled out for a killing and neither wanted it to happen in their city. I was the Ping-Pong ball, the hot potato, the ugly duckling. My feelings were hurt. Take a cold shower, I told myself, you always think better in the shower. Go ahead, you can whistle, sing, and talk to yourself. And maybe your memory will perform.

I was in the shower for more than twenty minutes before it came to me, first in black-and-white images of old photos, a young man, handsome, rugged-looking, wearing khakis and two big guns on his hips, and a heavy ammunition belt across his chest, standing on a hilltop with some other heavily armed young men, all swarthy and serious-looking. Then I remembered another photo of the handsome young man lying in the middle of an ancient town square, his body riddled, blood spreading in all directions from his curly-haired head. *Salvatore Giuliano*, bandit,

Sicily. *Now* it made some sense. Yes, it was the Mafia after all, as all the killings would indicate, the silent death of the spike in the ear, the spear in the chest, the stiletto in the back, all weapons of the Mafia.

I can't explain why I felt relieved, even though I certainly headed the hit list, but I knew I was not at the center of this murder rampage. It was Salvatore Giuliano, a man who had been dead for more than thirty years. I put through another call to Abbe and had her go into our old file room again, this time checking foreign entries. She was back on the phone in five minutes.

"I've got it," she crowed, reading from the card: "Giuliano, Salvatore, Sicilian bandit, murdered, 1949, in—I don't know if I'm pronouncing this right—the town of Castelvetrano. There are six reference sources on the card, all from your library. Do you want me to get to your place and dig out the books?"

"Not necessary, I know them by heart."

"That's what all this insanity is about, Jack? A dead Sicilian bandit?"

"Yeah." As I sat at the desk in my hotel bedroom, I looked up to the mirror behind the desk and saw a smile on my face. "I think I know what's in the damned library I bought from Lucan."

"For God's sake, what? This dead bandit's bones?"

"Better than that. Giuliano fought the fascists in Sicily for many years. He was sponsored by the local Mafia, who supplied his small army with weapons and cash. It doesn't matter to know it now, but Mussolini had tried to stamp out the Mafia as a rival authority in Sicily, its birthplace in the thirteenth century. The local dons used Giuliano to destroy Mussolini's Black Shirts, control local elections, and keep that hot little island in a defiant mood. After the war, Giuliano was of no more use to the dons. He was an anachronism and a problem. The fascists were no more and here was Giuliano, the popular leader of a small but powerful army of men, like Robin Hood and his band.

"He was so popular that many thought he would dominate local politics and, the worst fear of the dons, stamp out the Mafia itself. So he was murdered, his body put on display for all to see. They took photographs of him bleeding in the square, with policemen standing nearby, laughing. They made a circus out of it with vendors marching around the bleeding corpse selling wine and cheese. I remember one photo showing a group of children playing ring-around-the-rosy with Giuliano's body at the center."

"Disgusting," Abbe said. "But what does that have to do with the library you bought?"

"The *memoriales*."

"The what?"

"Sicilian for dairies. Giuliano kept diaries, three or four little black books, into which he poured everything he knew about his traitorous partner, the Mafia."

"But that's thirty years ago."

"And the *memoriales* are still missing. They're famous, or infamous, if you like—they've never turned up. The boys in Chicago still talk about them now and then."

"What boys?"

"Chucky Amansa for one."

"I've seen his name in the papers. He's part of the mob, isn't he?"

"They enjoy talking about history, those people. The past, like these diaries, is safe for them."

"And this character Amansa has talked to you?"

"About the past. If I were to write what he and his friends might be doing next Monday and cause them to lose money, they'd be planting dynamite under my house by the truckload. Yesterday is safe, tomorrow is death. It's the way they think. If you interrupt ongoing business, you die. Murder, extortion, drugs, anything they're involved in is just business to them. How many times have I heard it? This is our business, business, business."

"I still don't get it, Jack. These diaries were written more than thirty years ago. They wouldn't contain anything that could affect anybody today, would they?"

"I'm not so sure, pal. Giuliano's great dream was to someday go to America. He loved the United States. He even ran for election once, and in the leaflets he handed out in Sicily he offered a plan that would propose a union between the United States and Sicily."

Abbe laughed. "This guy was suggesting we make Sicily a state?"

"Something like that."

"What a nut."

"A lot of people in Sicily didn't think so, except for the Mafia. The old dons had great plans following World War II, a business scheme to control all illegal operations worldwide with the United States as the clearinghouse. They sent men to America, to organize the various Mafia families of every major city, especially when it came to international drug traffic—America was to be the big store for the hard drugs, a flow of narcotics that the Sicilian dons controlled in Turkey, Greece, and South America. All of these plans, all of the men who went to America and the rising young Mafia leaders of the American families, were known to Giuliano the bandit. And he wrote it all down in his *memoriales*, which he used to blackmail the Mafia and which is probably the real reason he was murdered. But the dons never got the diaries, no one did. Before Hugo Keimes died—"

"Keimes is dead?" There was shock in her voice.

"Murdered, today, you'll read about it later."

"Oh, my God, Jack, come back to Chicago right away."

"Later. Keimes sent me a note and mentioned Giuliano. Just the name. It can only mean that the diaries are somewhere in the library. That's what someone else knows and they're after it. I don't know exactly why, but someone is still alive, I think, who's mentioned by Giuliano. It's the only explanation."

"What the hell do you care if someone who can still be hurt is mentioned in an old diary? Is that worth getting killed over?"

"It wouldn't have been a week ago, but Carlisle Cashe got killed and Keimes, and then some goon tried to burn me to death today. And then there's old Lucan and Charlie. All of that makes it worthwhile now."

"Come home, Jack." Abbe said this softly, pleading, but she knew what my reaction would be.

"I'm going out of the country for a few days, pal."

"Where?"

"Paris. And, yes, I packed my passport."

"You think of everything," she said in a resigned voice. "If you need anything, call me—here or at home, any hour. And take care of yourself."

"I will." I wasn't sure I could even get out of my hotel room.

Within ten minutes I had booked a Concorde flight to London and a connecting flight to Paris; I was to leave the next morning. Then I dug out Chucky Amansa's home phone in Chicago and put through a call. There was apprehension in his voice when he answered.

"Yeah?"

"Chucky, this is Jack Journey."

"Journey? Oh, yeah, Jack. How ya doin'? Say, I been readin' about you and Charlie in the papers. What's it all about?"

"I thought you could tell me."

"I dunno nothin' about it."

"You'd tell me if you knew, right?"

There was a long pause, then he said: "Yeah, I'd tell ya,

Jack, really. But there's nothin' doin' with us on this, really."

"Who can I talk to in New York about it?"

"You in New York?"

"Right. Who can I see here?"

"About what? Somethin' that happened in Chicago? Those jerks don't know nothin' about what we do here . . . unless it's business for all of us. Now there ain't nothin' doin' with you here, so you're dealin' with whackos, see? Not us."

"I don't want to talk to anybody here about what happened in Chicago. I want to talk to them about the organization."

"Look, Jack, I trust you, you know, but don't call me up and ask me anythin' about the Outfit, 'cause you know what my answer is."

"I know—*you don't know nothin'*. I don't want to know about the next plane from Bolivia, Chucky, just some information on those old Giuliano diaries we talked about once. Remember, the Sicilian bandit?"

"Oh, yeah—them things." He laughed. "Ya callin' me from New York to talk about a fairy tale, huh?"

"Who do you know here who I can talk to about them?"

"We ain't got a club historian, ya know, Jack." He laughed mightily at his own feeble joke.

"That's my job, Chucky. Can you give me a name or not?"

There was silence.

"Chucky, are you there? I only want a little history, a little of yesterday. Are you there?"

"Yeah, yeah. I'm thinkin'. Okay—go and see a guy named Little Lou Victorine. Hangs out at a club called, let's see, a club called The Pink Alligator, in the Village. Lou loves to talk about the old days. But don't bring up no business and no murders, okay?"

"Fine."

"Just them goofy diaries, okay?"

"I appreciate it, Chucky."

"You're an oddball, Jack. You gimme a laugh." He laughed and hung up.

3

The Pink Alligator was one of those West Village bars that had been popular in the 1940s with the fat-lapelled advertising set. Its ancient oak bar looped in and out. The spreading mirror behind the bar was tinted pink and the walls were a darker pink and the half-circle booths were made of pink vinyl, which matched the many stools along the bar. On the walls were countless black-and-white photographs in cheap pink frames, bearing indecipherable autographs of second-rate singers, retired strippers, and unheralded chanteuses of another era. It was all mob, down to the threadbare pink carpet. But there was no alligator painted pink, stuffed or otherwise.

Little Lou Victorine, as Chucky Amansa had said, was there, sitting at the end of the bar, wearing a costume-shop double-breasted pinstripe suit, heavily starched pink shirt, French cuffs jutting forth, diamond-studded cuff links blazing. His gnarled manicured fingers gripped a copy of the *Daily News*. He pondered its sparse front-page copy, a massive brow knitted, pulling forward a scalp heavy with thick, oily black hair. As I approached I could see his thick lips moving as he painstakingly read the monosyllabic prose.

I sat down next to him. Victorine nodded upward to glance at me and then, with a puzzled expression, down the long bar area at the many empty stools.

"What'sa matter?" he grunted. "You gotta be ina crowd? G'wan—move it down the bar!"

"I'd like a few words."

"Yeah—well, okay. Screw you. Those enough words for you?" Little Lou slowly turned over his pawlike hand and rocked his thumb in the direction of the entrance. "G'wan —beat it!"

The bartender, a human steer with short hair, put down a glass he was washing and ambled up to us. "Whaddya want to bother customers for, mister? There's plenty of other seats. Whyncha move on down like a good fella?"

"Chucky Amansa in Chicago said you'd give me a few words," I said to Little Lou.

"Move on down, fella!" The bartender's tone was less plaintive.

"Hold on, Mickey," said Little Lou Victorine, interested.

Mickey shrugged and skulked away to his soaking wineglasses.

Little Lou flattened the newspaper on the bar, smoothing out its pages. "So what's this all about that Chucky tells you to see me, huh?"

They weren't cagy people unless they were doing their business, so I thought I'd put it directly to him, although I kept one eye on the front door and thought of a quick exit. "Some people have been trying to kill me—in Chicago and here in New York—over something they think I have which I don't."

Little Lou gave me a sideways sneer. "Whaddya got that anyone would wanna hit you for?"

"It's what I don't have, I told you. They think I might have the diaries written by Salvatore Giuliano, the Mafia diaries, as they're known."

"I don't know nothin' about no Mafia." He looked down at the front page of the newspaper, but he wasn't reading it. "Giuliano . . . Giuliano, no, don't know that guy."

"In Sicily, murdered in 1949, a bandit."

He lifted his head as I spoke, smiling in his recognition. "Oh, yeah, that guy. Very famous man, Giuliano, sure." He looked at me closely. "But that's old-time stuff, who'd kill you for something like that? Naw."

"For what might be in those diaries."

He hunched his massive shoulders and then let them down slowly. "Nothin' in there anybody doesn't know. Well, I think so—never saw 'em, those little books the bandit kept. But what could be in there? Nothin' to hurt nobody now, not—what is it—thirty years later, huh?"

"Somebody thinks they can get hurt and I'd like you to tell me if you think it's anybody in the Outfit?"

"That's crazy," Little Lou huffed. "Whadda we care about them old days and them little black books." He gave me a weak wave and a deep short laugh. "I mean, think about it. All them guys who this character Giuliano could've mentioned are either retired or dead by now. Carmine Galante knew them people over there—dead. Sammy Giancana in Chicago, I think he knew them guys, took trips over there—he's dead too. Albert, Vito, Lucky, Willie, Frank, all them guys are gone, so if this Giuliano mentions them, who cares?" He gave me a brotherly pat on the shoulder. "You got nothin' to worry about if that's your worry, see? All them guys are dead and planted." He winked knowingly. "They're in them history books now. You can understand that, right, Journey?"

"I didn't tell you my name."

"Yeah, yeah, but Chucky called me a little time ago and told me you was comin' over. Says you're a history guy or somethin', that what you do?"

"Crime history, I write a column for some newspapers."

"Yeah? Here in New York?"

"Staten Island is the closest paper running my column."

"Naw, I mean here—Manhattan." He poked the copy of the *Daily News*. "This is New York, Manhattan."

"So as far as Giuliano's diaries are concerned—"

Little Lou gave me another wave, more emphatic. "Naw, naw, we don't give a crap about them things and we don't want you for nothin'."

"How do I really know that?"

Little Lou pointed to a doorway at the end of the bar. "See that? It goes down some stairs. If we wanted you, Journey, you'd already be down them stairs." His affability disappeared instantly with a smile that turned grim. "And you'd never come back up them stairs, if we wanted you . . . never." He waited for that to sink in, and then added with a little smile: "No talk, no jokes, no info. You'd been down them stairs a minute after you walked in the joint, if we had you in mind for anythin'. I'll give you a little advice, Journey. Like Chucky says, you're dealin' here with crazies, political stuff maybe, I dunno. Look at that guy Hinckley shootin' the President, and that other kook knockin' off John Lennon. Shootin' down a millionaire like Lennon, can you imagine? Naw, it's the crazies, that's your problem."

He picked up the paper and began to struggle once more with its front-page story. It was over, Little Lou Victorine had spoken. The Mafia was not out to kill me, didn't care about Salvatore Giuliano's secret diaries, and thought my worries misdirected. It was the lunatic fringe after my scalp for reasons that could be found only in the minds of the insane. Or, just as easily, Little Lou in New York and Chucky Amansa in Chicago were lying and really intended to kill me after all. Why should they give me reasons? They never gave anybody else reasons.

"Thanks, I guess," I said, and got up, starting to go.

"Ah, listen, Journey," Little Lou said quietly, holding up the newspaper but looking at me. "You ain't thinkin' of goin' over there, are you?"

"Where?"

"Sicily."

"I hadn't thought of that."

"Don't even think of it." His dark eyes narrowed. " 'Cause if you go over there and ask a lot of crazy questions like you asked Chucky and me, well, them people ain't the same as us."

"I know, they're not Americans."

"That's right—you ask them guys over there one question, just one, and they blow your goddamned head off just to give their goddamned shotguns a workout. . . . Sometimes I think them guys over there are as crazy as the crazies we got here."

"Maybe it's their people after me."

Little Lou shook his head slowly with authority. "They stay outa here—for Chrissakes, them guys are foreigners. We catch 'em screwin' around in our country, we blow 'em away. They know that." He repeated it one more time so I would not forget. "It ain't us. We don't care. It ain't them. They don't care. It's the crazies."

I looked at my watch and saw that I had a half hour to meet Laura in front of the Haley National Bank. I started for the front door. When I reached it, Little Lou's deep voice boomed after me as he held up the paper to cover his face: "Go home to Chi. Say hello to Chucky for me when you see him."

VII

Death Dive

1

I was sick to death of the conspiracy that had entrapped me, goaded me forward, troubled and angered me almost every second in finding no real answers for the elaborate but artless murders that fell like rotten petals from dying geraniums. The Giuliano diaries did exist and were certainly part of that French library. The scratchings of a man dead for thirty years had caused the deaths of four men and had almost caused my own. But the Mafia had said it didn't want the diaries or me, which made it all the more maddening. There were no answers to be found in New York, I realized. Paris and Jean Rombout would have them.

When I returned to my hotel room, I made a transatlantic call to Frank Lovering, a man with whom I had spent three harrowing years in Europe as an agent for the United States. He was still with the firm and he would probably die inside the firm. Frank and I and a few others were the last of an old bunch that had been to Hungary, Czechoslovakia, and points east. To the mind that only knew the popular romance of such people, we were termed spies. But I had always preferred the word *agent*.

Frank's voice came on the line, distant and scratchy. "Journey? Jack Journey?"

"Yes—how are you, Frank?"

"Christ, I haven't heard from you in years."

"Two years."

"Something like that. What's up?"

"I'm coming over tomorrow. Thought you might like to meet me at Orly."

"Sure. On vacation?"

"Not exactly." I might as well let him have some of it, I thought. Why wait to spring anything at the airport? He could make up his own mind, beg off if he liked. "I might need a little help, Frank. I've got some problems."

"Do they have anything to do with the government?" His voice hardened with that line.

"No—just my own life."

"Your own life?"

"And its preservation."

"Christ, that sounds dramatic, Jack, but then you always had a flair for the theatrical. Sure, I'd be glad to help. I hope it's a woman, a good-looking woman."

"No, it's a library—books."

"Swell." He was not enthusiastic. "Say, Jack, are you high or something?"

"No, just meet me at the airport, will you?"

"Okay—give me the flight and time."

I gave him the flight number and arrival time from London. He told me he'd bring champagne and hung up.

A half hour later I was standing in front of the Haley National Bank. Crowds swarmed about me as I leaned against a marble wall and looked for Laura. She came out with a rush of people, and I grabbed her by the arm, pulling her to my side.

Laura gave me a long look without smiling. Apprehension danced on top of her words. "I wasn't sure you were still alive! We heard about the killing at the hotel and then this afternoon the deaths over on Ninth Avenue. It's on radio, TV. My God, Jack, what does all this mean? Have people followed you from Chicago?"

The look in her eyes was questioning, sincere. But I wasn't sure of her. She kept turning her head away from me to look up and down the street.

"Expecting someone else?"

"No," she replied slowly. "I'm just terrified for your safety. Can't we get out of this?"

"Let's get a drink. There's a little place a block from here."

We walked swiftly inside the rippling, sweat-dripping crowds, turning onto a small street and then into a lounge I had passed on my way to meet Laura. Once seated in a booth with high wooden backs, she leaned against the backboard, sighing, shaking her head.

"Why didn't you tell me someone was trying to kill you?"

"Why didn't you?"

"What? What does that mean?"

Hunching forward, I took her slender hands in my own, holding them firmly. They were cold, like ice. "I followed you last night out of the Oak Room bar at the Plaza. One of the men on the train, one of the two who was sitting in Bedroom D in the Pullman, went up to you. He talked to you."

Laura slid her hands out from under mine. "I didn't even know who he was. He said he remembered me from the train, that was all, and asked if I was alone."

"What did you tell him, beautiful?"

"What do you think?" She reached forward, put her hand inside my jacket, and fished out a cigarette from my shirt pocket, lighting it with a match that she threw indignantly into a small ashtray.

"I don't know what to think except to tell you that that man was in Bedroom D in our car."

"So?"

"And the porter told me he and his friend got off at Harrisburg and then he shows up in New York, at the Plaza, talking to you in the lobby. I *think* that looks a little strange, especially when the guy he was with in Bedroom D tried to shoot me today, and then burn me to death."

Her whole face went wide with surprise. "My God, then he was looking for you. And I thought he was just trying to pick me up." She reached forward, solicitous, wrapping her cool hands about mine. "You've got to leave New York, Jack."

"Later. Tell me exactly what that fellow in the lobby said to you."

"I told you."

"Tell me again, with all the commas."

"He asked if I was alone, said he remembered me from the train, said he was attracted to me, and wanted to know if we could have drinks. He struck me as a little drunk, a conventioneer who was a little drunk."

"He had no badge. They always wear badges to conventions so you know they have money to spend, are from out of town, and are safe lays."

She ignored my crudeness and plunged into her concern for me. "Do you want me to talk to the police about him, Jack, describe him or something?"

"I've already described him and his partner to the police. So he pitched you?"

For a moment, Laura looked disgusted. "He might have thought I was a call girl or something, who knows? He had seen us together and then me alone in the lobby. Who knows what a man like that thinks? That is, if he wasn't looking for you and was only on the make."

"Not a guy like that. Not in that business suit and that conservative tie. They spend their money in little German restaurants, buy economy cars, subscribe to *U.S. News & World Report*. They don't go looking for expensive girls at the Plaza."

"Then he was looking for you, like I've said."

A lean, elderly waiter came over and took my order for two glasses of white wine. He was about to place two menus before us, but I gently pushed these back. "We're not eating, thanks," I told him.

"Two glasses of wine, that's it? No dinner?" He stared down at me, annoyed.

"Right, just the wine."

He went off, tucking the menus under his arm.

"Do you want to tell me what's really going on, Jack?" Laura said this softly, slowly. There was no play in her voice. "I never believed that nonsense about researching train murders anyway."

"I'll tell you," I told her. I reached into my shirt pocket and found my cigarette pack empty. "I've got to get some cigarettes." As I stood up, I almost bumped into the waiter coming with the wine. He gave me a haughty look as I walked to the cigarette machine in front of the lounge. As I inserted the coins I could hear a faint, familiar voice coming from the closed telephone booth on the other side of the cigarette machine. I leaned closer and heard the voice say: "If that's what you want, okay, but I'm ready to crash. The guy's a walker and I'm stiff-legged. . . . Yeah . . . Yeah . . . I dunno, he's talkin' to some ritzy-looking broad in a booth. They was holdin' hands, nose to nose with the deep looks, all that crap."

I picked the cigarettes out of the tray at the bottom of the machine, then leaned around the machine to look upward into the glass of the phone booth. Filling the booth from wall to wall with his shoulders, his chin on his chest as he talked into the phone, so that the overhead light showed the sparse hairs of his crewcut, stood the police karate expert the fat lieutenant had assigned to follow me.

Standing up, I walked to the phone booth door and doubled it inward with my foot. The overhead light went off and the karate expert's head went up with an angry, surprised look. "She's not a broad," I told the cop. "She's a dame. Let's show a little class, huh?" With that I stepped back. The karate expert jerked the door closed and, looking at me, continued his report to the fat lieutenant, who was undoubtedly sweating at the other end of the line. I went back to Laura.

She was smiling at me over her wineglass, which was empty. Another two glasses, full, stood on the table. The buzz was on.

"I ordered another, Jack," she said dreamily. "I think we can use them."

With a quick tip of my glass I finished the first wine, then half of the second. "Fine, every nerve in my body cries out for anesthesia."

"Are you going to get drunk?" She kept her luscious smile going.

"No—that's too dangerous for me in New York."

"Oh, darling, you can get drunk anywhere."

"Not in a city where you have more enemies than friends."

She shook her head slowly to brush back that beautiful black hair. "You have friends, Jack." She put the second glass to her lips and drank heavily. "I'm your friend, Jack, your close friend."

I lit a cigarette and saw the karate expert go out the front door. He would hang around, tired, angry, doing his duty, not giving a damn if someone fire-bombed the lounge while I was in it. He would be down the street to report the explosion. He would do his duty.

"I'm glad of that, Laura, your friendship."

"It could be more than that. How do you feel?"

I drank some more wine. "Tired, a little hopeless, but wine does that to me, especially after a few killings."

"I mean about me."

She was making up her mind about something, wanted to get to the conclusion, a hazy declaration of love would probably do right now to justify her involvement with a man turned albatross.

"I like you a lot," I told her, "but you're too beautiful, too juicy to love. There'd always be a dozen guys running up to you in hotel lobbies. And I don't know anything about you, really. You've got a high-class job with one of the world's biggest banks and you flit about like some reigning beauty queen. I guess you like being on the move, everything kaleidoscopic, pick and choose friends, lovers, end it at the next airport. You'd get bored with me, squeezed between books and files, and try hard to have a good time. It wouldn't be Friday night with me, but Monday morning. I'm not on your schedule, beautiful."

The waiter came over, sullen, asking if we wanted another. Laura happily lifted her empty glass. He brought two more. The wine worked quickly on her, quicker than the wine she had sipped with me on the train, but then it was hot and at the end of a workday and here she was, sitting with a man pinpointed for murder. I didn't blame her. Get drunk, beautiful, get smashed, go blotto.

Laura placed her hands flat on the table, looking down at them, then up at me. "I've decided—it's going to stop."

"Our affair?"

She shook her head meaningfully. "All this nonsense about killings and death." She made a face. "It has to stop now, Jack, because it's so public that they can't bother you again. You see what I mean? It's in the newspapers, on TV now. You're too public to murder now, Jack. You're a personality now, Jack, and they don't kill personalities. You see how it is?"

I smiled at the ridiculous thought. "A lot of people have been more public than me—Martin Luther King, the Kennedy boys—and that didn't stop bullets."

"That was political, darling, people who live in the limelight. You're a private person—a very private person—who's become public because somebody has tried to kill you, you see, and this means—"

"That they'll go on trying to kill me until they get the job done."

"No, no, no," she said in a soft rush, "not if you just drop whatever it is you're doing and go back to Chicago and your books. I'm sure that they'll leave you alone, whoever they are, if you stop running after them."

"Running after them?"

She looked surprised, mouth slightly open, eyes enormous. "Why, isn't that what you're doing? Playing detective or something?" She laughed a low laugh and patted my hand. "Having your adventures? It's enough now, darling Jack. Time to stop charging into the jungle in search of panthers, don't you think?"

I saw it as her mind worked it out, the whole thing being too much, too deadly to face square on. Better to shun the reality, treat it all as a lark or, as the British might say, an escapade. The killings were mere mishaps that gobbled up other people. Too bad for the other people. They fell into mishap, that's all. They fell down a well, the old Black Hole of Calcutta where the Giant Rat of Sumatra got them. Bogeyman tales, fireside frights. Too bad. Time to go home now.

"I guess you're right," I said in what I thought was a convincing voice. "I'm not doing much good on my own."

Laura looked at her watch. "We must stop soon. I'm taking you to a party, get your mind off all these ugly experiences."

"A party?"

"A little cocktail party where people are nice. No killers, promise."

"That'll be exciting."

"Before we go, do you want to tell me exactly what all this running around means, darling Jack?" She finished another glass of wine.

I called the scarecrow waiter over and ordered two more. He was happier now; we were making up for the unordered dinners with the wine. His tip grew with each trip to our table, he knew.

I looked at Laura and trusted her then, but mistrusted my trust, thinking it was the wine. Stupidly, I opened up, saying: "Why not? I bought a small European library some months back. . . ." I told her the story as it had happened, Lucan's death, the poisoned drink, the chase and shooting in Chicago, the weird deaths in New York. I left out Giuliano and the Mafia diaries. That would have been too much. But I went on, and on, telling her most of it, as she listened carefully, holding my hand with fingers that began to feel warm. Of course, it was all a mistake.

2

The cocktail party Laura took me to was Jacquette's, as I should have known. His home was no home at all but one of those baroque mansions in the Fifties occupying a quarter of a block of prime real estate. Four stories of elegant brick shot upward into many gables, cornices boasted hard-carvings from the 1890s, gargoyles peered eerily downward from overhanging ledges. The reception room was large enough to accommodate a regiment on field maneuvers. A full orchestra played behind a hand-painted silk screen, on a stage at the end of the hall, and hundreds of the chic, the sleek, and the rich moved about like bees in a hive, buzzing and dripping honey.

A minute after we entered the hall, I grabbed Laura by the waist and moved her onto the marble floor, plunging into the dancers, doing steps I had not done in years, making her move with me, athletic angry dancing, I suppose you could call it. Fred Astaire would not have said hello to it. Laura didn't mind; she was half gone, dreamy, pliable. It was the wine. I held her warm, voluptuous body close to me as other dancers looked at us, arching their eyebrows. I held her tighter still as we slowed in the center of the dancing area, mashing her large round breasts into my chest, my hips moving back and forth with hers. I felt like a comedic dancer whipping about a cloth dummy tied to the ends of my shoes.

"Are you having fun, Jack?" Laura said into my ear, her head on my shoulder.

"Barrels of it. I hope I'm not too acrobatic for you."

"No. I like it savage," she whispered.

"Good." I waited for a moment and then, hitting the right note, tilted her backward in an exaggerated dip that made her laugh.

"Exhibitionist," I heard one woman say as she danced by.

"No—contortionist," I said to her before wheeling Laura away to some tables and chairs at the edge of the dancing area.

"Whew!" She mockingly fanned her face with her hand, then plopped down into a large wing-back chair. I sat down next to her.

"I'm damned hungry," I told her. "I haven't eaten anything today. Let's go to a restaurant and get about three hundred dollars' worth of food."

"Darnley has food, Jack. He always has lots of grand food at his parties." She stood up and took me by the hand, leading me through the well-dressed, thickly perfumed crowd, across the marble-floored foyer, where guests lounged, smoked, talked of money, and into a grand oak-paneled library crammed with first editions in Moroccan bindings. A huge table the length of a tennis court was laden with pheasant, turkey, ham, a hundred types of cheeses, caviar, of course, Beluga by name, bowls and bowls of exotic fruit, vegetables and relish trays.

"This is the greatest free lunch I've ever seen," I told Laura as I began to fill up my gilt-edged plate.

She followed me down the table, placing tiny fragments of meat onto her plate, a dab of this, a touch of that. She ate, of course, for her figure, not her appetite. That was fine with me; I would do the eating for both of us. Our plates filled, mine at least, we went to a small table and two vacant chairs near the cathedral windows that looked out on a lush garden enclosed by a high wall. The flowers in the garden shot up and outward in dazzling colors, all neatly rowed, with ground-covering neatly placed and vines neatly crawling up the neatly tuck-pointed wall. I ate ravenously, forking heaping mounds of potato salad and kidney bean salad and chicken salad.

"I've never seen you eat like this, Jack." Laura said, watching me.

"Hungry," I said between mouthfuls. "Haven't been this hungry—since I was in—the service." The plate was clean within minutes. Laura picked at her food, uninterested. She looked across the room and her face brightened. I followed her gaze to see Darnley Jacquette, Esquire, walking casually toward us, a benign expression adorning his handsome features.

"It looks as if you're having a good time," he said to me, extending his hand, which I took and shook once.

"You're the perfect host in the perfect house," I replied, wiping my lips with a cloth napkin embroidered with the Jacquette crest.

"I saw you two dancing for a moment but I'm glad you didn't keep up that pace. It would have worn out my other guests quickly. Do you mind if I join you?"

"Not at all," I said, waving him into a nearby chair. "It's your party."

"Just a little get-together. Some banking associates and friends." He pulled his chair close to us, sinking back, relaxed, ever affable. As he rested his tanned hand on the soft cushion of the chair, I saw the ring on his little finger. It had a curious ensignia on it, one I had seen before. Yes, now I remembered. The men in Bedroom D had worn the same ring, and, in the same moment, I saw the identical ring flashing on the little finger of the man who had poisoned my drink in Chicago.

I reached over and lightly tapped the top of the ring with my index finger. "An interesting ornament."

Jacquette held up his hand for a moment, sticking out his pinkie, as if drinking tea. "Just a sentimental item—a college fraternity ring. I don't like gemstones—too ostentatious."

Taking another mouthful of food, I turned away from him slightly to bend over my plate. Then I said without looking at him: "What fraternity is that?"

"Kappa Phi Kappa," he said in that resonant voice, "a business fraternity."

"For bankers?" I faced him, wiping my mouth with his monogrammed linen.

"Finance, yes, not specifically bankers."

"Brokers, bankers, people like that?"

"Like that." It seemed that nothing could remove the

smile from his face, a confident smile of powerful people, those who knew they would never be toppled from their thrones, knew they would never be poor, knew they were in control. You saw such smiles on the faces of kings and queens, in the old oil portraits of benevolent monarchs.

It was too absurd to think that Darnley Jacquette, richest man in New York, would be involved with those men from the train and the poisoner in Chicago. It was crazy, but I thought it anyway. I looked at Laura, whose eyes seemed to flutter for an instant, needing sleep. "I never joined a fraternity," I told Jacquette lamely.

"Why's that, Mr. Journey?"

"I thought most fraternities were jammed up with spineless pranksters."

"Spineless? You have an odd image of courage."

"I don't agree with people who move in crowds, gang motivation. Go your own way alone. Things go right, you don't have to thank anybody. Things go bad, you don't blame anybody."

"I like the old-fashioned ideas," he said in a patronizing tone.

"So do I," Laura said, reaching across the table to fondle my hand briefly. "I love collecting antiques."

"Now why do I get the idea you have no use for me, Mr. Jacquette?"

"I *don't* have any use for you, Mr. Journey, since you ask, but I meant no insult." He studied me, then said: "Have I insulted you?"

"Other than likening me to an ancient artifact, I guess not."

"Artifact?" asked Laura.

"An ancient tool used by prehistoric man," informed Jacquette.

"Most of us are tools, Jacquette, ancient or contemporary. Now take you—what kind of a tool would you be?" I studied him back.

He waited in smiling silence, bemused.

"Jack, please?" Laura gripped my hand harder as a way of asking me to stop.

"Oh, I don't mean anything, sweetheart, just curious about how Mr. Jacquette thinks of himself in the big, broad, bad scheme of things."

"I don't scheme, Mr. Journey. Schemes are for men without futures, for men—"

"How about just for men without."

Laura squeezed my hand harder. "Darling, will you take me home?"

"In a minute."

"I know you want me to play the uncaring financial ogre, Mr. Journey, the tyrant with the long black mustache who holds the mortgage and orders the widow and orphans from their ramshackle home. Sorry, I'm just a businessman. I have my own private ideas about the world and what should be done to it and for whom. My business is banking and most of the decisions in that field are made statistically, through giant computers."

"Machines, sure, very human."

"It has nothing to do with humanity," Jacquette laughed. "We are a nation of about two hundred thirty million in a world of billions. Have you any notion, let alone idea, of what those figures mean?"

"A lot of people."

"Statistics, not individuals. I know you champion the individual, that's fine. It means nothing, of course, but I think each statistic should feel human. This individualism is like a narcotic. Soothing to feel that you are a *person*, not a digit in billions of digits in computer systems that really run the world now. What do the computers care about individual effort and achievement, patriots who stay behind on some lonely road to defend someplace nobody wants anyway, heroes who jump off of bridges to save a drowning woman who might be dead of cancer a month later. They're all fine things to do, I suppose, but in a few years, after the television cameras have turned away, who remembers who did what and for what?"

"Oh, I'm sure some enterprising electrician will invent a computer that will store up all those trite tales of heroes and individuals so that they can be remembered," I said with as much sarcasm as I could grumble.

Jacquette toyed with the idea for a nodding moment, then replied: "That might be sold to someone, a bank of historic sentimentality on microdisk."

"I thought you'd see it as a good investment."

He eased his chair backward and uncrossed his legs. He was finished playing. "Mr. Journey, lamentable as it may be for idealistic college kids and steelworkers who raise the American flag in front of their bungalows every morning, there are no more heroes in this computerized world of ours."

"Good," I said firmly, "that leaves a lot more room for me."

Jacquette stood, wrinkle-free. "Good to see you again." As we shook hands briefly, he looked at Laura. "Don't keep my best aide up too late tonight. We've got a big meeting in the morning." He dropped my hand, took hers, and leaned down, pecking it. "Good night, Laura."

"It's a lovely party, Darnley, good night. Thank you." She watched him walk through the long length of the library.

I watched him too, looking for a mistake, an error in that faultless poise of his. As he reached the two huge doors of the library, just before stepping out of sight into the crowded foyer, he ran a hand over his college ring, twisting it around his finger as he went.

"Now where to?" I said to Laura.

"A penthouse with a view," she said softly.

3

The penthouse with a view was real, thirty floors up in the fashionable Forties, a private elevator from bottom to top. We stepped out to a wide marble area, appropriately dotted with exotic plants, then down into the sunken living room furnished in unmatched furniture.

"See, I told you," Laura said, turning on tall old lamps. "I do collect antiques. Everything here, from the sofa to the chairs, is antique." She walked quickly through the large living room to an elevated platformed area, turning on a heavy glass chandelier. "Look at this marvelous hand-carved table, Jack. It's more than one hundred years old. So are the chairs—rosewood."

"Lovely." I sat down in a stuffed chair that greeted my backside with groaning springs. "Even sounds old."

Laura pulled back a large sliding-glass door that led to a terrace. Light gusts of wind swept back the sheer curtains so that when she walked outside, they engulfed her. "It's a wonderful night, Jack, a cool light breeze. Come and see my view."

I got up tiredly and went through the billowing curtains and to the terrace. The view was impressive, an unobstructed vista of blazing city streets below and mountains of skyscrapers jutting upward like the peaks of Monument Valley all about us. The wind swept over and around us, cooling us.

"It's like your place in Chicago," I told her, "only bigger, higher, and more expensive."

She moved close to me, resting her head on my shoulder as she talked. "I've got a place like this in San Francisco too, but I don't get out there much anymore."

"Is that the Chrysler Building over there?"

"Uh-huh."

"Which way is the Algonquin?"

She pointed straight outward without looking, still close to me, holding tight with the other arm. "That way."

"Which way is the bedroom?"

Laura stepped back and smiled at me, then took my hand and led me down the terrace to another large glass door, which she slid back. We entered the dark bedroom, the light of the city dimly streaming after us. Laura flicked on a bedside lamp, one with a Tiffany shade and a brass base, then walked into a very modern bathroom.

"Antiques everywhere," I said, sitting on the king-size bed, which was covered with dark blue satin sheets. "Jacquette does all this for you, right, honey?"

"Not really," she said from the bathroom. She had closed the door to a crack and spoke loudly as she ran the shower. "The bank provides. We travel so much, it would be economically silly to take expensive hotel rooms."

"So it's economically cheaper to have a dozen penthouses."

"In the long run—yes. That's what our computer says."

I began to undress. "You punch that sort of thing up on your computer?"

"Oh, yes, Big Bertha we call her, she does everything, from evaluating investments to sending out our depositors' statements. Insert one little plastic card, feed sheets of information onto the scanner, and Big Bertha kicks out the answers and the copies, millions of them, all official, sealed, ready for mailing."

I walked naked into the bathroom, pushed back the molded glass door, and stepped into the shower beside her. She wore a shower cap and her curvacious body was coated with soap, some of which I scooped away from large breasts pointing at me, and rubbed onto my chest and arms. Then I put my hands on her shoulders, kissed her, tilting her head so that the water did not splash our faces, and turned about to soap down her back.

"It's still Jacquette, all of it," I said, fondling her more than soaping her down. "I'd hate being owned by a guy like that."

She stepped forward under the nozzle so that the soap washed off her back. "You'd hate being owned by anyone. But it's a system, really, Jack, and Darnley is only a member of a system. Because he lives in elegance and enjoys some privileges, *some* people think he's a manipulator, a power-hungry person—" She turned around and I turned with her as she soaped down my back. "Which he is not. He's a gentleman, not the stereotype you like to make him into."

"I never said he was a stereotype, more a prototype of things to come, the computer czar, lord of the statistics."

Laura put her arms around me, pulling me back with her under the spray. "Oh, you've got a computer obsession."

"Microchips, computer systems, video games, state-of-the-art triple-talk—software, hardware, nowhere. The whole electronic inhuman mess is creating a generation of unschooled, unread freaks."

As I turned to face her, her hands holding the perfumed little soap bar, she reached down, applying the soap in a massaging movement. Her eyes were cast downward to see what she was doing. I pulled her to me, kissing her.

"We've both come clean—now to bed," I told her, and broke away to rinse off.

Minutes later we were lying on top of the satin sheets with the cool breeze from the terrace drifting through the sheer curtains. Behind the curtains the lights of New York blazed like star clusters.

"Isn't this nice?" Laura spread out her arms so that one

fell on my chest. "That lovely air rolling over us. I hate air conditioning, never use it, just the open air."

"A lot of people down below are sweating their heads off because they don't have air conditioning. You have it and don't use it—kind of perverse."

She rolled to her side, facing me, looking upward at me. "I like having things now I never had as a child, as a teenager. Just having comfort and convenience is important to me, whether I use them or not. Having something I never had. I never knew what wealth was until I was in my early twenties, Jack. My family couldn't have been called middle-class. Can you believe my father had a black-and-white TV until I got him a color set a few years ago?"

"What does your father do?"

"He's retired . . . he was a switchman in a freight yard in Spokane, Washington. He's still there with my mother, my poor mother. We were always poor, lived in a back-of-the-yards tenement, four rooms. I shared a room with my sister. My mother did the laundry in our kitchen. The laundry!" She gritted the last words. "It was always hanging about, everywhere, no room, no money, no future. I thought that someday I'd throw myself down from the back porch to the concrete alley. I thought about that a lot, but the funeral expenses would have put my folks deeper in debt." She laughed weakly, propping her head up under a hand. "A good way to prevent suicide—permanent poverty."

"And now you're on top of the world, in the embrace of Darnley Jacquette's computerized system."

"My sister is a waitress in a Spokane lunch counter inside a bowling alley, serving chili. I'm here because I fought to go to school, worked like a dog to get through business college, got a job in San Francisco, the hardest town in the world to get a job in, and in a bank."

"One of Jacquette's banks?"

"An affiliate, but I wasn't *discovered* by him, if that's what you're getting at. I worked my way up the ladder, no sleeping around, either. I took special courses in the evening at Berkeley and worked up the corporate ladder. I saved the bank money and brought in computer systems that saved more."

"More computers, fewer tellers, less wages, right."

"Not that coldhearted, Jack. More jobs to handle the computers." She flopped back on the pillow, eyes on the ceiling, where shafts of light from the terrace were whipped about by the breeze-blown curtains. "I've earned the right to be in this place. Women my age who wanted a husband, a diamond ring, a house in the suburbs, kids—they have that and that's it. This is what I want and I want it as long as I can have it. In my purse I have every known credit card worth having, two cards alone that permit me to enter the nerve center of the greatest bank in the world. One of those cards sets the whole system to working. Only five people have a card like that."

"Staggering," I said, without being staggered.

"Oh, what would you know, Jack Journey? You're not living in the real world. I enjoy the trust the bank has placed in me, the authority it allows me to exercise."

I moved close to her, pressed my lips to her cheek, and said: "Does it beat a kiss?"

"No."

I placed my hand on her breast. "An embrace?"

"No."

I drew her hand downward to me. "How about this?"

She hummed and said: "You present a hard argument."

"Roll over," I told her.

"Why?"

"Roll over."

She rolled over, her bare backside, round and inviting, open to lascivious view.

"What are you doing?" Her voice was muffled by the pillow into which she had sunk her head.

"It's called caressing."

"More like probing."

Moving behind her, under, upward and outward, I tried to forget Darnley, his college ring, and the fraternity of thugs to which he might belong. I concentrated on Laura's flesh jiggling as I pressed against it in the dim light.

She talked into the pillow as I went at it: "I suppose—you think—I'm a—greedy—bitch?"

"Not at all." My legs went taut.

"Spoiled then—uncaring—selfish—"

"Never—occurred—to me—"

"I know—what—you—think—oh, oh—"

"Right now—anything—carnal—will dooo!" I pulled back, legs quivering, finished, satisfied with my weakness, grateful for being drained. I lay next to her, holding her as she sighed and gave a small shudder.

"How do you feel?" she asked in a whisper.

"Like I've been pretty greedy myself."

Laura inched next to me, putting her arm under mine, rubbing my back. "I like to be coveted, especially by you." She patted my back lightly, as if she were comforting a small child. "You've got to stop running around New York now," she said, her voice changing to that of a mother chastising an unruly boy. "Go home to Chicago and your work. I want you to stay in one piece." Her hand slid down and over my hip to my thigh. "I want this piece kept intact."

I didn't love her, but I was attracted to her selfishness. It fascinated me, made me wonder what caused it. Hate of poverty? Fear of the poorhouse? What kept that love of self going? Jacquette was using her the way he used everything else, of course, and she had long ago convinced herself that he was in real need of her piecemeal knowledge, her loyalty to his splendor, her gratitude for the antiques stores he had looted on her behalf. Hell, he had his computers for all that.

"Those fellows on the train, in Bedroom D—"

"Not again," she said, and moved away from me with an angry bounce, punching the enormous pillow to make a depression for her head. "I'm so sick of those horror stories, Jack."

I reached over to the bedside table, where I had put my cigarettes and change, taking a cigarette and lighting it, blowing out the smoke in slow rings that drifted upward in the dark. "Both of those fellows were wearing rings like the one Jacquette was wearing tonight."

"He always wears that ring," she said wearily. "It's a fraternity ring. He told you. Thousands and thousands of people have rings like that. God, Jack, are you saying Darnley has something to do with those men? That's ridiculous." She seemed to be drifting off to sleep.

"Probably." I decided to let her have what I had, which wasn't much anyway. "But Giuliano's diaries aren't ridiculous—they're real and that's what everyone's after."

Her voice came muffled with sleep. "What . . . diaries?"

"The Mafia diaries. They were in Sicily, got into the library I bought. That's what the killings are all about."

I watched her closely but she never moved an inch. Her back was to me but there was no nervous rippling of flesh, not a nerve jangled, not a finger twitched.

"The Mafia . . . has gone . . . to sleep . . ." she said almost inaudibly as she sank untroubled into slumber.

I put out the cigarette and lay back on the pillow, dismissing Jacquette as having had any connection with the killers. He was already Mr. Big, and generations beyond cheap murder. And that made Laura and her explainable selfishness innocent too. She hadn't responded to the name Giuliano at all. She was as sweetly innocent as a good night's sleep. I closed my eyes, telling myself that I had to get dressed shortly and go back to the hotel. I had a morning flight to Europe, I told myself, a flight to more madness. I'll just rest here awhile, I heard myself say in the back of my mind, a few minutes' sleep, maybe a half hour. That will be fine, that will be sweet.

4

I awoke fogbound, sweating, trying to remember an unfinished dream. Rolling over, I felt for Laura. She was not in the bed. The luminous face of my watch told me it was four in the morning, the dead of night. Half sitting up in the bed, I tried to adjust my eyes to the darkness. All was silent in the penthouse. I rolled out of bed and slipped on my slacks, then went to the bathroom. Laura was not there.

Going from room to room, turning on and off antique lamps as I went, I found she had gone. I threw some cold water on my face, then dressed. There had been no note, no explanation. The clothes that she had worn were not in the closet. Upon sliding back the mirrored closet door, I discovered that no clothes at all were present. I went to two bureaus and opened the drawers. All were empty. It wasn't hard to conclude that this elegant penthouse was not the residence of Laura Manville, executive vice-president of the Haley National Bank.

Turning off all the lights, I stepped out to the terrace, lighting a cigarette and looking over the sleeping city, dark now, silent, almost like a gigantic graveyard with towering tombstones of glass and granite. You never should have told her a thing about Giuliano, I scolded myself. A dimwitted move. No, no, she's all right. There's an explanation for all this, a perfectly good explanation. Yeah? Like what? She decided to visit her father in Spokane in the middle of the night? Or the sister—have a cup of chili in that bowling alley? It would be closed by the time she got there on a red-eye flight.

What you don't want to admit is that she went to Jacquette, not with any story but with her body, to be with him. She told you she was fed up with all the wild antics, the conspiracies, the Wild West adventures. She told you that, remember. She's had all she can take of you, vigilante. She went back to Jacquette and a safer bed, that's all. Do you blame her? Yeah, I do. I can't stand disloyalty. What's a person to do who wants to break it off with you—send you a two-week notice? I can't stand bad manners, either. Manners? You should talk about manners. After the way you treated Jacquette, you should be the top candidate for the Boor-of-the-Year award. I don't think I loved her anyway. Not much. Not any more than Gilbert loved Garbo, Gracie loved Burns, and Kukla loved Ollie. Now you're down to puppets.

As I was bending over the concrete wall of the terrace, which was no more than four feet in height, I heard a little noise behind me. Someone was in the bedroom. The noise I had heard was a small collision, as if someone had bumped into a piece of furniture in the dark. That wouldn't be Laura; she knew the place. I turned to try to look into the room from the terrace but could see only blackness behind the sheer curtain that jiggled and danced in the soft summer wind. I realized at that moment that I had the dim light of the city behind me and that I could be seen from inside the dark room, not well, but seen. In fact I was a fairly good target.

Maybe I was psychic. One of the curtains slowly bulged at the center as it came outward toward me, a small round object pushed against it, like the end of a iron pipe. More like a gun. I sprang from the terrace wall, shoving off with one foot, and landed against the penthouse wall. In that second the explosion sent a bullet past my face, igniting the sheer curtain, the flames eating outward from a tiny circle, and I could see a large man, trying to beat out the flames and get past the curtain and onto the terrace at the same time.

He had the gun and I didn't have a chance out here, I knew. A frontal attack was the only choice. I jumped in front of the burning curtain and, before he could level the weapon once more at me, leaped through the curtain, tearing it from its mountings, going under it and onto the man holding the gun. I drove him backward with my momentum. He was on his heels all the way to the king-size bed, which he fell on. I was on top of him, my right elbow jammed under his heavy chin, my shoulder pinning his left arm, both of my hands grappling for the gun in his other hand. I held the barrel flat against the bed, away from me with one hand, and pried his fingers loose with the other. He grunted and then dropped the gun, which fell to the floor.

Falling after it, he was on my back in an instant. I managed to sweep the gun far beneath the bed. You don't have to worry about that now, I told myself. But he had slipped both of his hands beneath my chin and was pulling backward in a crude attempt to break my neck. Working my shoulder over, I managed to turn about, shoving him as I did, toppling him onto his side.

The place was filled with smoke but had not caught fire. The curtain had burned away and the wind gusting into the bedroom drove the smoke over us so that we coughed at each other for some seconds. My eyes were running tears from the smoke, but I could see him get up and head for the living room fast. I got up and ran after him. He tried to turn a corner and make for the elevator, but I caught up with him, diving after his thick form, tackling him in the midsection, and we both crashed downward into the sunken living room. He heaved a great sigh and I thought he was through, but, using his legs to kick me away, he wobbled upward, full of fight. He came at me awkwardly, unprofessionally, arms raised high as if he intended to club me to death with his fists. I crouched and threw two or three jabs. My first went deep into his abdomen and he gasped for air. He was in lousy shape, this assassin. He was an eater, not a killer. I kept hitting but he kept coming at me idiotically, grunting and gasping, ineffectually charging. Christ, it must be Chuck Webner, I thought. But he wasn't that big, and he couldn't fight. He charged in fast and I went down and lifted an uppercut into the wattles of his neck. He groaned, stood still for a moment, then staggered backward, hacking and spitting in the dark, until he collapsed into a large chair.

As I stood in the dark catching my breath, I heard him moaning. I walked to a floor lamp and turned it on. Sitting in the chair, gripping its arms tightly and breathing through a fleshy pink face was the man from the train who had tried to shoot and burn me at Keimes's office. He stared at me with bulging eyes and sweat pouring from his balding head.

"You just don't give up, do you?" I said to him.

Between heavy breaths he gasped: "You—can't—get out—of here."

"What the hell do you want from me?"

"Nothing."

I walked to the curtains in the dining room and drew them back, then slid open the terrace door, sucking in fresh air. "If you don't want anything, then stop trying to kill me, you son of a bitch."

He stood up shakily, unknotting his tie, wrapping it about both fists to make a garrote. He looked at it for a moment, unsure of its strength. He pulled hard so that the tie was taut. Then he looked up at me with stupid determination and began to come forward, his step unsteady. His face was flushed beet-red and the pulsating veins running across his visible scalp stood out.

I held up my hand. "You're not going to try it again, are you?"

He staggered toward me, plodding steps, a grim stare.

"Cut it out. You're no hit man. You're liable to have a stroke any minute."

He kept coming, stepping onto the dining-area platform, going around the long antique table. I backed slowly out onto the terrace.

As if to screw up his nerve, he began to snap the tie curled about his large fists menacingly. I was out on the terrace now, close to the wall and a thirty-story drop. He was at the window, where he paused.

"You're too old for this, pop—now you'd better—"

"I'm stronger than you," he gritted. "We're all stronger than people like you."

"Rich man's son, huh?"

"It's got to be done," he said in a deep voice not unlike that which had once boomed down to Moses, I was sure.

I watched his feet as he edged them over the tracks that held the sliding terrace doors. He put his heels to the tracks. Just as he bent his legs slightly to propel himself forward, I jumped toward him, reaching out and grabbing the tie wound about his fists, yanking him to me and past me, sliding him across my chest. He went outward and over the wall with a little yelp, twisting in the air as I lifted his feet from the terrace floor. With one large hand he caught the inside ledge of the wall, clung to it until he could bring the other hand up and over, so that his thick fingers were curled around and under the ledge at the first and second knuckles, his arms crookedly spread over the top of the wall. But he could not bring himself farther up than to rest his chin on the outer edge of the wall. He stared at me with eyes full of fright.

"Pull me up," he said with difficulty because he could not work his jaw.

I walked to the wall and looked downward. He was too heavy to pull himself up any higher. I leaned on the wall. "You'd better tell me why you've been trying to kill me and why you've killed the others."

"Pull me up and I will."

"Tell me now."

"Can't—hard to speak."

"Try."

"Can't—pull me up, for God's sake."

"I don't think so. You'd only lie to me and then when you got your second, third, or fourth wind you'd try to kill me again. No, I don't think so." I reached over the wall, pressing my hand between the outer wall and his body, slipping fingers into his inside suit-coat pocket. I grabbed a slim wallet and pulled it up. It was empty, not a business or credit card, not a single dollar. Then, as I stared down at the man, I noticed the fraternity ring on his pinkie, the same as Jacquette wore. I pried his little finger free from its curled position on the corner of the ledge. Holding it straight with one hand, I worked the ring off and put it in my pocket.

"Now you're a goddamned thief," he said through clenched teeth.

"Routine. Just collecting evidence."

I walked to the elevator and hit the button, but it did not light up. Putting my ear to the crack of the brass doors, I heard no cable movement. I hit the button again and again. No light, no movement inside the shaft.

The man hanging from the ledge could see me at the elevator. "It won't work—we fixed it," he said loudly.

A quick check of all the doors told me that there were no stairs by which to escape. I went back to the terrace, standing before the man clutching the ledge, struggling vainly to lift his heavy body upward, grunting, straining.

"God—pull me up," the heavyset would-be killer grunted.

He had said that I could not get out of this place. That meant there were others around, waiting to see if he had done his job. If not, the second team would have a go at it. I walked down the length of the terrace, looking downward into space. There was a short L-shaped area at the end of the terrace. Looking over the wall, I could see an iron ladder riveted to the side of the outer wall. This went downward for several floors to an iron catwalk on the side of the building. The catwalk met a fire escape that zigzagged downward to the street. I eased myself over the wall, clutching the iron ladder. I let myself down until only my head was still over the wall to look at the man dangling from the terrace ledge.

He painfully twisted his head in my direction, scraping his chin on the ledge. "Please—pull me up."

"You were strong enough to murder a lot of people. You ought to be able to pull yourself up."

"You're murdering me."

"I could have pushed you off already. If you fall, you've murdered yourself. Who knows? You might have a chance to pull yourself up."

He didn't have a chance in hell.

"My feet are in the air!" he said through grinding teeth.

I started down the ladder, then raised my head up again, seething. "Just think of what you did to Hugo Keimes with that acid and the knife, and that poor guy you burned to death. It's about time one of you went. Think about what you've done, then drop dead."

"Pull me up—please, pull me up. Tell you everything."

"You've already told me all you're going to say. Well—chin up!"

I went down the ladder fast, feeling the wind rushing all about me. I got to the catwalk and felt guilty about the guy on the ledge, then I thought about Keimes and the others and went over the catwalk without remorse. It was an ancient thing, rusted and groaning under my weight. As I went quickly down the stairs the iron slats banged and the rust fell through in showers beneath my feet. I went downward, downward, floor after floor, then stopped, breathing hard, to rest. The street still looked like it was a mile away. Suddenly, high above me, six or seven floors perhaps, a heavy steel exit door was flung open, banging against the building's wall.

"He's down there on the fire escape!" someone yelled.

I moved quickly, downward, downward, two steps at a time, gripping the thin handrails, sliding along them, gathering rust so that the palms showed orange. There was a dull popping noise and then a crash of a bullet into iron and a high, whining ricochet. Then another and another, all around me as I raced downward, high-shrieking metal against metal. They were above me, shooting straight downward through the open fire escape, hoping for the best.

They didn't come down after me, only shot downward through the open grates. The bullets whined and whizzed and bounced off the rusty iron, kicking up iron dust everywhere. The street was coming up fast to meet me and I rushed downward to it as if to greet an old friend. Bullets were now pinging off the concrete of the street as those above tried to lean over their high perch and shoot inward at me. That didn't work either. I got to the bottom landing of the fire escape, then let myself down the descending ladder to the street.

Pressing against the wall of the building—solid brick, no

windows, only the fire escape and the lunatics above firing
at me—I worked myself down the street, then sprinted up
to the corner, bullets dancing in my wake. I turned the
corner and ran for a block, then slowed to a walk, scanning the empty streets for a cab. The whole town was
dead. All that shooting and not a soul came running, not a
cop came whistling, no sirens, nothing. Where the hell
was that karate expert assigned to protect me? He was at
home, of course, practicing body chops on his wife and
kids.

Hell, they can catch me on the street this way. It will be
easy for them. I walked another half block, looking every
which way for an errant cab. Then I saw one turn the
corner, slowly heading my way. I jumped into the street,
waving both arms, like a man on a desert island frantically
signaling to a smoking speck on the horizon. The cab
eased over to the curb. A young man leaned over from the
wheel to scrutinize me through the window.

"Where you headed?"

"Algonquin Hotel."

He thought about it for a moment. "Okay, hop in." He
pushed a lever in front and the locks on the back doors
clicked upward. When I got inside, I took out my handkerchief and tried to rub the rust from my hands.

The cabbie drove along slowly, eyeing me in the
rearview mirror. "Have an accident?"

"No—I've been painting the town orange." I opened
the window and let in the cool air. I looked up to see the
sky beginning to brighten. We turned the corner and I
sank back into the seat. We were going right past the
penthouse address where Laura Manville didn't live and I
had almost died. I sat up and stuck my head out the window.

"What'sa matter?" asked the driver.

"Just getting some air." I looked upward as we passed

the apartment building. Very high up, as the sky turned pink behind him, I could see a man dangling from a ledge, struggling, legs squirming for a foothold in nothing but air.

VIII

Into the Tomb

1

Tired and grubby, clutching at terrible images of revenge—chiefly my hands around Laura Manville's beautiful white throat—I deplaned at Orly to find Frank Lovering waiting for me at the end of the customs ramp. With a grin, he held out a hand. The other was wrapped around an unopened bottle of expensive champagne. It was good to see that friendly face smiling so that his neatly trimmed mustache was spread wide.

I shook his hand and patted his stomach. "You've put on weight, Frank."

He stepped back and looked me up and down. "And you look like you've lost some—and you could use a shave."

"And a shower."

He swept a long arm toward the corridor leading to the main terminal. "Right this way to the showers." As we walked down the corridor I noticed that there was a bit of a stoop to Frank's lanky frame, and gray had crept subtly into his dark hair. As we entered the main terminal my eye caught a headline on the front page of the *Herald*. I bought the paper and glanced at the story as we continued walking. The headline read: BANKER DIES IN MYSTERIOUS 30-STORY FALL. I stopped dead still and focused upon the lead paragraph of the story: *Michael Pautz, 58-year-old executive vice-president of the McVicker's Bank of Brooklyn, N.Y., died this morning from injuries received after falling thirty stories from a 45th Street penthouse apartment leased by his bank.*

"What is it?" Frank said, leaning into the paper.

I pointed to the story. "It was almost me."

Frank straightened with a somber look. His voice was flat and official. "What the hell is going on, Jack?"

"All this week I've been a murder target." I held up the copy of the *Herald*. "It's been reported. Haven't you been reading the papers?"

"No—I just got back from a vacation in the mountains when you called. I had turned off the world." He stood silent for a moment, giving me the intelligence agent's study. "I don't like this, Jack." He took the paper and we started to walk, reading the story of the falling banker. "No, I don't like it a bit." He gave me another look, saying: "What are you dragging over here—murder?"

"Maybe my own, I don't know. I do know that it probably started here with a Paris bookdealer named Jean Rombout. So far it's caused five deaths that I know about." We reached the entrance, and stood outside at the taxi stand. I noticed that it was much cooler in Paris, balmy, in the seventies. "I need your help, Frank," I told my friend. "I want to find this guy Rombout."

"I don't know." He shook his head.

We got into the first taxi in line and Frank told the driver to take us to St. Germain-des-Prés, where he had an apartment.

"What don't you know?"

"About getting involved. You, more than most, know my position with the government. And this isn't a government matter."

"I still need your help. How about making it a matter of friendship?"

He handed me the bottle of champagne limply; it had gotten warm. Frank slapped the paper against his knee and said softly, "You push this guy?"

"He fell, he didn't need any help. He tried to make mashed potatoes out of me on a New York street."

"I don't know."

"To hell with it, then. We'll have a few drinks and I'll find this Rombout myself."

"Sure you will, and probably get killed doing it." He turned an angry face to me. "That was always your problem when you were over here—doing things on your own, going your own way. You made it more hairy than it really was then and it was goddamned hairy enough."

"We'll have a few drinks."

"You were always taking chances, crazy stuff, like how you got that Hungarian code once, and—"

"Why don't we drop you off at your place and I'll go on to the George V?"

"And that time you were supposed to deliver that bag of money in Vienna to that doctor. Just drop off a bag of money and leave, but oh, no—it develops into spy drama." He spat out the last two words.

"What did you expect me to do? The doctor was dead inside his house and the sister who answered his door wasn't his sister, and there were two guys in the pantry with howitzers. I know—I should have been an obedient little agent and delivered the goods—and be found dead right next to the doctor."

"You didn't have to go barging in there, banging away

at those guys. You could've left the money and reported it and we would have handled it from there. But not you—"

"Christ, Frank." I turned away from him. "That was fifteen years ago. Those guys are a long time dead and you can bet the KGB isn't up nights mourning them. Forget it —we'll have a few drinks and I'll be on my business here."

Frank grabbed the champagne, leaned over, and began to unwrap the gold foil at the top. "Business—yeah. I can imagine what kind of business." He twisted away the wirework at the top of the bottle and slowly worked the cork out. There was no pop. "That thing with the doctor in Vienna." He gave me a sideways look with a little smile hanging on it. "You got a medal but you should have gotten a one-way ticket to Leavenworth, you know that?"

"They wouldn't have liked me at Leavenworth."

He took a short pull at the bottle, then handed it to me. "You're lucky, but that doesn't go on forever with any-one."

I took a drink of the champagne. It was like swallowing warm vinegar. We sat in silence for some minutes as the taxi drove through the suburbs of Paris. Then Frank leaned forward and told the driver to go to the George V. He sank back and said: "I'll go one more time with you, just to see if you can stay alive. I know a guy at the Sûreté, a friend, named Devol, Inspector Marcel Devol. I'll call him from the hotel while you check in and get cleaned up, and we'll meet you in the bar." He held up his hands, palms toward me. "One guy, this man Rombout, one good look for one guy and that's it, okay?"

I held up the bottle of champagne and tipped it in his direction, toasting, before swallowing again. It tasted bet-ter this time.

Inspector Marcel Devol looked more like a broker than a cop. Everything about him was drab, except for a colorful tie with tiny roses on it, undoubtedly his personal swipe at the police bureaucracy that engulfed his life. We sat at a small table in the hotel bar and he looked at Frank before speaking to me, as if to be reassured that I was safe to talk to.

Frank led him comfortably into it, taking the responsibility for the conversation. "My friend Mr. Journey is looking for a bookdealer named Jean Rombout, who he says has disappeared. That right, Jack?"

"According to what I know."

"Why are you seeking this man, Mr. Journey?" Devol asked dully.

"I bought a library of used books from him through some American bookdealers and he didn't deliver. I want my books."

Devol turned down his thick lips at that, gave Frank a quick glance and said: "This man Rombout has not disappeared. He is dead. His body was found last week in the Bois, under some shrubbery." He watched for a reaction, but I registered no shock; I had expected that kind of news. Frank had not. He rolled his eyes in an exaggerated manner.

"How was Rombout found?" I asked Devol, surprised at the details he volunteered.

"Horrible death—murder, of course, but not mere murder." He warmed to the subject, enjoying the role of keeper of the facts. "This man Rombout had been tortured, sliced hundreds of times—there were cuts all over his body and the murderer did not respect his privates—with what must have been a razor. A brutal, sadistic killing, the kind"—he enjoyed saying this part—"one might expect to happen in your country."

"Yeah—I'm sorry the franc has dropped in value against the buck too."

"Jack—" Frank shoved his glass of wine away from him, annoyed.

"All right, Frank. I just don't like flying three thousand miles to hear how bloodthirsty my country is." I turned to Devol. "And what have you found out about this murder?"

He shrugged. "We have found the body. We detained a man walking through the park but some distance from where Rombout was discovered. He was on an evening stroll, he said. We interviewed him and sent him home. He had no connection with the dead man, none whatever, didn't know him. That's all."

"Who was this suspect?"

"He said that was all, Jack." Frank was impatient to drop the matter and my problems with it.

Devol smirked knowingly. "It makes no difference to me to tell him," he told Frank. Then, folding his hands, speaking his words slowly, he said to me: "The man we detained is not a suspect. We thought he might have seen someone, that's all. An officer stopped this man a great distance in the park from where the body had been found some minutes earlier. He is a businessman, well-to-do, the kind of man whose background and reputation demands respect. He is above suspicion."

"What does this pillar of society do for a living?"

"Living?" Devol laughed. "He is the director of a very large bank, Mr. Journey, a millionaire, a philanthropist." The inspector laughed again. "Hardly the kind of maniac who would slash a person to death."

"And this banker was strolling through the park in the middle of the night?"

"It was the beginning of the night," corrected Devol. "It was a short walk for him. His limousine was nearby with his chauffeur and male secretary inside, waiting for him to finish his constitutional. Do you find it uncommon for rich people to exercise, Mr. Journey?"

Frank Lovering gave Devol a long stare, lifted his wine-glass and drained it, then put it down slowly. "Jack—that man who fell from the 'penthouse in New York was a banker, right?"

I withdrew the ring that the man in the penthouse had worn and tossed it onto the table so that it rang out like an imitation penny when it struck the marble top. "I took this away from the guy in the penthouse, the man who tried to kill me. I took it off his finger and ran for it because the place was crawling with people after my scalp."

Inspector Devol stared down at the ring, not touching it.

I skidded it toward him with a flick of my thumb. "See if this esteemed banker you detained for an interview wears a ring like this."

"What does it mean?" Devol looked at me, then Frank, then back to me.

Frank pushed in tight at our little table. "Tell him Jack, and tell me, too. Tell it all."

I told them what had happened in Chicago and in New York, leaving out no details, knowing that Devol savored them as does any professional cop who lives from detail to detail, item by item, stock clerks with badges itemizing the shoelaces of the murdered.

When I had finished, Devol sat back and nervously fingered the small knot at his tie. "And all of these amazing things in America are somehow tied to the death of Jean Rombout, you say?"

"Yes, and I'd like to look at his shop and warehouse."

Curling his lip officially, Devol said: "The place is under police seal. It is guarded during our investigation."

"I'd like to see it."

"We are still investigating," he repeated, stern and stiff.

"Maybe we could take a look?" Frank asked him in a quiet voice.

"Is the United States government asking this?" Devol arched his eyebrows with the question.

"No," Frank said, "only me. I'm asking for my friend here."

Devol reached out a stubby finger and ran it around the tip of his wineglass, which he had not touched since the waiter had placed it in front of him. "No interference." He raised the stubby finger and waved it widely, slowly, like a metronome in front of the both of us. "You touch nothing."

"Of course not," I said.

"This is police business," he said solemnly. "The case is undetermined."

"We understand," Frank said understandingly.

Devol stood up, buttoning his suit coat. "I will allow you a look, that's all." He leaned over the table and scooped up the ring I had thrown down. "I would like the loan of this."

"Fine," I told him, and put some money on the table for the drinks.

The inspector crooked his arm, holding up that stubby finger of authority once more. "And please, gentlemen, no advice."

2

The offices of Jean Rombout were what I expected them to be, small, dirty, cramped with files, old desks. His warehouse consisted of the second and third floors of a ramshackle brick structure on a Montparnasse side street. Inspector Devol led us past a plainclothes guard loitering outside—they casually waved to each other—and into the office. Another plainclothesman clomped down the spiral staircase in the corner of the office, coming from the second floor.

Devol waved his arms at the cabinets and desks, saying: "Well, here is the office. There is nothing to look at really. We, of course, have gone over Rombout's personal correspondence within the last month or so, his financial records, all the important data. We, of course, found nothing that pointed to this man's murder."

"Did Rombout live here?" I asked.

"Upstairs, in a back apartment. Nothing much. A small bedroom, kitchen, utility apartment."

"Hermit's hovel," I said, and went to a well-worn metal file cabinet, pulling open the top drawer. "Do you mind if I look at his shipping ledgers?"

Devol was swift in moving to the cabinet, almost closing the drawers on my fingers. "Not permitted, Mr. Journey. Touch nothing, remember?"

"Then you do it."

"What?"

"Pull out his shipping ledger."

Devol gave me a vacant look.

"The ledger that shows what books he shipped customers."

Frank was sitting on top of a cluttered desk, smoking a cigarette. He stood up, ground out the butt, and said: "Look, Jack—all you said was that you wanted to look at the place. He's done that for you."

"The books are upstairs," Devol said, and pointed to the ceiling. "Would you care to see the books, there are lots of them."

"I've seen a lot of books before. I'd rather see that ledger."

"Not permitted."

It was no use. I would have to tell them about the

diaries. "I'll trade a look at the ledger for what I think is
the reason why Rombout was murdered. Fair enough?"

"Anyone can have reasons for such things." Devol was
playing the polite cop to the hilt, offering nothing. He
looked at Frank, who walked over to the cabinet.

Frank tapped the cabinet with his knuckles. "Maybe
you could give him a look. Who knows? My friend's theories might have some value."

It was a smart remark. The word *theories* was irresist-
ible to the French cop; unlike any other cop in the world
the French investigator indulged in theories as endear-
ingly as a cop in southern Alabama would fondle a rubber
truncheon. And Frank knew it. He had been in France
long enough to know it.

"And what is this theory?" Devol quizzed as a patronizing smile played about tight lips.

"I believe that somehow Rombout got hold of the diaries kept by the Sicilian bandit Salvatore Giuliano—"

"Those are mythical," Devol put in. "That is an old
story, those diaries."

"They fell into his hands, I believe, when he bought a
library from a widow of one of your inspectors in the
Sûreté."

"Who?"

"I don't know his name. I never ask for names when I
buy crime libraries, only the books. Rombout may have
gotten the diaries in this private library, or some other
way, and secreted them in the library. And I think the
diaries contain dangerous information, that they have
caused Rombout's death, and the deaths of others in the
States."

"Fantastic," Devol exclaimed, shooting up his arms and
letting them slap to his side. "A plot out of Dumas."

"At least Balzac," I said. "Now, what about the look at
the shipping ledger?"

"No, the theory is preposterous, unworkable."

Frank scratched the back of his head, then said to Devol: "He gave you this theory, crazy or not, why not let him have a peek at the ledger, Devol?"

He looked at my friend as if Lovering had lost his senses. "And you give credence to such fantasies—Giuliano has been dead for decades. The diaries would be meaningless . . . if they did exist."

"The Mafia diaries do exist," I said. "It's the only explanation. Why was Rombout cut to pieces? You yourself said it was torture. They want those diaries."

"Aha—the conspiracy, the underworld federation, the Mafia." He waved a limp hand in my face, disgusted with the idea. "You Americans are obsessed with this Mafia, you have a complex about it—you fill up your newspapers with these witch tales and make movies about it."

"Silly, isn't it?" I said. "But we're such a childlike people, as you know, and put great store in fantasies."

"Yes, dreamers, impractical people." He gave Frank a sideways glance, then said to me sarcastically: "America—land of opportunity—to you that means anything is possible. Where do you get such notions? Eh?"

"From a statue standing in New York Harbor," I said, knowing this would probably do it. "Something some Frenchmen shipped over to us children of whimsy about a hundred years ago. Any other country would have made it a man, but not the French. They sent a woman, very tall, elegant, beautiful. It's the one woman every American is nuts about."

Before Frank turned his back on Devol, I saw a grin about to break wide on his face. Devol didn't smile. He stared at me and rubbed his chin slowly, leaning on the file cabinet. Sticking out his foot, he caught the handle of the third drawer of the file cabinet and dragged it out. Then he pulled out the ring I had given him and held it up to me. "I'm going to see if there is a match of this." He pointed downward to a large black leather ledger sitting in the open drawer. He walked to the front door of the shop, saying to the plainclothesman sitting sleepily on the last step of the spiral staircase: "Let them look at what they want." He opened the door with a flourish. "I would like to talk to you further, Mr. Journey. I will call your hotel."

"Thanks."

"*Every* American is 'nuts' about her? Eh?" he said with a smile.

"Crazy for her."

Devol shook his head and went out. I leaned down and yanked out the ledger, putting it on the desk and quickly opening the heavy cover and turning the pages.

Frank stood next to me, laughing. "How could you pull that on him?"

"I didn't pull anything," I said, scanning the pages, "it's true."

"What is this?" Frank jabbed a finger at the thin type-written pages bound into the ledger.

"These are bills of lading with names and addresses. I'm trying to figure out his system." I pointed to abbreviations typed on the right-hand corner of each bill, then went by date to the time I figured he would have sent the New York shipment. "Here it is. To Hugo Keimes. See the letters up here in the corner—CR—that's the crime library, but it wasn't a crime library."

"So now what do you look for?"

"Archaeology." I scanned the pages before and after the one showing the Keimes shipment, writing down what seemed probable. "I've found them, Frank, four of them. See here, all of them marked ARCH. Rombout shipped four archaeological libraries about the time he sent off Keimes's shipment, two to Germany, one to Spain, and one to Austria." I held up the sheet of paper I had been writing on, waving it. "This will give us the answer."

"*You*—it might give *you* an answer. What the hell does it mean anyway?"

"The New York bookdealer Hugo Keimes received a shipment of archaeology books, in German, instead of my crime library, even though Rombout labeled them crime books. He switched the libraries, don't you see? That's how he hid the diaries. One of these clients getting the archaeology books got my library instead and I received— or Keimes did—his library. I don't know why Rombout made the switch—perhaps to throw off those looking for the diaries—but he did. One of these birds has the crime library . . . and Salvatore Giuliano's *memoriales.*"

"This is more involved than that Hungarian-code caper of yours all those years back."

"That was only the KGB. This is the Mafia."

"Now what?"

"Drop me off at my hotel, then get some sleep. I'm going to call these four wizards of archaeology."

It took an hour and a half of frustrating phoning from my hotel room to get through to those receiving Rombout's shipments, three of them, the two in Germany, the one in Spain. These customers had gotten their archaeology books. The Austrian shipment had gone to a Dr. Hans Zunker of Salzburg. His housekeeper informed me that he had gone hurriedly out of town, packed some crates and left with them, and, no, she had no idea where Dr. Zunker had gone. So it was Dr. Hans Zunker who had the diaries and my crime books. It had to be. But where had he gone? The Alps? Great, get out your snowshoes and your Saint Bernard. They've probably gotten to him by now. These people were not stupid, and they were quick, awfully quick.

Archaeology was not my field. I had to know someone who knew about these bone-diggers. I did, barely remembering: Professor Handler, University of Chicago, staying in New York. I dug out his card from my wallet and looked at the archaeological association he had listed on it. He'll help you out, sure, especially after the way you insulted him on the train. Oh, bet on it.

I made the transatlantic call, expecting no answer. The operator got a night watchman at the association building. I had her put me through.

"Harvey speaking," said an old man's voice.

"Yes, Harvey, I'm calling from Paris, France. It's urgent that I get in touch with Professor Handler."

"He's gone, left late this afternoon. Be back in the morning."

"I must reach him at his hotel."

"Sorry, we don't give that out."

"I told you, Harvey, this is urgent."

"How urgent?" There was no urgency in his tired voice.

"He's won the Paris sweepstakes at Auteuil today, several million francs."

"Wow!" Harvey came to life. "I didn't know Professor Handler went in for that kind of stuff—why, the sly old duffer. You with the sweepstakes people or the press?"

"I'm on the committee making the payment. Unless I confirm his winning number tonight, the money will go to a French bus driver."

"Are you kidding?"

"Professor Handler's hotel, please."

"I dunno—we got strict rules here—"

"I don't think Professor Handler would appreciate being out a fortune, Harvey, because you wouldn't bend the rules a little bit. But I'm sure he *would appreciate* your helping me to inform him of his good luck, and I'm sure he would find a way to show you his appreciation, Harvey."

"Professor Handler? He brings his lunch here in a paper bag. Naw, he wouldn't give me a nickel. Why, that old guy doesn't even spend change for a bus, walks over here every day from the Warwick and that's a long walk. Naw, why should I? He ain't gonna take care of me. Hell, give it to the bus driver."

The Warwick. "Thank you, Harvey. Have a nice evening."

"Sure, mister, and I'll tell the professor you called . . . when he shows up tomorrow morning."

Ten minutes later I got Professor Handler on the line from his room in the Warwick.

"Mr. Journey—how pleasant to hear from you. Are you in New York? That sounded like a long-distance operator."

"Very long distance. I'm in Paris and would like some information, if you can provide it."

"I'll do what I can, but I can't imagine what I could bring to your line of work."

"I'm doing some historic crime research, felons of ancient Egypt."

"Hmmm, intriguing."

"Yes, and I understand a Dr. Hans Zunker is quite knowledgeable in Egyptology, correct?"

"Zunker, yes, I know him well. Old friend. But his specialty is South American relics. He's in Salzburg, you know."

"Good—I'm planning some columns on South American primitives gone bad. But Dr. Zunker is not in Salzburg. His housekeeper tells me he's left town, no forwarding address."

"Strange," mused Professor Handler. "Hans is very conscientious about things like that. You always know where he is."

"Do you have any idea where he might be?"

"No, perhaps on vacation. It's that time of year, Mr. Journey. You know he has a few exhibits here for our showing. Just a minute." The Professor muffled the phone somehow, but I could hear him talking to someone, as if calling to someone far off. Then he got back on the line, saying, "You know, it occurs to me that Dr. Zunker might go to Innsbruck, his favorite retreat. He likes the Goldene Rose Hotel very much, goes there when working out problems sometimes. I went there once with him, oh, many years ago, a charming place, rustic. Did you know that Lord Byron used to stay at the Goldene Rose? Marvelous old hotel with fireplaces in the rooms, a grand dining hall. I remember—I remember how low the ceilings were in that hotel, and the quilted beds sloping downward. Very Austrian, Mr. Journey. You ought to try it sometime."

I heard a slight click, as if someone had picked up another receiver at the professor's end of the line. A little heavy breathing went with it. "Well, thanks for your help, Professor. I think I'll try that hotel."

"Oh, yes, Mr. Journey, do, and let's hear from you when you get back to town. Perhaps we can still have lunch."

I heard someone on the extension cluck their tongue in disgust.

"Good-bye, Professor, and thanks."

"Good-bye, Mr. Journey, enjoy Europe."

"And good-bye, Miss Stulka," I said, "enjoy New York."

I heard one click, but the line remained open, the other person on the extension listening in silence for a moment. Then, before hanging up, Miss Wanda Stulka said: "And you go to hell!"

3

I called the Goldene Rose Hotel in Innsbruck expecting nothing. The impossible happened. The hotel did have a Zunker registered, not a *Dr.* Zunker, just plain old Hans Zunker. Yes, he had a suite but was unavailable. He was to have no calls, according to instructions he left at the front desk. That was fine with me. I planned on a personal appearance.

As I put down the phone, questioning whether or not to call Frank on this before booking a flight to Innsbruck, sudden exhaustion swept over me like warm bath water. I went into the bathroom stripping my shirt and soaked a towel in cold water, which I placed around my neck. I splashed cold water on my face and sat on the edge of the tub dripping, contemplating the flight to Austria and what I might find, but I was worn out and sick to death of playing sleuth. It wasn't a matter of choice anymore, I reminded myself; I was so far into it that the only way out was to get it all, have the answers, the solution, as Inspector Devol would officially put it. Chances were that I would wind up dead first, mutilated and awfully dead like the others. It made me angry to think about it, but even the adrenaline coughed up by the anger seemed incapable of creating more energy.

The phone on the bedstand began to ring. I thought about letting it ring, lying down on the bed and letting the phone ring me to sleep. I got up and, walking slowly, reached the bed and lay back on the rose-printed coverlet. The phone kept ringing. It was Frank or Inspector Devol or Wanda Stulka with the raspberries, I thought. I didn't care. I'd see them all in the morning, everybody in the world. None of them mattered, not even the Mafia. I was too damned tired.

But the phone rang on shrilly. "Persistent bastard," I mumbled, rolling over, eyelids squinting open, as I reached for the phone. It wasn't Frank or Devol on the line. It was an American voice.

"Mr. Journey," it began, "we'd like to see you now."

"Who's we?"

"Those concerned with the Giuliano diaries."

"Why so polite? Your last appointment with me was at the edge of a thirty-story terrace. You didn't call then to ask me to take a dive."

"Mr. Pautz was a fool," the voice sneered. "That wasn't our intention."

"And Laura Manville's intentions—what were they?"

"She was only doing her job, reluctantly, I might add."

"Yeah, I saw how hard she fought against setting me up."

"You've only yourself to blame for what's happened. Without your theatrics—"

"Can that, buster. Say what you want to say."

"We'd like to meet with you in an hour, to resolve all this violence. The violence must end, Mr. Journey."

"It's all coming one way—from you. And I have a pretty good idea how you'd resolve the matter. Planting me headfirst in a barrel of concrete. Correct?"

"No, that's all over, Mr. Journey. That's not necessary anymore. You know almost as much as we know. But you know it and that's worth money."

"You're the other fellow from the train, aren't you, the one with the glasses."

"Yes."

"How much money were you thinking about?"

"A great deal."

"How much is a great deal?"

"What do you need?"

I thought for a moment about Edmond Dantes, the

Count of Monte Cristo. He had unlimited funds with which to take his revenge, he had had enough. "How about a couple of million?"

"Two million dollars?"

"I don't mean pesetas."

"That's unreasonable. An eighth of that sum perhaps. But we must talk about it."

"Go to hell—why should I talk to you?"

"Because we have the diaries now, and all you have is information."

"And names."

"That won't mean anything without proof, without the diaries."

"You're lying—you don't have the diaries. If you did, you wouldn't be on the phone with this kid's game."

Then he hit me with it, a triple checkers jump: "Don't bother going to Austria, Mr. Journey. Dr. Zunker won't see you. Now, would you like to settle matters peacefully and in a lucrative manner, or go on this way until you're dead?"

"I wouldn't like that, neither would my dog and some of my friends."

"Quarter of a million, cash."

"For what? I've got nothing you want."

"You have a check from Lewis Lucan of Chicago and a letter or two from Mr. Keimes of New York, both deceased bookdealers. Those items could lead back to Jean Rombout. Miss Manville, for some reason, did not take them from you when she had the opportunity. We'll take those items in exchange for the money."

"A quarter of a million—you can come up with that kind of cash in the middle of the night?"

"In ten minutes."

"This I've got to see."

"Then you accept?"

"Where do we meet?"

"Behind the Invalides in an hour." He hung up.

I called Frank at his apartment and told him about the call.

"Don't go over there; it's a trick to get you out. I'll get in touch with Devol."

"No, I'm going. Tell Devol. I'll see you there."

"Jack, listen to reason—"

"In about forty-five minutes." I put down the receiver, slipped on a fresh shirt, and dug out my .38, for which I had no bullets. And they would know that, wouldn't they? The man who called had been on the train and had gone through your luggage and had taken the bullets. Remember? Hell, you can get bullets anywhere. Not at midnight in Paris at the George V.

Putting on my sport coat, I left without a tie, but I did check to see that I had Lucan's check and the two notes from Keimes in my wallet. So that's what they'd wanted all along—paper. In the lobby I jammed the check and the two notes into a hotel envelope, addressed it to myself in care of the U.S. Embassy, and put a stamp on it before dropping it into the mail slot. A cool night greeted me as I stepped outside. The doorman piped a taxi over to me and I told the driver to take me to the Invalides. He drove away slowly into the light traffic. He turned about as he drove, remarking: "The building is closed at this time of night."

"It's lit up, right?"

"Oh, yes, many lights around the building. It is one of our great monuments."

"I know—Napoleon's tomb."

"Yes, Napoleon, but the building is closed."

"Go there anyway. I only want to see it lit up."

"Most people like to go inside."

"I've been inside before, years ago." I put my head back

against the seat and closed my eyes for what I thought were only a few seconds. Then I jumped forward when I heard the driver shouting at me.

"You, sir! Hey, you, sir!"

I rubbed the instant sleep from my burning eyes. "What is it?"

"The Invalides, Napoleon's tomb." He waved at a domed building with magnificent columns before us. "All lit up, as you can see, sir."

"Isn't that a pretty sight?"

"Oh, yes, sure. Now where do you wish to go?"

"This will do." I gave him the fare and a tip and got out.

The driver called after me, "But, sir, as I've said, the building is closed."

"I believe you. But I think I'll check the locks to make sure no one is tampering with Bonaparte's body."

The driver wore a cap that shrouded his eyes; I could see only a long slack-jawed face turned to me in silence. He then drove off slowly and I quickly made my way around the building to the rear. Beneath a high lamp stood a man in a brown custodian's uniform. I walked directly up to him, my hand in my pocket, holding my .38.

The man lifted a single finger to the bill of his cap and touched it in a short little salute. "This way, Mr. Journey." He opened the door behind him. I went inside, standing in the middle of a long narrow hallway with a low ceiling. "Follow me, Mr. Journey." I walked behind him, keeping pace with his jaunty gait, listening to the hollow sounds our footsteps made down the dimly lit corridor. We reached another door, which the man in the custodian's uniform also opened. "Please step inside, Mr. Journey."

I stopped before the opening and could see little. All was dark inside.

"I'll get the lights in a minute," the dapper little man said from behind the door.

I took a step inside and then tried to go back into the corridor, but the door came rushing forward, striking me and sending me into the room backward as the heavy door slammed shut. I tumbled down to a cold marble floor. I reached out my hand and felt an enormous block of marble at my side, found a ledge in it, and used this to pull myself up.

The lights went on above me, searing bright, coming from a domed ceiling, flooding a large circular room, a colonnade of marble pillars that held up a circular walkway above and a high marble balustrade. At my feet in a circle around a huge red porphyry sarcophagus, etched in elegant Italian marble were names that greeted my shock: "Jena, Wagram, Friedland, Austerlitz, Moscow." All them were Napoleon's battles. Jesus, I was inside the tomb!

I went to the small door through which I had been hurled. It had been locked by the little custodian. There were no other doors leading into the sunken tomb. I studied the pillars leading up to the high balustrade where visitors normally stood to look down upon Napoleon's resting place. There was no way I could climb upward and out.

I stood in silence for what seemed hours, but they were only slow minutes of apprehension. Then came echoing footsteps, heavy and casual, making their way to the tomb on the floor above. Slipping behind one of the pillars, I looked upward as I brought out my useless .38 and held it at my side.

The footsteps stopped at the edge of the balustrade across from me. Above stood a distinguished-looking man with thick gray hair wearing a dark suit. He stared silently down at the sarcophagus. He was joined by a tall, large man dressed in a traditional tan chauffeur's uniform, complete with cap. Through the openings of the balustrade I could see that he was wearing shiny black boots, an archaic getup but it all seemed correct in this setting.

"Mr. Journey, are you there?" called out the gray-haired man.

"I'm here," I said, and stepped slowly from behind the pillar, using it to half shield my body so that my right arm holding the .38 was hidden.

"Did you bring those items, the check and the letters?"

"Where's the man who spoke to me on the phone?"

"He had business elsewhere. Show us the items, Mr. Journey."

His stentorian voice echoed down to me, calm, an in-charge voice.

"I have them here." I patted my breast pocket with my free hand. "Where's the money?"

The gray-haired man nodded to the chauffeur, who held up a small paper bag.

"A quarter of a million in that little thing?"

"Thousand-dollar bills, two hundred and fifty of them, Mr. Journey."

"I thought thousand-dollar bills were out of circulation."

The gray-haired man smiled benignly. "Not for us." He nodded again to the chauffeur, who tossed the bag in my direction so that it fell at my feet. I used my foot to kick it close to me without moving away from the pillar, sliding down along its line and picking up the bag, which was open at the top. It was full of thousand-dollar bills.

"Now the items, Mr. Journey, and all of this is ended."

I dropped the bag of money and laughed; he really meant it. They meant to pay me off and walk away from all the bodies. Simple as that. "Sorry, but I neglected to bring those items."

The gray-haired man's expression changed from placid

self-confidence to a scowl. "We had a deal," he boomed. "You accepted a deal, Mr. Journey!"

"I changed my mind. A quarter of a million is not enough."

"What *is* enough?"

"I need twenty million dollars right away. I've got bills to pay."

"You have *bills* to pay?" He repeated the words, dumbfounded.

"Bar tabs in Chicago, and I make a lot of long-distance calls, things like that. Yeah, it will have to be twenty million right away." I kicked the sack of money to the center of the tomb. As it skidded across the marble floor the money spilled out, leaving a trail of thousand-dollar bills. I was using up time, of course, figuring Frank and Inspector Devol would be along any second. I was wrong.

With his fists clenched on the railing of the balustrade, the man stared down at the money, eyes wide, face drawn. He spoke not to me but to the money. "We trusted you to keep your word, to keep the deal you made. When you make a deal in our profession, you keep it. If you don't keep it, the world goes to hell. That's two hundred and fifty thousand dollars down there, Mr. Journey." Then he said with the voice of an angry parent: "Now you pick up that money and keep your end of the bargain! You do that right now!"

"I think I understand you . . . the whole bunch of you," I said, easing back behind the pillar. "I thought you were fearless, impervious to interference when you walked in here, and pretty stupid, to keep a rendezvous with someone who would be insane to meet you without bringing along an army of cops. But *you are* blind to that. It's inconceivable to you that I didn't want your lousy dough, that I'd come over here to find out just how nuts you guys are, who you are, and if you'd pay the money and merely expect me to walk away with it and keep my mouth shut. But here you are, bold as brass—you thought you made a deal, that no matter what you do, you can make a deal and that ends the problem. That's the mentality, all right. And I also understand the playacting for the Mafia. You're not the Mafia at all. I don't know quite what you are, but it's all been set up to look like Mafia, cornball setups to put it all on the Outfit. Obvious—too damned obvious—all this ridiculous Mafia-style killing."

"The methods worked," the man with the gray hair responded.

"Red-flag stuff. A spike through the ear, a spear through the heart, a stiletto in the back. You had me thinking Mafia with those broken-down techniques, but they were obvious, maybe so obvious that I failed to recognize them. Now this—Napoleon's tomb in the dead of night. That's obvious too, as if you ripped it out of a crime history book." He was about to speak, but I waved him silent. "France has historically been the mortal enemy of Italy and Sicily and that goes back to what . . . the thirteenth century, when the battle slogan of Sicilians fighting invading French was *Morte alla Francia Italia anela!*"

"Death to the French is Italy's cry," the man translated with a knowing smile.

"Yes, and the initial letters of the words of that slogan make up the word Mafia, an archenemy of *this* man"—I pointed to the sarcophagus containing the bones of the diminutive French conqueror—"and he of it. And I'm brought to this place so that the old legend will have meaning in my death, if I didn't take the deal and you had to kill me—more Mafia smokescreen. God, you guys are corny. No self-respecting Mafioso would stick you with a penknife."

The gray-haired man unclenched his fists and gripped the side of the railing. "Mr. Journey—did you contact the police? Were you so foolish as to contact the authorities? You knew who you were dealing with, didn't you, that we always keep our end of any deal? Didn't you know that? We thought you learned that in New York. If we intend to kill you, we kill you. If we deal, we deal. Now, pick up the money and live up to your agreement."

"Come down and pick it up yourself! Or you can wait up there until my friends arrive and take a trip over to the Sûreté."

"You *did* contact the police!" The gray-haired man became livid, his face flushed red in an instant. It wasn't a matter of the police closing in on him, that he might have to face murder charges. His self-centered rage of the powerful, his authority, had been challenged. Someone had told *him* what to do, and worst of all, his money wasn't working for him, his money was useless. He turned to the chauffeur and said, "Kill him."

Reaching into his large coat pocket, the chauffeur brought out an automatic. He was about to level it at me when I jumped out from behind the pillar and pointed my .38 at him.

"I'm aiming straight at your forehead, bozo. You can get off a shot, maybe, but I'll drill that thick head of yours in the same second."

A little laugh came out of his boss, who said: "Shoot him, Maxel, there are no bullets in his gun."

"If you believe that, Maxel," I said, holding my arm stiffly upward at the chauffeur, "you'll believe that he'll send that money over there on the floor to your widow after I kill you."

"He has no bullets," the other man hissed.

"How do you know?" the chauffeur asked his boss as he rested his automatic limply on the railing without aiming it.

"They were removed from his gun some time ago. Now kill him."

"Toss that gun down here to me," I told the chauffeur, "or I'll blow the top of your head into that dome."

The chauffeur gave his boss a quick, nervous look, then threw down the automatic so that it clattered at my feet. I picked it up, put my .38 away, and held the automatic on the both of them.

"He was right," I said to the chauffeur. "No bullets, but I'm sure you weren't so careless." I patted his automatic.

The gray-haired man shook his head, lowering it onto his chest and unbuttoning his coat.

"Stand still," I told him.

He slowly turned away from the railing. "You're either mentally unbalanced, Mr. Journey, or an alcoholic." He kept turning, pivoting slowly so that his right hand was disappearing from my sight.

"I'll shoot if you move another inch!" I shouted upward.

"Your brain was undoubtedly afflicted at birth," came his calm voice, and he kept turning. Then he dropped like a rock to his knees, pulling out a small automatic, aiming this through the pillars of the balustrade and firing quick rounds. I jumped backward as the bullets smashed into the marble floor, chipping away at the glorious names of Napoleon's old battles. One of his slugs tore into the pillar I managed to slip behind.

I rolled to the other side of the pillar, gave him a glimpse of me, as he expected, and he chipped the other side of the pillar, and then I came back again to the same side while he shot the other way. I dropped in the open to my knees and, holding the big automatic level with two hands, fired off three shots. The bullets blasted through the small pillars where the gray-haired man crouched.

As the bullets struck him, the older man bolted upright and half climbed to the top of the balustrade for one clear shot at me, and I shot him square in the chest. He fell forward into space, a look of utter amazement on his face, so that he crashed like a pulpy sack of tomatoes thrown from a great height onto the top of Napoleon's sarcophagus. His blood ran over the sculptured top of the granite block and down its sides and onto the marble floor of battles.

Above, rock still, holding onto the balustrade, was the chauffeur. Slowly, mechanically, he climbed up on the balustrade and stood on the railing.

I stepped over and out so that I was almost directly beneath him. "Get off of there before you get hurt."

His eyes were watery and he worked his mouth back and forth like a cretin groping for words. Then he spread out huge arms and bent his knees, springing outward and downward at me. I shot him in midair, and stepped aside as he hit the floor. Unlike his boss, tranquil in death, the chauffeur slowly doubled up in agony, holding his midsection, crying. "You've killed me."

"What did you expect?"

"I had . . . to do . . . something. I worked for him . . . for twenty-three years."

"Yeah, I know, loyalty. Who killed Rombout, you?"

He moved his head slowly, eyes at the top of the lids in the direction of his boss. "He did. I cut him. He killed him."

"Why?"

"He had the diaries, wanted millions for them."

"So Rombout was a blackmailer. And you killed him for the diaries, right?"

"We never got them . . . but there is a man . . . from America going to get them now . . . in Austria. He knows what you know . . . about where they are." He tightened himself into a ball.

"How did he find out about Zunker?"

"We found out, followed you since you arrived here
. . . please, may I have a doctor?" His voice was getting
weaker.

"Sure, any minute now." I knelt down next to him, not
too close. He was a large man who might have had that
extra burst of energy. "How did you find out?"

"Got into Rombout's place. I took care of the detective
. . . didn't kill him. . . . The American . . . tore out
the pages of the ledger . . . so he knows. He's gone . . .
to Austria. Please . . . please get a doctor." His voice was
down to a whisper. He was dying and there was nothing I
could do for him except lie and weasel and cheat with
words, which is what I had been doing successfully for a
long time now. The chauffeur bubbled up some black
blood. "I'm going—going." And he was gone.

I sat down next to the dead man. Then I looked up,
feeling eyes upon me, and saw many heads along the
round balustrade. Frank was there, and Inspector Devol
and others. They came down through the ground-floor
corridor and through the only door. With them was the
dapper little man in the brown custodian's uniform.

"He's the one who ushered me in here," I said, pointing
to him.

"He's the male secretary," Devol volunteered. He nodded and two of Devol's men took him out through the
door. Devol walked to the gray-haired man whose arm
dangled down at the side of the sarcophagus. "The
banker, Henri Bertouillon . . . above suspicion . . .
and he put one of my men in the hospital tonight!" He
held up the man's hand, which showed a familiar pinkie
ring. Devol brought out the ring I had given to him and
held it up alongside the dead man's ring. "It matches," he
said laconically, then dropped the arm, which banged
against the wall of the sarcophagus.

Frank sat down next to me.

Devol looked sadly about at the carnage, and the blood-specked scattered money, the shattered marble in this hallowed place, then turned to me in utter disgust. He said: "I ought to charge you with desecrating a national monument." He walked over to me and took the automatic out of my hand. "We heard the chauffeur make his statements to you. And the secretary has also told us about the same thing. And the other American is on his way to Austria. So your conspiracy is real, a living thing, eh?"

I stood up and Frank stood up with me. I said to him: "I need to get to Innsbruck."

"So do I," Frank said. "This *is* government business now."

IX

The Diaries

1

All planes frighten me, or the thought of turning over my life to a stranger, the pilot, frightens me. Having little trust in my fellow human beings these days, it was impossible for me to trust a kid ten years younger than I was to fly my tired body at supersonic speeds over the mountains to Innsbruck. Yet I went. Frank and I sat in the large plane as it whined through the cloudless night, burning its way southeastward.

To look down was to look back and get dizzy, so I looked over the pilot's shoulder, peering ahead into distance that became instant memory, landscapes that rose into towering peaks and vanished beneath us, hills, plateaus, the mountains again, and mountains beyond. I closed my eyes and tried to sleep, but the speed was always there humming about me, and the distrust, as I nodded in and out of consciousness.

Breaking the silence now and then was the sharp static-filled crackle from the pilot's headphones and distant voices coming abruptly to life, dying in a mechanical click. The pilot was from Youngstown, Ohio, and had been only six years old when John F. Kennedy was shot. *H. Viculian* was stenciled on his helmet. I think he said his name was Herbort or Hubert, something distinctive.

Frank leaned forward and talked to the pilot, who held up his left hand, making a circled "Okay" with his thumb and index finger. Frank sat back and nudged me. "It's all right. We contacted the police in Innsbruck. They have a guard on Zunker at the hotel. The only way your friend with the glasses will get in there is to blast his way by the guards."

"He won't do that—not his style."

"Then you'll get what you're after maybe, Jack. And when you do, you'll turn it over to me, right?"

"Why should I do that?"

"Because if this fellow going after Zunker in Innsbruck is an American, it's our business. He was involved back there in Paris with assaulting a French policeman and he's tied in with those Frenchmen who killed Rombout. That's United States business, Jack."

"I guess so."

Frank patted my knee and sat back in the seat, his body cramped. "You know, I've often envied you over the years since you got out of the service."

"What the hell is to envy? I have to work my ass off to make a buck. You're on the public teat."

"I continue to live inside of a rule book." He sighed. "You go around stomping it. It's because you're your own man mostly. I know you have to be judicious in what you write for that column, but you pick and choose your friends, your residence, the restaurants where you eat, the bars you drink in. For me, all that is dictated by my job. Yeah," he said through an even heavier sigh. "You got out, I stayed in. You went on to have a real life. I hung back, an apple that never dropped from the tree."

"You're a poet, Frank."

"Sure, and you're a free man."

"No freer than any other American citizen."

Frank turned awkwardly in the large leather seat we shared to look at me square on. "Do you realize just how *free* that is? Take a look out that window. You're in Europe—"

"I figured out that much."

"And you're flying over the Alps in one of the world's fastest jets, a citizen of the United States, being taken into another country to settle a business transaction gone wrong." He laughed.

"I don't think I'd be here unless you—"

"Yeah, an American citizen. We won't let you get cheated, robbed, kidnapped, or killed—if we can help it. We spend millions on you, boy." He turned and faced forward. "Yeah, you do as you please, shoot down your enemies and then go out to dinner." The teasing in his voice disappeared. He was solemn now. "And we clean up the mess and bury the bodies. I guess that's why I envy you. I don't like being a goddamned janitor in a suit."

"Why don't you quit?"

"What would I do? Become a security consultant?"

"You make good money, take vacations, have an important position with the government. That means a comfortable retirement."

"If I live that long. Do you know how many of us from the old days are gone, Jack?"

"I haven't kept track."

"There's eight of us left—eight out of fifty young men who were going to save America by crawling around in the dark with young men from Russia, cutting each other's throats over codes, ciphers that were obsolete the next month. Eight. That's it."

I put my head against the leather padding of the seat. "I thought there were more than that."

"None of them died of old age, if you remember. When you left the service, there were twenty-three of us left, and—what is it? Fifteen years later? Now we're down to eight and that includes you, and you're the only one who left the service."

I had heard this from him before. And I had answered the same way: "The odds of getting killed in the service are high. And killing others, higher. That's why I got out. You can resign. You could quit tomorrow, tonight when we land, if you like. You know that."

Frank pointed to a shimmering cluster of lights that came into view as we hurtled over a mountain range. "That's Innsbruck," he said, then added: "Quit? Then what would I do for fun?"

The city of Innsbruck came up fast, a town of not more than one hundred thousand souls. It was all yellow with soft old light that showed its ancient wonders of looming church steeples built by Franciscan monks four centuries ago, the university buildings off to the right, thick-walled buildings with powerful arches, and the glittering Fürstenberg Palace.

"It's an architectural marvel, this place," I told Frank as we made our descent and the pilot cut our speed.

Frank peered straight ahead and said: "Their airstrip can just take this baby by a few feet."

"Thousands of people come here each year," I instructed, "just to look at the Hofkirche."

"What's that?" He really didn't want to know and kept his eyes glued to the airport that appeared before us, and the lighted runway at which we aimed. The pilot was busy talking to the control tower, talking in a calm, crisp voice, unconcerned with danger. *He* knew he was in no danger whatever because he was twenty-six years old. At that age there is no danger, no death. The noise from the plane's flaps and the cutting back of the engines made it difficult to talk, but Frank and I struggled on, as a way of beating back the mistrust and the fright it brought. So, while gripping the seat tightly, I shouted like an idiot: "It's a church, hundreds of years old!"

"Good!"

"It has a monument inside of it to Emperor Maximilian the First!"

"Swell!"

I could see Frank stiffen in the seat, holding on for dear life as we shot downward to the runway, seconds from touching the sweet earth. "It's an elaborate monument, done by Peter Vischer in the fifteenth century!"

"Who's he?"

"The artist who built the monument!"

We hit the runway and bounced downward to a dribble. The pilot reversed his engines with a blasting whine and we were thrust against our seat belts, which were over our laps and chests. We were at a standstill inside of a minute. My watch showed it to be 4:00 A.M.

Frank went limp, sighing, and looking at the palms of his hands, which were soaked with sweat. So were mine.

"How long did it take this Vischer to complete the monument?"

"Many years, I think."

"That's too long for a dead emperor," he said, unfastening his belt.

An Austrian police captain met us near the runway. He was standing outside a large car that looked more like a limousine than a police squad. He wore a smart uniform and almost clicked his heels when shaking Frank's hand, the hand of the United States government. He gave me a curt nod and a brief handclasp and then ushered us into the back of the car. Once inside, he gave orders to the driver to take us to the Goldene Rose Hotel. Next to the policeman at the wheel sat another officer, who held a carbine between his legs.

As we sped into the old city the captain explained: "I have placed two guards inside the hotel, they are in civilian clothes." He smiled at this, as if to tell us how professional he was. Then he told us: "It's best not to disturb guests with uniformed men. This is a country that dislikes uniforms, gentlemen."

"Understandable," Frank replied. "What about Zunker?"

"He is perfectly fine, in good health. Nothing at all the matter with him. I spoke to him personally after receiving the call from your embassy, Mr. Lovering. Of course, he said he has no idea what this is all about."

"What about his room?" Frank asked the police captain.

"His room?"

"We asked you to place a guard in his room. With him."

"Oh, yes," the captain said slowly. He shook his head. "Dr. Zunker wanted no part of that, gentlemen. He is an old and respected man in Austria. Teaches archaeology."

"You didn't put a man in his room?" Frank's voice stiffened.

"We respect the wishes of our intellectual leaders in Austria, gentlemen." The implication was that in the United States we treated intellectuals with the kind of disdain we showed to dogcatchers, which, of course, was right.

"You have to tell him to get a guard in that room, Frank."

"I know," Frank shot back at me, angry over my telling him how to do his job. "I want your man up front to call on the radio and send a guard into Zunker's room, now—right now."

"But why—what does it mean?"

"It means that one of your leading intellectuals is about to be murdered."

The captain snorted a laugh. "I'm no fool, Mr. Lovering. Your people in Paris said he was in danger." He pursed his lips, a satisfied look on his lean face. "And I took the necessary precautions." He slapped his hands together. "I have a man in the hallway, outside Dr. Zunker's room." He put a finger to his eye and threw it outward in a straight line. "That man has his eye glued to the doctor's door, you see?"

"He should be in the room," Frank said lamely.

"The hallway will do," the captain said smugly. "This is Innsbruck, Austria, Mr. Lovering, not New York City or"—and he drew out the word, looking over to me—"Chicago. That is where you are from, is it not, Mr. Journey?"

"Chicago, Illinois, that toddling town, the Windy City, Big Shoulders, yes."

"Of course, that's what your embassy people in Paris said—Mr. Lovering of your government from Paris and you, Mr. Journey, a journalist from Chicago, Illinois." He spoke to us in the manner of a guide trying hard to entertain tired tourists. "Well, no harm will come to Dr. Zunker here. Now, in Chicago, Mr. Journey, perhaps it is customary for people to go charging up and down hotel hallways —even the better hotels in Chicago—shooting at the guests, but that is not the case in Innsbruck, I assure you."

We were deep into the city now, winding through the twisting streets, all empty and silent, the large car humming over cobblestones. Old towering streetlamps adorned with iron filigree threw down yellow patches of light in our path. The driver was taking his time.

"Can't you go faster?" I asked the captain.

He gave a little twist of his head and a Simple Simon smile. "Speed limit, Mr. Journey. We don't speed in Inns-

bruck." Then he was thunderstruck with what he thought
to be a joke. "Where is the fire?"

"Yes," I said to him, "we *do* say that in the States—
good." I leaned close to Frank and whispered: "This guy is
a bumbling idiot. Get him to step on the gas."

"Could we go a little faster, please," Frank asked the
captain.

"Certainly," nodded the captain. "You will find us coop-
erative." He put his head over the back of the front seat
and spoke softly to the driver. The car jumped forward,
going at least five miles per hour faster. The captain re-
sumed the position on the seat facing us, nodding. "We are
now doing the maximum speed under the law." He
looked at a cheap watch on a lean wrist. "It should be only
a matter of minutes now and you will see Dr. Zunker, do
whatever it is you must do, say what you must say, and
then we will be glad to return you to the airport."

We went into a broad street, crossed several large
squares, and came to rest in front of a massive building
with thick brown walls. Above an arching entrance was a
sign in old Austrian script reading: GOLDENE ROSE HO-
TEL.

"And now for your little rendezvous, gentlemen," said
the police captain as he politely swung the car door wide
for us.

2

We walked quickly into the lobby of the Goldene Rose
Hotel, a lobby not dissimilar to the Algonquin's, with oak
paneling, heavy couches, and overstuffed chairs, all
empty except one. A man, sprawling in one of the chairs,
his head resting on his arm and wearing an Austrian police
uniform, came to life when hearing us enter. He got up

sleepily and approached the captain, saying: "Nothing unusual, sir. Everything quiet."

"You see, gentlemen?" said the captain. "Everything is quiet."

Coming from behind the desk was the hotel's night manager, a tall young man with sandy hair, a neat suit, and a glad hand. He shook the captain's hand and said: "Dr. Zunker is sleeping now. He requested that he not be disturbed. He is very tired."

I walked to a table next to the front desk. "Are these the house phones?"

"Yes, but no one can be disturbed at this hour," said the pleasant-faced young manager, moving to the table with Frank and the captain. "That's our policy."

As I picked up the phone, the manager gently rested his hand on it and lowered it back into the cradle.

"Dr. Zunker left word—"

The police captain said: "It is important we call the doctor now. These gentlemen have come all the way from Paris to see him." He lifted the receiver of one of the phones. He added in a reassuring voice to the manager: "It's only for a few minutes, a few questions, and then these gentlemen will allow the doctor to go back to sleep."

The young manager made a face close to a grimace and the captain ignored it, holding up the receiver, speaking into it with the voice of authority: "Dr. Zunker's suite, please. Yes, I know, but this is police business. I? I am Captain Runkelhaus, Innsbruck police. Who are you? I see, now put the call through. What? Don't be silly—put the call through. I *told* you who I was. That's ridiculous—how can I show you my identification when I'm talking to you on the phone—where are you? Where is the switchboard room?" The captain placed a hand over the mouthpiece of the phone. "Am I speaking to a hotel employee?"

The manager nodded. With a quick thrust the captain placed the phone into the hand of the manager. "You tell your operator to put this call through now—she knows your voice."

The young man pursed his lips at having to violate hotel protocol, then spoke into the mouthpiece. "This is the manager—yes, yes. That was Captain Runkelhaus on the phone. Now do as he asked and ring the Zunker suite."

"Bureaucratic bullshit," I said to Frank.

"Not so loud," he whispered back. "You're in another country."

"Yeah—Freedonia, all we need is the Marx Brothers."

The manager suddenly beamed at the captain and announced in triumph: "It's ringing."

"Good," replied the captain. "Give me the phone when the doctor comes on the line."

I took Frank aside and said: "Tell this wooden-headed cop that unless we get up to those rooms right now, Zunker may never answer another phone. Tell him!"

"God damn it, Jack, this is Austria. They have their own ways of doing things. We don't even know if Zunker is in real danger. What do you want to tell him—that some assassin is stalking a broken-down archaeology instructor because he got the wrong books in the mail?"

"It's still ringing," announced the manager.

"How many times has it rung?" asked the captain.

"I've counted twenty rings."

"Perhaps the doctor is in the bathroom?"

"Will you listen to this insanity, God damn it!" I said to Frank. "Get that bird's room number and let's get the hell up there!"

"Take it easy. There's a guard on the floor, sitting at the end of the hallway with his eyes glued to Zunker's door, remember?"

"I've counted thirty rings now," said the manager dutifully.

"Let it ring," ordered the captain.

Frank finally moved over to the captain, saying: "I suggest we go up and personally check on Dr. Zunker."

"Pound on the man's door in the middle of the night?" the captain huffed. "An affront to the man's dignity. Do you realize that Dr. Hans Zunker was nominated for the Nobel award? Do you?"

"Did he win?" I asked.

"The nomination was sufficient to make him a hero of Austrian culture."

The manager was shaking his head, alarmed now. "Fifty rings—I've counted fifty rings. Perhaps he's in a deep sleep."

"Or he's dead," I said to the captain. "At the hands of a killer."

"I have a guard on that floor, a good man, watching the hallway," exclaimed the captain.

"Then let's go up and see *him.*"

"Sixty rings," said the manager, astounded, as if announcing the underwater level of a submerging sub being depth-charged. "This is irregular—very strange."

"We will go up," concluded the police captain. He led us to a hallway off the lobby while the manager stayed at the phone, continuing to announce the number of rings to us as we moved into an elevator where a pretty young woman sat on a stool next to the operating lever. "Fourth floor," ordered the captain. We jerked upward slowly in the dilapidated elevator, its gears grinding, cables clunking.

The captain and the officer from the lobby stood in front of us. I whispered to Frank: "Do you have your gun?" He nodded. "Good, because Devol kept mine in Paris."

"Good," Frank said. "That way you'll stay out of trouble."

We came to an agonizingly slow halt on the fourth floor and stepped out, the captain leading us down the hallway, where we turned a corner to another hallway. He came to a dead stop, jolted by the sight of an empty chair at the end of the second hallway. "Where's the guard?" he asked his subordinate.

"Franz was here twenty minutes ago," the officer told him. "I personally brought him a cup of coffee. He was sitting in the chair and I took it to him."

The captain moved swiftly down the hallway, almost at a nervous trot. "I told him not to move from that chair—to stay in that chair."

"Maybe he went to the men's room?" volunteered the officer.

"Go—check the men's room," the captain half shouted.

The officer turned around and ran down the hallway. The captain went up to the chair, which was leaning against the wall, and kicked it so that it slid forward and down. "I *told* him not to leave this spot."

"What's Zunker's room number, quick," I said to the captain.

"I must find the guard," he said angrily, looking down another hallway.

"To hell with that—the room number?"

"What's the number?" Frank asked.

"Four-oh-five," the captain said lamely, now perplexed. He began to walk slowly down the other hallway. "I must find the guard. He'll have a proper explanation, I'm sure."

We didn't wait for an explanation as we ran back down the hallway, stopping at Room 405, and tried the door, which was locked. Frank banged on it loudly. No answer.

I pressed my ear to the door. "I can hear the phone ringing . . . faintly."

Frank anxiously glanced up and down the hallway.

"To hell with those tin cops, Frank. Blow that lock away."

He drew out his gun slowly, hesitantly.

"Shoot it open."

Frank stood with the gun half pointed at the door lock. "Christ, Jack!"

"Go ahead!"

"I'll get a passkey."

"Yeah, and you can also call down for a mortician."

Frank shrugged, pushed me away from the door, stepped back and fired two shots, loud popping sounds. The lock was blown away and the impact of the bullets from the .45 drove the door inward a foot. I rushed in front of Frank, pushing open the door and going into the suite. It was big and gloomy, heavy drapes drawn over the windows. Papers and books were strewn about on top of the heavy chairs and sofa of the sitting room. Against one wall several large crates were stacked. I went to these, looking into them, pulling out book after book.

Frank was at my side. "What the hell are you doing? Let's find Zunker."

"My library, here it is." I held up a book. "All crime books, in French."

"Great, now you can open up a bookstore."

I put the books down and walked across the sitting room to a closed door. "This must be his bedroom." We could hear the phone ringing inside the room, louder. I slowly turned the knob of the door. It opened. Pushing it back, we saw Dr. Hans Zunker, a wizened little old bald-headed man, sitting upright in a large bed, several pillows propped behind him. The bedroom was blazing with lights, every one of them turned on. Zunker stared straight ahead at us, motionless. At the side of his bed the phone rang and rang.

"Dr. Zunker? Dr. Zunker?" I said to him, but he did not respond. We took a few steps closer. His large blue eyes were fixed straight ahead.

"Is he dead?" Frank asked quietly, surprised at the thought.

"Looks like it."

We walked on paper toward him. The entire bedroom was covered with sheets of paper and books turned every which way.

Then Zunker's large blue eyes blinked. At the foot of the bed, we could see that he gripped the sheet over him with both hands, which were knuckle-white and trembling. He opened his mouth slowly, thin, quivering purple lips that said nothing.

"What's the matter with him?" Frank said. "Is he having a fit?"

"Dr. Zunker," I said calmly, "we're here to help you."

His lips went on trembling; he kept his body rigid.

"Have you had a visit from anyone tonight?" I moved to the side of the bed. Dr. Zunker continued to stare straight ahead at Frank. "From a man wearing glasses—an American?" I leaned over, putting my face close to his. "It's all right, we're here to help you." Then he slowly moved his eyes from dead center to the right, back to dead center, then to the right, over and over, rolling his eyes. I stood up and jerked sideways to look at another door. I waved Frank over.

With a quick twist I turned the handle and shoved the door inward and open. It banged against the side of an old bathtub with ornate legs on it, legs sculptured in the form of hooves. Switching on the light, I walked into the bathroom, brushing past a plastic shower curtain drawn in a circle around the tub and imprinted with golden roses.

I took a step, then with lightning speed Frank pushed me hard. At the same second there was a movement be-

hind the shower curtain. A moment later a bullet plowed
through the curtain, singing past the back of my head as I
plunged forward and struck the tiled wall. The bullet
crashed into the mirror above the bathroom sink, shattering it into large shards that exploded outward, downward,
so that the pieces clattered into the sink and onto the tiled
floor. In the next second Frank, standing in the bathroom
door, fired into the curtain, shot after shot, making a little
circle with the gun so that his spread of bullets would find
the mark. He emptied the clip and we stood for some
seconds in silence.

Standing next to the wall, I saw a large shadow behind
the curtain sway back and forth slowly, then fall heavily
downward, a wet thump into the bathtub and a hand
clutching outward between the curtain opening, grabbing the edge and pulling the curtain downward, along
with the circular frame above it, so that it all rested on top
of a very dead man. We could hear rushing, gurgling
water. Only the hand jutted out from beneath the plastic
curtain. I reached down and held up a small lifeless finger,
showing Frank the pinkie ring on it, the same as that worn
by the French banker, the man in the New York penthouse, and Darnley Jacquette.

Frank put the .45 into his pocket, then knelt next to me
and we pulled back the plastic shower curtain. Beneath it
was the other man from the train, the one wearing gold-
rimmed glasses, a balding tall man in his mid-fifties. His
expensive suit was punctured with holes that seeped
blood. In his fall he had struck the bathtub faucet, and
water was splashing over his face from the tap, splashing
onto his glasses, through which he stared with dead eyes.
The water spread over his face and mixed with the blood
from his wounds, all running into the drain next to his
head.

Gripped in his other hand were three small black

leather volumes tied with a cheap string. I pried his fingers loose and took them. Frank reached inside the dead man's coat pocket as I stood up and walked into the bedroom, saying: "Ten to one the son of a bitch is a banker!"

Dr. Zunker turned and looked up at me from his pillows. I patted his shoulder. "Everything is all right now, Doctor. You'll be taken care of, they'll give you a safe escort back to Salzburg. By the way, Professor Handler in New York says hello." He didn't respond. I walked toward the sitting room, untying the little volumes as I went. "And I'll take all these crime books off your hands too, if you don't mind."

As I walked into the sitting room, the Austrian police captain rushed forward from the hallway door, his officer next to him. He was beside himself, raging: "I found Franz —tied up like a hog! In a utility closet—like a hog!"

Frank stood in the bedroom next to Zunker, and called out: "Step in here, captain. The man we were looking for is in here, in the bathroom."

The captain ran forward into the bedroom, then the bathroom, a useless revolver drawn. Frank stepped into the sitting room. I sat down tiredly in a chair and began to turn the pages of the little volumes slowly, savoring each pen-scratched page. Frank walked over, holding the dead man's wallet, reading from an identification card: "Howard L. Orrline, executive vice-president, Travers Exchange Bank of Akron, Ohio."

I looked up at him, to see him staring down at me in disbelief.

"When did you become a clairvoyant?"

"It had to be," I said, waving the three volumes at him. "They're all in here and a lot more."

"Are those the diaries? The real diaries?"

I opened the cover of one of the diaries and read: "*Memoriale di capo Salvatore Giuliano.*"

"I didn't know you could read Sicilian."

"Enough to know what I have here. Besides, Giuliano wrote a lot of this in English. He always wanted to become an American citizen. I guess he thought these would be his passport."

Frank reached out and took the diaries. "Death decree is more like it."

"For a lot of people." I stood up and gently took the diaries out of Frank's hands. "Private property—they came with my library over there." I handed them back to him with a smile. "But you can make a copy for the firm. I'm sure somebody will want to interview the people mentioned here. They'll all be wearing the same fraternity ring."

3

"According to Dr. Zunker's statement to the police," Frank said, holding up an official-looking form, "he got Rombout's shipment about two weeks ago, called him in Paris and was told that it was a mistake. Then Rombout called him back and told Zunker—just before he went for that little ride in the Bois—that the library contained important secret papers—he didn't specify what—that were dangerous and these were to be shipped to Rombout somewhere else. He, Rombout, would call Zunker back and tell him where to send the library. He never called because he was dead and Zunker read about the killing and panicked. Not knowing which book in the library was being hunted, he brought the whole damned works with him to Innsbruck.

"It must have been a bad time for the old man, sifting through all the books, trying to find which one would cause a murder, perhaps his own. That's why they were scattered all over the place. He said he hadn't slept in days, going through the books. Typical academic. Instead of going to the police, he decided *he* would find what it was that caused his friend Rombout's death, *then* he would turn over the deadly book to the authorities. He, Dr. Hans Zunker, would solve things. Christ, he almost got himself killed—like you. Why?"

"Because everybody's a detective." I sagged in a chair in the Innsbruck police station, where the captain had given us a small room to work out Frank's report. Frank sat at a desk, his eyes drooping, begging for sleep. Sunlight annoyingly poured through a high arched window.

I watched, half awake, as Frank turned the pages of one of Giuliano's deadly diaries. "You'll find all the old Mafia boys in there," I told him, "and their American counterparts, just after World War II when the world was safe for democracy and worldwide crime. Luciano, Marcello of New Orleans, Gambino of New York, the Mafia overlords in America of 1949."

Frank put down the book and rubbed his eyes. "Doesn't mean a damned thing anymore. They're all dead."

"Or deposed."

"Or in retirement."

"Like Joe Bananas or Tony Accardo, sure," I said. "But there's another set of names in there, good old-line American names of people who are—or were until recently—very active. Michael Pautz, the guy who took that thirty-story fall—Howard Orrline, the guy in the tub—Henri Bertouillon, the man at Napoleon's tomb—and others, a Chicago banker named Walter Cubbedge, who was just dying to get hold of a check sent to me by one of the victims, and the great Darnley Jacquette of New York. And more."

"Jacquette, I know—big-shot banker. But who are these fellows, if not members of the Mafia?"

"The real power behind the Mafia, my friend. All of

these fellows were young banking executives in 1949, geniuses of finance, a postwar brains trust in the United States and Western Europe. All of them were selected by the Mafia and given enormous amounts of money by the Mafia dons in Sicily and through their American counterparts. They were groomed and coddled and financed to take over the world banking system, or as much of it as they could control. A small group in their profession, but dedicated. Giuliano learned about it from the dons who sponsored him, and wrote it all down, every name."

Lifting a cup of cold coffee to his lips, Frank said over the rim: "The banking system, for Chrissakes—"

"Yeah, to wash the Mafia billions, mostly from world-wide drug traffic. Billions of loose dollars that had to somehow, the dons knew way back then, be put into the legitimate flow of world cash, so that it could be used to buy up legitimate businesses, property. And Jacquette and his fraternity friends did that, and are doing it still. And they would have gone on doing it, had it not been for a down-and-out Paris bookdealer with too much larceny in his heart."

Frank tapped the top of one of Giuliano's diaries. "How do you think Rombout got hold of these? Were they in the Frenchman's library?"

"God knows. Maybe someone had them stored in an attic in Sicily and they got misplaced and were sold with some old books and these spine-broken tomes went into the used-bookstore system and wound up in the Frenchman's collection. Rombout got them, read them, and recognized some of the names of the bankers. Bankers meant money to him and he tried to take over the vault."

"And they were going to give you only a quarter of a million for these babies."

"Rombout's own greed got him killed. They would have

paid him off—you heard the chauffeur back there in Paris —and he could have lived in luxury. But, oh, no—he had to have millions."

"They would have killed him eventually," Frank said, then looked at his watch. "We've got to get out to the airport. That plane is waiting to take us back to Paris."

"I'm ready."

He started for the door, then stopped. "One thing that gets me—why the hell didn't these banker boys go to the Mafia when they heard from Rombout that he had the diaries, and let them take care of it?"

"You don't know the Mafia, Frank. The bankers couldn't go to those people. They would have disappeared and been replaced." I snapped my fingers. "Overnight. They were too vulnerable to go to the Outfit, so they decided to settle matters themselves, and make the killings look like Mafia hits as a shield against their true identities, to put the murders on the very organization that originally sponsored them."

"Disloyal bastards, aren't they?"

"They computed their odds, checked their balance sheets, and thought themselves statistically correct. They control the money, they are the real power. It's just that they were amateurs at killing. One badly staged bump-off led to another. Amateurs!"

"Like you."

"With me it was an accident. All I did was buy a library."

The Austrian police captain met us as we stepped from the office. He gave us a curt nod, then said: "If you don't mind, gentlemen, I'll have one of my men drive you to the airport. I have much to do. Dr. Zunker must be taken back to Salzburg and I will be accompanying him. Then there is the body of the American at the hotel. I must arrange for shipment to the United States with your consulate. *Quite* a lot of work to do."

"Some town, Innsbruck," I said to him as we were leaving. "Archaeology professors in jeopardy, armed guards in the best hotels, dead men in bathtubs. I ought to pinch myself to make sure I'm not in Chicago."

He watched us go out with a glare.

The captain's car was waiting for us at curbside, door open, officer at attention. The minute I sank back into the deep-cushioned seat, I closed my eyes. As we drove off I opened them for a moment to see Frank's head against the back of the seat and his eyes closed. We talked that way, sightless, hoping sleep would come.

"Thanks for shooting that guy, Frank."

"I don't want to talk about it," he answered through a yawn. "I'll get hell for it in the end."

"You'll get a commendation. All I'll get is harassment from a Chicago cop who is convinced I drove a billing spike into a man's ear. But now I can explain that and why I ran like hell, explain it and prove the explanation."

"Jack—you shouldn't have run at all."

"Uh-uh. Run and someone runs after you, sometimes the real culprits, but they ran too fast, caught up, passed me, got out in front where I could see them. I planned it all."

"Sure you did, Jack."

"That's what I'll tell anyone who genuinely wants to know."

He was silent for a while and I thought that he had drifted off, but then he said: "I know you. You like getting yourself into box canyons . . . to see if you can escape."

"Yeah . . . that's me . . . just a thrill-seeker."

I was slipping downward into sleep when I felt the police car surge ahead. I sat up and looked at the speedometer in front of the driver, the same one who had driven us in from the airport six hours earlier. Then I collapsed back into the seat, with eyelids coming down like iron gates. I was too tired to fear the flight back in the supersonic jet. I was too tired to talk, but I did manage to say: "Can you believe it? *Now* the damned driver is speeding."

Frank answered with a snore.

X

At the Top

1

We flew into New York on Sunday. I saw Frank's people and I agreed to turn over the diaries to them within twenty-four hours. Actually, *they* had Giuliano's literary keepsake but loaned the *memoriales* to me for a wire job I agreed to perform, one that gave me great pleasure. I had slept ten hours in Paris before returning with Frank. I was refreshed, angrier than at the start because I had answers now and would not have the Lucan murder around my neck. And I also had my library, which I had shipped from Innsbruck to Chicago. I was ready for revenge.

It wasn't sweet. I didn't want Laura's head on a platter; she had cut into me deep, striking a vein and panning nuggets from what I thought to be an abandoned mine. And the pain made me angry. I had to find release. I would let the anger reveal itself to the tiny microphones Frank's people would plant on me early Monday morning when I faced Laura's distinguished employer, Darnley Jacquette. One setup deserved another, certainly.

Frank and I stayed at the Waldorf that Sunday night. It

was early in the evening when I made my call to Laura, finding her at the number she had given me when we got off the train a million afternoons ago. Her conversation on the phone did not match her beauty; it was standard fare, a cliché of concern.

"Jack, my God, I've been so worried," it began. "I haven't heard from you and then that man falling from the terrace—"

"Where did you go, my little cul-de-sac?"

"That night? I had to leave, Jack—I had to leave. I want to explain about that penthouse. It's a company place, they have lots of them. Many people use them, people I don't even know have keys to that private elevator."

"I want to see you, Laura."

She was silent.

"I want to see you tonight, Laura," I repeated.

"Where are you?" she finally asked.

"At the Waldorf, Room 614. Come over. We can talk it out."

"Give me an hour."

"Take two. See you, beautiful."

Room 614 was not the room where I was sleeping, but one that Frank's people had set up with cameras and microphones. They had moved my clothes there, neatly hanging them in the closet, neatly folding them into the drawers of the bureau. I was scattered about everywhere inside of Room 614, they had seen to that, loose change on top of the bureau, my cigarettes on top of the desk, my shaving equipment in the bathroom, my robe draped over the chair next to the bed, slippers at its side.

I was brushing my teeth, standing in my underwear in the bathroom, looking into the mirror, wondering who it was before me with foam on his lips, when I heard her knocking at the door. I wiped away the toothpaste and draped the towel around my neck. I looked back into the

mirror and knew that man well now; in that moment I
was appraising the face and physique of a new porno star.
And at age thirty-nine, think of it.

As I walked into the large bedroom I stopped and
checked the places where Frank's men had placed their
sophisticated little wireless cameras. One was in the overhead light fixture. One was inside the mouth of a comic
theater mask on the wall, another was planted at the top
of a mirror above the bureau, peeking through hand-
carved filigree. They were live, all of them, with attached
microphones. I stood by the main light switch, flipping it
on as I said aloud to listening ears and watching eyes:
"Camera, lights, action—I'm ready for my close-up now,
Mr. De Mille!" Then I sauntered to the door, feeling low.
Ever since Abscam, these federal boys insisted on putting
everything on film. What Laura might say about Jacquette
and his banker friends and the Mafia they slept with
would hold up in court if it was on film. And I would be on
film with her, for the record, for corroboration, stark naked.

She stood in the hallway, lovely, her face expressionless,
dark eyes smoldering. She wore a business suit of deep
gray, a light blue silk blouse, pearl-gray high heels. Slung
over her shoulder was a light blue bag. Laura Manville's
ensemble was perfectly matched as usual.

For a second I thought I would close the door in her
face, somehow save her, but I told myself that there was
nothing left to save. She was Jacquette's woman, always
had been. I was someone who had to be serviced for
business reasons, killed for business reasons.

"Come in, beautiful," I said, reaching out into the hallway, holding her hand and leading her inside. I slammed
the door hard, which was the signal to the surveillance
men to keep the film running. As I followed Laura
through the small entranceway and into the bedroom, a

strange question came to mind: Would they film all this in color or black-and-white? It didn't matter. I wouldn't ask for prints.

Laura walked to the window, pulled back the curtain for a moment to look out at the street. God knows who was waiting for her down there. Then she turned, gave me a nervous smile, and came forward to me, putting her arms around my waist, her head on my shoulder.

"I didn't know what happened to you," she said slowly. "I left so hurriedly I didn't even get a chance to write a note."

"I got the message," I said, putting my arms lightly around her, rubbing her back.

"Then when I read about that man the next day and there was no trace of you, and I made a call to the Algonquin, and they said you had checked out—I was so confused that I got drunk."

Holding her away from me, I gave her a smile. "You got drunk? But you don't drink, sweetheart."

"Oh, God, Jack, I got sick-to-my-stomach drunk." She looked deep into my eyes. "Yes, drinking bourbon, can you imagine it? And I was so terribly worried about you . . . disappearing like that, and I thought that the police might be after you. It was all so very melodramatic." She put her long cool fingers to my face, holding it. "Where did you go?"

"Europe, to Paris." Of course, she already knew that. I slipped her purse from her shoulder and threw it on the chair. She put her hands to my waist, then worked them up beneath my undershirt, going upward on my chest, rubbing. I pulled them away gently and took off her short suit jacket.

Her hands went down to the side buttons of her skirt, which she quickly unfastened so that it slid downward to the floor. As she did this I worked the buttons of her blouse and she took it off, putting it on the chair, then stepped back out of the crumpled circle of her skirt, scooped this up, and, snapping it out as a washerwoman would snap a freshly laundered bath towel, placed it flat over the back of the chair. She grabbed the strap of her bag and pulled it upward, then walked back to me and kissed me.

"I'm *so* glad to see you, Jack," she said. "I've got to freshen up." She held up her bag and took out a small makeup kit before putting the bag on the chair. Then she walked into the bathroom, high heels clattering on the floor tiles, and closed the door.

I went to her sling bag and picked it up, taking it into the entranceway, behind the closet door, away from the cameras. There were two items in that bag I wanted that had nothing to do with my agreement with the government people, something I had told them nothing about. It was my own way of getting even, and making sure that the Mafia diaries would never be lost again. Deep inside the large blue bag I found what I was digging for, a leather holder containing two thick plastic cards with strange-looking indentations on them, a series of numbers on each, really, like embossed letters on a dinner invitation. Only this was an invitation to the American public to feast on infamy.

Slipping the plastic cards into the inside pocket of my sport coat, I returned the purse to the chair, went to the bed, stripped and sprawled. There are no cameras, I told myself, no eyes watching and ears listening, but the nagging thought of their real presence sent a shiver over my naked body. There was only the sound of the humming air-conditioner in the bedroom and the faint gurgle of running water inside the closed bathroom. The water stopped running and I could hear Laura clack toward the door. She opened it stone naked, and the sight of her large breasts bobbing, full hips swinging as she walked toward me, made my blood race.

She stood at the foot of the bed, appraising me, smiling downward with deep red full lips, her long black hair falling over graceful shoulders. She bent down and removed her high heels, then, with one knee on the edge of the bed, breasts swaying, moved on top of me, enfolding her arms about mine, soft warm flesh I had almost died for.

She began slowly, working back and forth, riding high, breasts jutting above me, head thrown back and to the side, facing the bureau mirror, looking at me in the mirror and talking to me that way as she rocked in wet passion.

"I had nothing to do with what happened to you, Jack. Believe me."

"I believe you," I answered, moving with her.

"I love you, Jack. Believe me."

"I believe you."

"It's foolish to keep pretending. Darnley wanted you out of the way. He had me get on that train to follow you. We followed you to the airport and then to the train. I was supposed to drop cyanide into your drink on the train. I couldn't, I love you. Believe me."

"I believe you."

She moved faster, rocked harder, but kept eyeing me in the mirror. She could not look down directly at me; she needed the distance of the mirror, the illusion that it was someone else over there on the bed, some other impaled woman. I ignored the device, looking up directly at her turned-away face, addressing her profile.

"I took you to the company penthouse so that they could talk to you. That's what Darnley told me, it was only going to be talk—no hurting—only talking sense to you."

"Darnley lied to you. They tried to kill me."

"I know." She blinked her eyes and they became watery and spilled over at the edges when she shut them hard, so that the tears went over and down either side of her high cheeks and across the planes of her face. "I know, I know, I know," she said in a deep hurt voice, and each time she said it, she pressed hard against me. She stopped, turned her head to me, then sank forward, crushing her breasts into my chest, rocking on me slightly, pushing her cheek next to mine. "I didn't want to see you die, I love you," she said, half into the pillow.

I moved her head up with my hand so that it was flat across my face and so the microphones would more easily pick up her words. "It's all over, beautiful, I've got Giuliano's diaries."

Her response to this was to begin rocking on me again, harder, faster—sex would beat back the bad news.

"Did you hear me?"

"I heard you, darling," she said almost in a whisper. "And I'm glad. I'm glad you've won."

"Won? What?"

"That means Darnley won't try to hurt you anymore. He can't. You have what he wants now—it's been driving him crazy, those diaries. I don't care. I'm quitting him. I gave him my notice when I heard about the man falling from the terrace."

"Quit? A job like yours, all the money in the world? Power and money, seated at the right hand of Darnley Jacquette? Quit that?"

"Yes, it's all rotten." She eased off me, going slowly to my side, rolling onto her back to lie next to me. Her stomach quivered nervously. We lay there staring at the ceiling, and I held her hand as we looked straight at the overhead light where the hidden camera peered down at our nakedness.

"I'm quitting because nothing is worth bloodshed, especially yours, darling Jack."

"I believe you."

"You sound like you don't." She said this with an urgent voice, turning her head toward me to search my thoughts. "Jack, darling—please, please, please, please believe me!"

"Oh, I do, beautiful. I believe every lie you tell me. That's how far down I've gone for you. But I have an old-fashioned problem."

"What's that?"

"I can't stand betrayal. Any kind of betrayal—emotional, sexual, fraternal, any kind. I guess it's a sickness in a world where betrayal is just good business."

She rolled over on her side, blinking at me. "A betrayer. And that's all you think I am?"

"No—you're also one hell of a great lay." I rolled off the bed and stood up, putting on my shorts, wiping the sweat from my chest with a towel emblazoned with a huge *W* that stood for the Waldorf. She sat up in bed, drawing her knees into her breasts, putting her chin over hands that were folded over the knees. "I want you to go back to Jacquette and tell him I'll make that deal now—tomorrow morning, at ten sharp, in his boardroom at the bank. I want you there with him and anyone else involved. I'll bring the diaries and we'll talk about price, real money, not the quarter of a million they threw at me in a sack in Paris."

Laura didn't respond, only stared ahead at nothing over her knees.

"You shouldn't mind me asking you to do this, beautiful." I put on my undershirt, then went for my slacks, talking to her from the closet. "You can take your pick tomorrow morning. Me and the dough I collect from Jacquette, or stay with Jacquette, who's always going to have more dough than me."

"I don't love Darnley Jacquette," I heard her say as I stood behind the closet door getting dressed. "So money can buy you?" she said, and I could hear her moving about in the bedroom. "I didn't think that of you, Jack."

"No, money can't buy me—but millions can."

"So you still want the two million?" she said in a hard voice.

I closed the closet door to see that she had already gotten completely dressed, down to the bag that was slung over her shoulder.

"That's what I told them in Paris, beautiful, two million. Of course, you didn't know about that—you were guzzling bourbon and wondering, no doubt, how my brains would look splattered all over Forty-fifth Street after falling thirty floors."

She marched up to me, past me, going to the door. "The only thing *you love* is being right." She reached for the doorknob and I caught her hand, held it, drew it next to my chest. "I think Darnley will pay you the two million. If you take it, you go alone, not with me."

"Don't hand me that, Laura. You're not concerned with penniless but proud people. You're not concerned with codes of honor, or human life. Penthouses and priceless antiques, homes among the chalets in Aspen, a long, very rich life on top of the mountain, sure. You'll stay with Jacquette because you never had any intention of leaving him." I pushed her away from me and opened the door. "He's your man. You're his baglady."

Laura stepped into the hallway, eyes blazing at me.

"Make sure Jacquette and company are present tomorrow morning at the bank. Ten sharp. I'll be there to pick up the cash."

"He'll be there all right," she said angrily to me, her shapely legs spread in a fighter's stance, tight against her skirt. She gripped the strap of her purse with a fist. "You'll get your *money.*"

My hand was resting on the edge of the door and I gave

it a shove, stepping back. The door slowly closed in her face, cutting off her furious stare.

2

The rear entrance of the Haley National Bank had a walk-up area with two stainless steel doors. To the side was the guard's room, fronted with bulletproof glass. Inside, a single guard sat with his feet up on the desk, holding a paperback copy of a Zane Grey western, *Riders of the Purple Sage,* I think. I stood before the window to be identified, but he did not move. It was almost 7:00 A.M. and no one was expected at this entrance at this time of day, that was obvious.

The guard dabbed a finger with spittle and slowly turned a page of the book. I tapped on the glass and smiled down at him. He squinted and pulled his legs from the top of the desk. He clicked on the intercom. "What do you want?"

"Computer inspector."

"For Bertha?" He nodded. He pushed a knob that sent a stainless steel drawer out to me.

"Right." I dropped one of Laura's magic plastic cards into the drawer and the guard drew it inside. He picked it up, looking at it as if he understood what it meant. There was no name on it, only the etched numbers. Then he reached to a slot and dropped it in, watching a green screen that kicked up a series of numbers, and then another series of numbers appeared, matching the first set exactly. He punched a button and the card shot out. This he returned to me through the drawer. He nodded and pushed a red button on the desk, and the giant stainless steel doors opened before me.

I walked inside as the guard went back to Zane Grey. The deserted corridor of the bank's computer center was empty but white with indirect light. I walked along a corridor paneled in clear large glass. On one side, visible for the awestruck eye, was a huge computer, bank after bank, row after row of banks, connected by huge cables. At the end of the corridor were two large glass doors, with heavy metal stripping. There was an electronic box above the doors and a slot next to it. I stepped onto a mat before the doors and the electronic box lit up with the words INSERT I.D. I slipped the plastic card the guard had returned to me into the slot. The glass doors separated and the card bounced upward to me out of the slot.

Entering the computer room—it was as long as a basketball court—I went to the main control panel, sitting down before the large screen. A manual hung from a hook and I read through it briefly. I set the scanner flat before me for legal size, took out the second book of Giuliano's diaries—where he had written down Jacquette's name and others, the part where he stated that these would be the Mafia's future bankers—and placed it squarely inside the duplicating area. Then I punched out the word STATEMENTS on the keyboard. The word came up on another small screen on the face of the control board. Taking the other card I had removed from Laura's purse, I inserted this into a slot in the computer above which was a window marked EXECUTE. I punched up on the keys the words SAME COPY and UNIVERSAL DISTRIBUTION. Then I hit the large green button to my right on the control panel.

The entire board lit up, red and white lights blinking as the instructions were fed into Bertha's waiting brain. The computer sucked the card down the slot and kicked it back up, the window above the slot now reading IN PROCESS. The banks of computers stemming from the one where I sat all began to hum and whir and sing, little lights flashing red and white as one bank of computers set the next one in motion.

I got up and zigzagged through the maze of computer banks, at the end of which was a huge duplicating system, which fed down from racks that rose to the ceiling all manner of blank paper—from deposit slips to bank withdrawal forms. Feeding now at blurring speed were legal-size depositors' statements, shooting through a series of fast-moving conveyor belts, down from storage racks to a speed printer, which copied the material I had placed on the scanner at the control board in blinding speed, thousands of copies a minute, whipping out the printed copies onto another conveyor system that automatically folded the statements and fed them into envelopes that roared into the system from another series of conveyors, all pre-addressed and postmarked. Robot fingers edged the envelopes of a wet roller system, then sealed the envelopes. At the end of this system was another automated mailing-bag system, a huge one, bags coming down on a mechanized runner, spread wide automatically by robot arms before the mouth of the computer system, which disgorged thousands of sealed statements into each bag, filling each and sending it along to make way for another empty bag and another and another. I gloated at the sight of it, Darnley's priceless computers undoing Darnley.

The bags, once full of statements, were carried by hook along the conveyor line, upward and then over, so that they were heaped into a huge bin that faced the back of the bank and a loading dock where the mail trucks would come.

Grabbing a sealed envelope, I checked its contents and smiled. I put this into my pocket and walked the long way to the control board, waiting for Bertha to finish her job. It took a little less than thirty minutes before she exhausted her lists of depositors and sent through the last statements, then closed down, one system after another. On the large screen before me the words EXERCISE COM-

PLETE appeared. I punched the button marked TERMI-NATE and the computer went dead. Then, using the phone next to the control board, I called the post office.

I picked up the volume of Giuliano's diaries, slipped this into my pocket, and started to make my way out. I had enough time to meet Frank for breakfast before going up to see my old pal Darnley Jacquette.

3

We sat in a small French deli around the block from the bank. I munched on a fresh croissant and sipped my coffee. "Funny, I was in Paris and didn't eat a croissant until I got back here."

Frank lunged into business. "You understand, now, that you're to return those original diaries to us after this meet with Jacquette."

"Want a piece of my croissant?"

"No, damn it. Jack—this is serious. Those guys could still kill you."

I popped the last of the croissant into my mouth. "No, they won't. Too dangerous for them. They'll try to pay me off, that's all."

"Fine, then give them the diaries, take the money, and get the hell out of there. We need the money for evidence. Are you comfortable with the wires?"

"I don't even know I'm wearing them." I knew, all right. I had a wire under my shirt, taped to my chest, one taped to my right leg, and one on my left arm. "How powerful are these things?"

Frank grinned. "You know those mikes umpires and referees wear at football games?"

"Yeah."

"That powerful."

"Well, I don't want them to hear me in Yankee Stadium, chum."

"It's all fed back to us in a room we've got three floors below. Just get Jacquette to talk, give you the money, and tell you all about it, and then get out of there." He drank some steaming coffee, blowing on it before he sipped it. "And no tricky stuff, Jack, no theatrics, okay?"

"Right. But I want to be sure those original diaries don't get lost after I turn them over to Jacquette."

"We'll pick them up five minutes after you drop them in his lap."

"And that none of your people lose them."

He put down his coffee hard, spilling it. "You know better than that!"

"No, I don't. Better people than those working for the firm and the Bureau and the Secret Service and all of them have gone into the tank. That guy Jacquette will spend millions, and millions of dollars can buy a lot of people. Some take a lot less—hell, we had an attorney general in Illinois who went into the tank for five thousand dollars, only five thousand and his whole career was over. Millions buy a lot of people and on any level."

"Not that many people, Jack. Washington knows all about this. We're up to our ears with insiders on this one."

"How about the President," I joked. "Is he in on it too?"

"Don't joke about the President, Jack. He's got enough worries."

I leaned forward. "They're not getting away with anything on this, Frank. I'm going to make sure of that."

"Just pick up the money, get Jacquette to implicate himself, then leave, and we'll do the rest. Get the money and leave. Then we take over. When you leave, you come down to Room 1110. Got it?"

"Can't miss," I said. "I think I'll have another croissant. Want one?"

4

The fourteenth floor of the Haley National Bank Building was unlike any other. Only one elevator stopped there and the operator had to call up to clear me for the floor. We rode up slowly and the doors opened onto a foyer lush with oriental carpets, Persian wall tapestries, and oil paintings. Seated at the end of the foyer was a lean-bodied blond woman, her yellow hair swept back into a severe bun. She wore glasses that made her eyes look exotic. The little desk she sat at was clean, except for a small intercom and a telephone. Behind her was a wall of walnut paneling glistening with heavy wax, and double walnut doors with giant brass handles on them.

"I'm Journey," I told the blonde.

Her hand went out to the intercom, a finger pushing down a lever. "Mr. Journey is here," she said in a noncommittal voice. A voice came back at her: "Show Mr. Journey in, please." It was Jacquette.

The blonde stood up, going up and up, to a height in her high heels of at least six feet, plus. "This way, sir." She went to the double doors and pulled one back, using both hands to grapple the huge brass handle. I walked inside an oblong room filled with a thirty-foot table edged with deep brown leather chairs. The chairs were filled with silent men, all in their late fifties, all well dressed, all wearing that fraternity ring. As the heavy door behind me slowly closed, I spotted Darnley Jacquette. He sat at the end of the thick, well-polished table, presiding, of course.

He spoke down the distance of the room to me. "We'll make this meeting short, if you don't mind, Mr. Journey?"

"What? And I've got all kinds of parlor tricks stored up."

"We're only interested in the diaries, Mr. Journey," Jacquette said. "Put them on the table." He turned his lion's head an inch to the left and said: "Mr. Cubbedge—the briefcase."

A beefy, red-faced man in a pale blue suit at the end of the table next to me reached down and brought up, from between his legs, a handsome briefcase. He placed this on the table in front of me, clicking open the locks and slowly lifting the lid of the case to show me neatly packed rows of thousand-dollar bills.

I walked over to the case and ran my finger across the stacks of bills, never taking my eyes from Jacquette. "How do I know you're giving me two million dollars here?"

"Count it," said the man who had produced the case.

"Are you Walter Cubbedge, the Chicago banker who was trying to get me to turn over Lucan's check to you?"

"I'm Walter Cubbedge," he admitted quietly. "Now, if you'd care to count the money, be pleased to do so."

"Be pleased to do so," I repeated. "Such old-world phraseology, courteous talk from the cultured, the civilized. Wonderfully civilized people, all of you." I leaned on the open top of the case for a moment, then slammed the lid shut, clicking the locks into place.

Walter Cubbedge reached up and placed a small gold key on top of the briefcase. "This will open it." I put the key in my pocket.

Two chairs down from Cubbedge sat a familiar face staring blankly at me. Beneath the face was a dark business suit, the same as the others, except that I knew this man as the murderer of my friend Cashe.

"Where's your valet's costume, you son of a bitch."

His stare was steady at me, but a smile crept up the corners of his thin mouth. I'd get him later, I'd get the whole goddamned smug bunch later, in just a little while, some sweet, fat minutes later.

"Now the diaries, Mr. Journey," Jacquette said.

I took out the three slim volumes, weighing them in my hand. Jacquette stood up and came around the table, walking slowly toward me as the men in their seats eyed him. I threw the volumes down on the table and the eyes of the men seated there darted to them, hungrily eyeing them. "I believe this is what you vultures were in search of."

Jacquette reached the end of the table and snatched up the diaries. He held them in both hands, going over the pages rapidly, a confident smile growing on his lips. He half turned to the anxious men at the table and reported softly: "These are the originals." Then he gave the brief-case a little nudge in my direction, saying: "A reasonable transaction for a man wanting to stay alive, and one that will assure you a comfortable life."

I walked to the bank of windows that ran around the room on three sides, looking down for the back entrance. I followed the windows down the length of the room, as the men in their chairs turned to look at me. At the end of the room, where Jacquette had sat, I could see the bank's loading docks. I said without looking at any of them: "Of course, there are copies of the diaries in Washington right now."

"What?" shouted the man nearest me.

"Jacquette—you told us that this man—" began another at the top of his voice, half rising out of his deep brown leather chair.

"One minute!" Jacquette thundered, and walked swiftly to my side. He then said so that only we could hear: "What are you saying? That you're not taking the money?"

"I didn't say that." I could see postal trucks beginning to arrive at the bank's dock, one after another, backing up to it, and swarms of men in gray going onto the dock, taking out keys and opening the huge mail-bin doors. Mailbags spilled down on them and the postmen grabbed them, two at a time, and began to throw them into their trucks.

"Journey," Jacquette said in a whisper. "I want you to turn around and tell these men that our investment in you is safe, that there are no more copies."

I nodded and turned around to face the nervous executives sitting around the table. "Your day, gentlemen, is over. You're a disgrace to the banking profession . . . if that's possible. You've killed your way into a bad situation and then you tried to buy your way out, and now the diaries themselves are exposing you." I faced Jacquette. "What the hell did you expect me to do? Trust you?" I laughed in his face. "Not for two million or two hundred million. You and your friends are going into the trick bag, not the same way you brought down Lucan and Keimes and my friend Cashe, but down anyway. Maybe, after Washington starts to throttle you by those fat necks of yours, the boys over in the Mafia will take care of you. Sure, they'll reach all the way inside your cells and take care of you and it won't matter how much money you shove through the bars at them to keep them off your necks."

"He's crazy, Jacquette!" one of the men shouted. "What are you going to do about him?"

"None of this guarantees you a longer life than this morning, Mr. Journey."

"Is that a death threat?"

"You bet it is." His face never lost its composure, only the words came out with a bite, as if from a different man, a separate tough man inside that polished exterior, that affable body.

"Are you going to murder me the way you did Lucan— shove a spike in my ear?"

"Perhaps."

"Or maybe the way you killed Carlisle Cashe, with a

spear—or a stiletto in the back, the way you gave it to Keimes, or slashed to pieces, the way your people gave it to Rombout in Paris?"

"Whatever way we kill you, Mr. Journey, will be the method that most pleases us."

"Then you've got a hell of a job on your hands, Mr. Bankroll. Look down here."

Jacquette looked out the window and downward to see the scurrying mailmen loading their trucks, some of them already leaving the dock, trucks going outward into the city.

"So? One of our mail deliveries."

"No—this one is *my* mail delivery." I pulled out the depositor's statement I had taken off the computer line about two hours earlier. I handed this to Jacquette, then jerked a thumb at the mailmen below. "Looks like you'll also have to knock off about a million of your depositors along with me, Jacquette." I made my way down the length of the table as he stood there, looking over the statement. I got to the end of the table where the money sat and looked back at him.

Jacquette read the printout in his hands with trembling lips.

"What is it, Darnley?" asked the man closest to him.

"A depositor's statement . . . from the bank . . . dated today," he answered. His voice was full of wonder, then he glanced back out the window at the departing postmen. He read aloud from the statement: *"Memoriale di capo Salvatore Giuliano . . ."* He moved to the end of the table, slamming down the statement. "God damn you, Journey—did you make copies of this . . . have you been in our computer room?"

"Yes," I answered, working hard to contain the bubble of triumph. "You were right about your computer—it's a beauty, no giant greedy corporation should be without one. Worked like a charm. I sent out the diaries—only important pages, mind you, the ones mentioning important people, namely yourselves—on statements to each and every one of your depositors. But you all have a few long days to run for it. You know how notorious the mails are."

"Why, for God's sake, have you done this?" Jacquette was screaming now, red-faced, twitching and out of control, which was gratifying to see.

"To protect myself, to make sure that it all got out." I reached under my tie, unbuttoned my shirt, and pulled out the tiny mike, speaking into it: "There's no telling what might happen to the diaries, even in hands of our agents." Then back to the bankers: "This way everybody stays honest and the diaries are made very public. You want to kill me? You'll have to include your depositors." I picked up the briefcase and headed for the huge swinging door, putting my back to it, moving out slowly, watching the table of petrified men closely. "I wouldn't worry about it, though. Probably only about fifty thousand of those depositors read Sicilian—that'll cut down the odds."

I slipped out the door and let it go back slowly. There wasn't a sound on the other side of it. As I turned in the foyer and started for the elevator, I saw Laura standing by a side door, standing and staring at me. I pressed the elevator door, then gave her a sideways look. "You better start running, beautiful."

"Did you take the money, Jack?"

I held up the briefcase and gave her a little smile.

"What about the diaries?"

I nodded toward the big doors. "They've got them, but not for long. I think you'd better start running, Laura. I'm giving you a chance by telling you that, a break, even though you didn't give me one."

She moved to my side and said: "I'm going down with you."

The elevator opened. I backed into it, putting out a hand, pushing her gently back from the door. "No. Use the stairs."

"Jack, please—"

I nodded to the operator, who shrugged and began to close the doors. "It's only fourteen floors," I told her through the narrowing space. "A lot less than you gave me once."

5

"God damn you, Jack!" Frank was shouting, "what the hell kind of crazy stunt was that—running the goddamned diaries through the bank computers?"

"Can you hold it down, Frank? I'm talking to Abbe in Chicago." I held the receiver close to my ear as I watched Frank's people assemble the tapes they had gathered from my wires and tediously count the two-million-dollar bribe. "Go ahead, Abbe, how's Henry?"

"Shedding . . . all over my apartment. Jack, when are you coming back?"

"We're going to look like idiots with those goddamned bank statements sent all over the world!" Frank yelled. "Some friend you are—God damn it, this is government business!"

"And the government is the people, Frank. I just wanted the people to have a peek at something you'll probably stamp top secret an hour from now. And under that stamp the Jacquettes will squirm with high-priced lawyers, and maybe weasel out."

"When are you coming back, Jack?" Abbe was saying over the phone.

"In a couple of days," I told her. "I'm going to take the train back to Chicago."

Frank stood at my side, still burning. "I'm not taking responsibility for that bonehead play, Jack. You're in real trouble. You can't use the mails like a newspaper—"

"Jack—why don't you fly back—faster," Abbe encouraged.

"I want to relax on the train, no calls, no worries, just bad food and a bumpy ride, that'll be fine."

"Washington will be all over me for what you did," Frank droned on.

"Hold on a minute, Abbe." I put the receiver on my knee and said to Frank: "Look, you got what you wanted —a bunch of well-dressed killers over in the federal detention center behind bars. You've got the evidence—" I pointed to the money on the table, which four men were counting, and to the technicians working on the tape. "Now you'll have a solid conviction and the praise of big-bellied bureaucrats everywhere. All I did was inform the public—that's my job as a journalist. Now let me finish my call, will you?"

"Thank God you're out of the service," Frank said, and walked over to the money to stare down at it, hands on hips, his back to me.

"I get in on Wednesday," I told Abbe. "Meet me at the train, will you?"

"Why?" she said. "I've got work to do."

"To hell with the work, meet me at the station, and bring Henry, and ask Charlie to come down, arm sling and all. And ask the cops to meet me too, Ackerly and Brex. And call Champ Rimmel and anyone else you can think of—be down at the train station at ten in the morning. We'll have a party. And get a Boy Scout band."

"What—a Boy Scout band, did you say?"

"Have them on the ramp when I get off the train. The

minute they spot me have them strike up 'When Johnny Comes Marching Home.' You got that? I can't stand coming into a train station with no one to meet me."

"See you on Wednesday, Jack," Abbe said without promising the band, and hung up.

Frank walked me to the elevator in silence. I held out my hand and he took it.

"I'll come over for a real vacation next spring. We'll do up Paris."

"I can't talk to you now, Jack." He looked at the floor. "I'm too angry."

"Okay, talk to me next spring."

He was still looking downward at the floor, but he gave me a short wave good-bye as the elevator doors closed between us.

By the time I reached the street I had begun to feel bad, not for Jacquette and those other financial cutthroats, but for Laura, who had schemed her way out of a miserable existence, climbed unsurely upward into a power structure she had always been taught was the ideal American dream come true. And now she was going to prison, along with Jacquette and the others. The feeling got worse, knotty in the throat, as I walked out of the front entrance of the towering Haley National Bank Building.

I stood there, immobilized by the thought of Laura in drab-gray prison dresses, queuing in chow lines, entering a stuffy cell night after night, an airless, dark place. My gaze was at the gutter of the street, transfixed with the grim images of Laura's future.

"It can't be that bad, fella," I heard a voice say.

"What?" I was looking into the face of a hot-dog vendor who stood next to his pushcart.

"I said it can't be that bad, can it?" He wore an idiotic grin on his broad face.

"It's as bad as it can be, I suppose."

"Naw, it ain't, never," said the stoic vendor, and he flipped up the lid of the container holding hot dogs floating in scalding water. Steam shot upward into his face as he jabbed a dog into a fresh bun and pasted it with mustard and dropped on some onions. "Here, fella, have one on me—really, take it, it's free, on me."

"Free?" I smirked.

"Sure, g'wan, take it. Pick you up. I ain't chargin'."

I took the hot dog and bit into it, chewing slowly. It was delicious. "Thanks," I said, and began to walk away.

"It's okay, fella."

I held up the hot dog and said: "You know, this is the nicest thing that ever happened to me in New York."

As I started to walk away, chewing up the dog, I heard him say: "Whaddya—crazy? A hot dog?"

"It is," I said to myself. And I meant it.